Hand Me Down World

Also by Lloyd Jones

Swimming to Australia

Biografi

This House Has Three Walls

Choo Woo

The Book of Fame

Here at the End of the World We Learn to Dance

Paint Your Wife

Mister Pip

The Man in the Shed

Hand Me Down World

A Novel

Lloyd Jones

BLOOMSBURY
NEW YORK · BERLIN · LONDON · SYDNEY

Published by Bloomsbury USA, New York

All papers used by Bloomsbury USA are natural, recyclable products made from wood grown in well-managed forests. The manufacturing processes conform to the environmental regulations of the country of origin.

LIBRARY OF CONGRESS CATALOGING-IN-PUBLICATION DATA

Jones, Lloyd, 1955–
Hand me down world : a novel / Lloyd Jones.—1st U.S. ed.
p. cm.
ISBN-13: 978-1-60819-699-9 (hc)
ISBN-10: 1-60819-699-2 (hc)
1. Mothers of kidnapped children—Fiction. 2. Women immigrants—Fiction. 3. Voyages and travels—Fiction. 4. Human trafficking—Fiction. 5. Psychological fiction. I. Title.
PR9639.3.J644H36 2011
823'.914—dc22
2011005633

First published in Australia by The Text Publishing Co.; in New Zealand by Penguin New Zealand; in Great Britain by John Murray Publishers, a Hachette UK company; and in Canada by Alfred A. Knopf Canada, a division of Random House of Canada Ltd., 2010.

First U.S. Edition 2011

1 3 5 7 9 10 8 6 4 2

Printed in the U.S.A. by Quad/Graphics, Fairfield, Pennsylvania for Anne

part one: *What they said*

one

The supervisor

I was with her at the first hotel on the Arabian Sea. That was for two years. Then at the hotel in Tunisia for three years. At the first hotel we slept in the same room. I knew her name, but that is all. I did not know when her birthday was. I did not know how old she was. I did not know where she came from in Africa. When we spoke of home we spoke of somewhere in the past. We might be from different countries but the world we came into contained the same clutter and dazzling light. All the same traps were set for us. Later I found God, but that is a story for another day.

If I tell you of my beginning you will know hers. I can actually remember the moment I was born. When I say this to people they look away or they smile privately. I know they are inclined not to believe. So I don't say this often or loudly. But I will tell you now so that perhaps you will understand her better. I can tell you this.

The air was cool to start with, but soon all that disappeared. The air broke up and darted away. Black faces with red eye strain dropped from a great height. My first taste of the world was a finger of another stuck inside my mouth. The first feeling is of my lips being stretched. I am being made right for the world, you see. My first sense of other is when I am picked up and examined like a roll of cloth for rips and spots. Then as time passes I am able to look back at this world I have been born into. It appears I have been born beneath a mountain of rubbish. I am forever climbing through and over that clutter, first to get to school, and later to the beauty contest at the depot, careful not to get filth on me. I win that contest and then the district and the regional. That last contest won me a place in the Four Seasons Hotel staff training program on the Arabian Sea. That is where I met her.

There, instead of refuse, I discover an air-conditioned lobby. There are palms. These trees are different from the ones I am used to. These palms I am talking about. They look less like trees than things placed in order to please the eye. Even the sea with all its blue ease appears to lack a reason to exist other than to be pleasing to the eye. It is fun to play in. That much is clear from the European guests and those blacks who can afford it.

We shared a room. We slept a few feet away from one another. She became like a sister to me, but I cannot tell you her middle name or her last name, or the name of the place she was born. Her father's name was Justice. Her mother's name was Mary. I cannot tell you anything else about where she came from. At the Four Seasons it did not matter. To show you were from somewhere was no good. You have to leave your past in order to become hotel staff. To be good staff you had to be like the palms and the sea, pleasing to the eye. We must not take up space but be there whenever a guest needed us. At the Four Seasons we learned how to scrub the bowl, how to make a rosette out of the last square of toilet paper and to tie over the seat a paper band that declared in English that the toilet was of approved hygiene standard. We learned how to turn back a bed, and how to revive a guest who had drunk too much or nearly drowned. We learned how to sit a guest upright and thump his back with the might of Jesus when a crisp or a peanut had gone down the wrong way.

What else? I can tell you about the new appetite that came over her like a disease of the mind. She forgot she was staff. Yes. Sometimes I thought she was under a spell. There she was, staff, and in her uniform, standing in the area reserved for guests, beneath the palms, taking up the precious shade, watching a tall white man enter the sea. She watches the sea rise all the way up his body until he disappears. The tear in the ocean smooths over. She waits. And she waits some more. She wonders if she should call the bell captain. All this time she is holding her own breath. She didn't know that until the missing person emerges—and in a different place. He burst up through another tear in the world and all of his own making. This is the moment, she told me so, she decided she would like to learn to swim. Yes. This is the first time that idea comes to her.

After eighteen months—I am aware I said two years. That is wrong. I remember now. It was after eighteen months we were moved to a larger hotel. This was in Tunisia. The tear in the world has just grown bigger. This hotel is also on the sea. For the first time in our lives it was possible to look in the direction of Europe.

Not that there was anything to see. That didn't matter. No. You can still find your way to a place you cannot see.

For the first time we had money. A salary, plus tips. More money than either of us had ever earned. On our day off we would walk to the market. Once she bought a red-and-green parrot. It had belonged to an Italian engineer found dead in the rubbish alley behind the prostitutes' bar. The engineer had taught the parrot to say over and over *Benvenuto in Italia.* Thanks to a parrot that is all the Italian I know. *Benvenuto in Italia. Benvenuto in Italia.* We had our own rooms now but I could hear that parrot through the wall. *Benvenuto in Italia.* All through the night. It was impossible to sleep. Another girl told her to throw a wrap over the cage. She did and it worked. The parrot was silent. After a shower, after dressing, after brushing teeth, after making her bed, then, she lifts the wrap, the parrot opens one eye, then the other, then its beak—*Benvenuto in Italia.*

On our next day off I went with her to the market. We took it in turns to carry the parrot back to where she had bought it. The man pretends he's never seen the parrot and carries on placing his merchandise over a wooden bench. She tried to give the parrot to a small boy. His eyes grew big. I thought his head would explode. He ran off. The parrot looked up through the bars, silent for once, looking so pitiful I was worried she was about to forgive it. But no. In a tea house the owner flirted with her but when she tried to gift the parrot he backed off with his hands in the air. In the street a man stopped to poke his finger through the bars. He and the parrot were getting on. But it was the same thing. They were happy to look, to admire, but no one wanted sole charge of that parrot. She began to think she would be stuck with that parrot forever.

I took the cage off her and we boarded a bus. The passengers were waiting for the driver to return with his cigarettes. I walked down the aisle dangling the cage over the heads of the passengers. Some fell against the window and folded their arms and closed their eyes. One after another they shook their heads. Back in the market people talked to the parrot, they stuck a finger through the bars for the parrot to nibble, they cooed back at the parrot. It turned its head on its side and gave them an odd look which made everyone laugh. But no one wanted to own a parrot. She asked me if I thought there was something wrong with her. Because how was it that she was the only one who had thought to own a parrot?

We returned to the hotel. It wasn't quite dark. We could hear some splashing from the pool. Some children. People were sitting around the outside bars. She took the parrot from me and set off to the unvisited end of the beach. I followed because I had come this far, and the whole time I had been following, so that now, just then, I did not know what else to do with myself. Down on the sand she kicked off her sandals. She placed the cage down and dragged one of the skiffs to the water. Had she asked for my advice I would have told her not to do this thing. Now I regret not saying anything. I was tired. I was sick of sharing the problem. I wanted only for the task to be over with. As she pushed the skiff out the parrot rolled its eye up at her, to look as though it possibly understood her decision and had decided it would choose dignity over fear.

In the night the wind blew up. I stayed in bed. But I can say what happened next because she told me. She also woke to the waves slapping on the beach but dozed off again without a thought for the parrot. The second time she woke it was still early. No one was up when she walked across the hotel grounds. She found the skiff hauled up on the beach. The cage was gone. Further up the beach she found the damp corpse of the parrot on top of the smouldering palm leaves. The groundsman was raking the sand. When she asked him about the cage he looked away. She thought she was going to hear a lie. Instead he told her to follow him. They go to the shed. He pulls back the beaded curtain. On the bench she sees the thin bars of the cage. The cage itself no longer exists. The bars have been cut off. She picks up one—holds it by its wooden handle, presses the sharpened point into the soft fleshy part of her hand. Well, she took the sticking knife as payment for the cage. That's the story about the knife.

She told me once that as soon as you know you are smart you just keep getting smarter. For me it hasn't happened yet. That's not to say it won't. When the Bible speaks of eternity I see one long line of surprises. It's not to say that that particular surprise won't come my way. I'm just saying I'm still waiting. But she got there first when she was promoted to staff supervisor. Now it was her turn to tell the new recruits that they smelt as fresh as daisies. You should see her now. The way she moved through the hotel. She would change the fruit bowl in reception without waiting to be asked. She says 'Have a nice day', as she has been taught, at the rear of the heavy white people waddling across the lobby for the pool. When a guest thanks her for picking up a towel from the floor she will smile and say 'You're welcome', and when told she sounds just like an American she will smile out of respect. The tourists replace one another. The world must be made of tourists. How is it I wasn't born a tourist? After four years in the hotel I could become a tourist because I know what to take pleasure in and what to complain about.

White people never look so white as when they wade into the sea under a midday sun. The women wade then sit down as they would getting into a bath. The men plunge and then they swim angrily. The women are picking up their towels from the sand as their men are still bashing their way out to sea. Then the men stop as if wherever they were hoping to get to has unexpectedly arrived. So they stop and they lie there with their faces turned up to the sky. When a wave passes under them they rise like food scraps, then the wave puts them down again. I used to wonder if these waves were employed by the hotel. I wondered if they too along with the palms had been through a hotel training course. 'Look how gently the sea puts them down,' she said. Look—and I did. 'See,' she said. 'There is nothing to be afraid of.'

One of the floating men was called Jermayne. He happened to catch her watching the white people at play in the sea. Not this time, but another time. I wasn't there. But this is what she told me. I hadn't set eyes on him yet so this is what she said about Jermayne. He was a black man. Yes, he had the same skin as her and me but he hadn't grown up in that skin. That much was easy to see. He had a way about him.

I remember asking her once—this would have been back at the other hotel on the Arabian Sea. We'd been lying there on our beds making lists of things to wish for, and I said, 'What about love?' Everyone needs loving. That too is in the Bible if you know where to look. I said, 'Don't you want to lie down with a man?' She burst out laughing. Now, under the palms in the hotel ground,

I asked her the question again. This time she looked away from me. She focused—as if there were so many ways of answering that question she couldn't decide on just one.

But with this man I can see she is interested. When I see her with him I stop whatever I'm doing to watch. She starts playing with her hair. Now she produces a smile I have never seen before. When I reported back to her what I had seen she said I had been blinded by wishfulness on her behalf. She said Jermayne had offered to teach her to swim. 'Well, that's good,' I said. 'That way you are bound to drown.' See how negative I sound. I don't know why that is. Why did I decide I didn't like Jermayne? Maybe instead of being smart I have developed some other kind of knowing.

Maybe it was his confidence. Maybe it was his unlived-in blackness. Maybe I just didn't like him. Does there have to be a reason? Then—I will say this here, just place it down for the time being. I thought I saw him. No. What do I mean by 'thought'? I did. I saw him with a woman. They were crossing the lobby in a hurry. But after that I didn't see her again. I decided she must have been another guest, entering the lift when he did, because the next day it was just Jermayne in the breakfast room.

When I saw them together, my friend and him, there were two Jermaynes. One is with her—that one she can see. But at the same time there is another Jermayne. This one is standing close by looking on and smiling to himself like he knows her thoughts before she does. He saw her reluctance to get in the pool whenever guests were using it. He read her like an open book. He had to insist—she laughed him off, pretending she didn't want to get wet after all. It was the same at the pool bar. Before Jermayne she had never had a drink with a hotel guest. Never ever—no, no, no, and the barman knew it, the stars knew it, the night knew it, the palms stood stunned in the background, and the little droplets splattering the poolside reminded everyone of the silence and the rules. She said Jermayne made it feel all right. Then it began to feel more and more right. She was no drinker. He had to explain what an outrigger was—the boat and the drink, and after that cocktail she said her thoughts drifted off to the parrot and its night out on the skiff and didn't drift back until Jermayne started to talk about his upbringing. An American father, a German mother. He grew up in Hamburg but now lived in Berlin. He had his own business, something with computers.

She is getting down off her stool when he reaches for her hand, then he leans over her and kisses her lightly behind the ear. A group of tourists were laughing like jackals at one end of the bar. She looked to see if anyone had seen. No one had—but Jermayne had, he had seen her looking, seen her eyes looking for trouble, for blame. He smiled. He told her to relax. She was safe. He wouldn't hurt her or do anything that would get her into trouble. That's not my calling—that's what he told her. He said now listen—and she did.

The next day—it was after her shift—I saw them paddle a skiff out to the artificial reef. I saw them pull the skiff up the beach and walk to the ocean side. This was her first swimming lesson. I didn't see any of it. This is just what she told me, and this was a good deal later, months later following the events that I am leading up to.

Her first swimming lesson begins with Jermayne walking into the sea up to his waist. He looks around to see if she has followed.

She hasn't moved from the sand. He tells her there's nothing to be afraid of. If he sees a shark he will grab the thing by its tail and hold it still until she has run back to shore. She is afraid, but she enters the water. The whole time she doesn't take her eyes off him. To do so, she feels, will see her tumble into an abyss. So, there they are walking deeper into the sea. She is also walking deeper into his trust—that is also true. The rest is straightforward. She did what he asked her to do. She lay down on the sea. She turned herself into a floating palm leaf. She felt his broad hand reach under her belly. Then she begins to float by herself. Every now and then her belly touches Jermayne's ready hand. Then, she said, it was just the idea of his hand that kept her afloat. I have never put my head under the sea so I can only go on what she said about it pouring into her ears and up her nostrils. I thought, I will never do that. I will never ever allow the sea to invade me. But she'd done it all wrong. That's the point—what she wished me to know. She'd forgotten to take a breath.

Jermayne gave her buoyancy. He taught her how to float like a food scrap. But it was a Dutchman who properly taught her. He never used the words 'trust me'. If he had she would not have listened. He would say 'like so…' and demonstrate the frog kick and the crawl. I haven't learnt those strokes myself, just the words. Frog kick. I like that. I'm not sure about the word 'crawl' any more, especially when I look out at a sea that is as vast as any desert. She tried to show me these things by lying flat on a bed. That's where she used to practise her strokes when the guests were using the pool. I had to pretend the bed was the sea. But I did not want to swim. Besides, what I have just said belongs to another story.

What I meant to say is this. With Jermayne it was all about her trusting him. And she did. Some of the things I will say now are what she told me. I was not there. How could I be? But this is what she said. When he asked her if she ever felt lonely, she had to stop and think. It had never occurred to her that she might feel lonely. I often wonder about that magic. Where does that feeling come from? If we don't know the word for our wants maybe that is better. Anyway, they are out at the pool bar. Everyone has moved inside. They are by themselves. Perhaps the barman is there. I don't know. After asking if she is ever lonely he touches her hand, moves his hand to her arm, now her neck. He asks if he can come to her room. 'No,' she tells him. She is the supervisor. She would have to sack herself. 'In that case,' he says, 'come to my room. Come and lie with me.' She looks around in case someone overheard. 'Trust me,' he says.

In Jermayne's room there was just the one embarrassing moment—there may have been others which I have since forgotten, but this is the one that has stuck. At some point he asks her if she would like to use the bathroom. She's surprised that he should ask. Why would he? Does he know when she needs to pee? Then she realises why he asked. It's because she has stood there rooted to the spot staring in at the white lavatory. It was the marvel of being in a guest's room without rushing to clean the toilet bowl and tie a paper band around it to declare it is hygienically fit for use. Or to spray the door knobs so the room will smell nice or to punch the pillows and turn up the bed.

She stayed the night—well not quite because she woke to the noise of the generators. There had been a power cut. She got out of bed and dressed and returned unseen to the staff quarters. I know she stayed with him the next night, and the one after. Then Jermayne flew back to Germany. He said he would ring. I did not think he would. But I underestimated him. Sometimes I would see her on the phone in the lobby and I would know it was him calling across the sea. A month later he was back, this time for a shorter stay, and it must have been during this period that she became pregnant. I was the only one to know. At first I should say, because eventually there is no hiding a pregnancy.

Jermayne came and stayed another two times. The last time was for the birth. The hotel gave her time off. Jermayne rented an apartment in a nice neighbourhood on the other side of town from the market. I visited her there once. It was nice, quiet. There were no flies. He insisted she stay there with him. For a short time they lived as man and wife. She rang me once at the hotel. She said she just wanted to hear my voice, to be sure we still occupied the same world. She was visited by a doctor. She had never seen a doctor. He took her blood pressure and her pulse and put his hands where a midwife would. Jermayne was there, holding her hand. She listened to him ask the doctor questions. Many, many questions. Until he was satisfied the baby would be a healthy one. She had never known anyone to show so much care. When her waters broke there was a taxi waiting to take her to hospital. That Jermayne thought of everything.

They hadn't talked about what would happen next. I was sure Jermayne would take her to Germany. There she might start a new life. She was willing. I sensed that. She hoped that was what Jermayne had in mind. She never did ask. She did not want to burden him with a surprise. Of course she hoped it would not be a surprise, that the plans she saw clicking away behind his eyes involved her. He was with her at all times, even for the delivery, and before, too, breathing with her, holding her hand.

Many hours later a baby boy is clamped to her breast. And there is Jermayne with a bunch of flowers. There are forms to fill out. Jermayne has thought of everything. Some of the forms are in another language, Deutsch, she sees. She checked with Jermayne. He explains, it is like taking possession of something. You have to sign for it. Like signing in for a room. So she did, she signed where he indicated on the forms. After two days in hospital a taxi brought her back to Jermayne's apartment. He'd been out to buy baby clothes. He put her and the baby to bed. At night they lay with the baby between them. Once she asked Jermayne to come and lie next to her. She wanted to feel his hand on her, like the times when he was teaching her how to float. He turned his head on the pillow. A car's headlights found the window and in that single moment she saw him with his eyelids closed.

He insists she stay in bed. She has to mend. She tells him nothing is broken. But he doesn't hear. Jermayne has to do things the Jermayne way. He doesn't hear what he doesn't want to hear.

One morning she woke to the sound of the shower running. It was very early, yet when Jermayne comes out of the bathroom he is fully dressed. His face alters a little to find her sitting up in bed. He puts on a smile. Yes. A nice smile. A smile to calm the world. He puts a finger to his lips to shush her. They don't want to wake the baby. He sits on the edge of the bed. He bends down to tie his shoelaces. She watches him doing this, wanting to speak, to ask what he thinks he's lost because now he's walking from one corner of the apartment to another. Now he's found it. A baby carrier. It's the first time she's seen it. Now he comes to his side of the bed and picks up the baby. He presses his nose to its belly. He always does that. She likes it when he does that. Jermayne will be a good father, a loving father.

The baby stirs; its eyes are still fiercely shut when it opens its mouth and makes a waking noise. At last they can talk. He says it is time for the baby to get some air. He doesn't want to take him out when the sun is up. It will be too hot. He stresses to her the importance that he get used to different air. So he will take the baby for a short walk. Not far. He doesn't want to tire him out. Just as far as the gardens at the end of the road and back. He holds the baby out to her. 'Kiss Mummy goodbye,' he says. She kisses the baby's cheek. Then she lies back, head on pillow, hands on her belly, eyes closed. Then she reaches a hand into the space beside her. How strange it is to find that space empty. How quiet the apartment suddenly feels. It feels wrong. She tries keeping her eyes closed but it is no good. There is nothing to mend, no tiredness to collapse into. That's when she gets out of bed. She walks to the window. Maybe she will see Jermayne and the baby, and she does. There they are—well, the top of Jermayne's head. There is also a taxi. The back door opens and a woman gets out. Jermayne hands over the baby and the woman cradles the baby in her arms, rocks the baby, looks at its face for a long time, then she lowers her face into the bundle. Jermayne holds the door of the taxi. He looks up once to the windows of the apartment. Now the woman and the baby get in the back, followed by Jermayne, the door closes, and the taxi moves up the street.

The rest I don't know. I don't know how she spent the hours waiting for Jermayne to return. I don't know what her thoughts were. But, for only the second time in my life, there is a phone call for me. I hear the whole story, and when she comes to the bit about the strange woman waiting by the taxi I know who that woman is; it is the same woman I thought I saw with Jermayne months earlier. They crossed the lobby together. She went into the lift ahead of him. At that moment I felt quite sure they were together. In a hotel you quickly learn who is alone and which ones are couples, and which ones are unhappy. And when you change their sheets you know more still. I never saw that woman again. And remember, at breakfast there was just Jermayne.

But as soon as I hear about the woman getting out of the taxi I see the woman walking slightly ahead for the lifts, and I see Jermayne gesture with his hand for her to go in first, and I see, as if for the first time, the woman open and close her purse, and as the lift doors are closing I see her turn to Jermayne. This is information that sits inside my mouth. Perhaps one day I will spit it out and tell her. But as she is telling me about that woman getting out of the taxi I hold my tongue and at the same time I feel a prickly heat cover me from head to toe. This is my cross to bear. But listen to what I say to myself. If I tell her, I feel I will lose a friend. Because if I tell her she will think she has lost a friend. A friend would have shared such information. Why did I not say something at the time? She will want to know. And I don't know what I might say. Now I do know. I would have said I wanted her to be happy.

It was another two days until my day off. I walked across the city to the apartment. It was very hot. No one else was out. There were cars. But no one was walking. I was walking because I had only enough money for the trip back to the hotel in the taxi.

I was expecting her to be upset. I'm not saying she wasn't. But most people when they are upset will cry or wave their arms about. Not her. She was still, very still. Still as a hotel palm on one of those hot breathless days. I gave her a hug but I can't say I felt flesh, not breathing, living kind of flesh. She lowered her eyes away from me. She would not let me see her or get near to how she felt. Perhaps there was no way of getting closer. I only know she was glad I was there to bring her home to the hotel.

The hotel managers were surprised to find her back on the roster. Like everyone else they had imagined she would move away with Jermayne. They thought of her story as a good luck story. A bit of star dust had fallen out of the sky and landed at her feet. That's how they saw it. I backed up her miscarriage story. The management were kind. They gave her time off. One of the women gave her a hug. A man we hardly ever saw, he had something to do with laundry, he gave her flowers. Soon she was back in uniform, back to supervisor, but there was no going back to that person she had been.

She did not smile at the guests. She looked right through them when they made their little complaints. She did not care. I saw her take a skiff out to the artificial reef. She did that by herself. I would like to have gone out there but she didn't invite me and I didn't ask because these were pilgrimages. I could see her quite clearly, walking up and down that shoreline looking off in the direction of Europe.

One afternoon while I am looking at that solitary figure on the reef Mr Newton from management comes up behind me and whispers in my ear. How would I like to be made supervisor? Well I am still that person today. I don't know what tomorrow will bring. I am happy. I believe in love. I would like some of that to fall out of the sky and land at my feet one day. But before I bend down and pick it up I will be sure of what it is first.

two

The inspector

The boat she paid for stank of fish. She never saw the pilot. There were crew—a few men, always with their backs turned to her—and the others. It was at night and so it was hard to know exactly how many of them there were. But then cargo doesn't ever stop and think to count.

To pay for her berth she had hotel sex with foreigners—counting the Dutchman who had taught her to swim. She had saved money of all denominations and currencies. Some she thought must be Chinese, but also euros and pounds and American dollars. She rolled these notes over and over into a cigar which she slipped inside of herself for safe keeping.

For hours there was just the slap of the sea against the bowsprit. The cargo sat huddled. People from different parts of the continent. No one speaking for fear of being overheard. The danger is around them, thickly layered, ears filled with good hearing, eyes able to pierce the darkest night. They sit with their bundles of belongings. They sit on top of their emptied bowels. They haven't eaten for hours, half a day or more. They have been advised it is better that way.

The slowing of the boat made everyone sit taller. Heads turned. Those seated opposite peered back across her shoulder. That's when she turned and saw the coastal lights of Europe. From the area of the stern there came a loud splash. She watched a black face scramble and clutch a buoy at the side of the boat. The man was still hugging it as the boat pulled away. Now, for the first time, she heard the instructions. Another boat would be by to pick them up. They aren't to worry. They can expect to be in the sea for upwards of an hour. They should hang onto the buoy and wait. There is no need to be afraid. It will work to plan just as it has so many times before. She was reminded of the hotel voice used to placate guests—gentle, reassuring, smiling. The water will soon be back on. It won't be much longer before the electricity is restored. A repair man is on his way to your room. Of course you may drink the water if you so choose but it is not advisable.

There was a splash. Another body writhed in the unfamiliar, and, as before, a pair of frightened eyes receded into the night.

An older man sitting further along the gunwale quietly announces he cannot swim. He is sitting with a box of belongings on his lap, his long peasant arms thrown over it. No one said anything and no one turned to look at the splash he made.

She can at least swim. The Dutchman used to sneak her into the hotel pool at night. He told her to lie in the water and to pretend it was a bed, then he had shown her how to move her arms and to think that the thing she was reaching for lay continually beyond her grasp.

A face wearing a black woollen cap crouches near her. As the boat quietly comes around she sees the buoy. She had taken off her sneakers and is bending down to pick them up when a hand shoves her and she falls on her side into the sea. Briefly, miraculously, she doesn't seem to get wet. She is in the water but it isn't in her. It was just for a split second, something for hope and amazement to cling to. Then all at once the water seeped through her clothing and she thrashed around in the sea at the shock of it until she felt the hard plastic of the buoy.

The boat moved away, and the night and a sense of the void walled up around her. In the unseen distance she heard another splash. From the boat the coastal lights had been clear. Now she can't see them any more. The sea is in the way, heaving and dragging her around the buoy. The buoy is difficult to hold. It is too big, too round. She has to settle for hanging onto its anchoring rope and changing hands whenever one arm tires.

How long was she in the water? What is time under those circumstances? What is an hour? What is ten minutes? Time can be measured in other ways. By the cold. By fear. By the length of time it takes for flesh to turn numb and then to rot and come away from her bones. She began to doubt the words of the crew. Or else something had happened. That was more believable because whatever was supposed to happen rarely did.

She saw the sun rise and draw itself against the sky. The last of the blinking lights died. The sea bulged up, and the line of Europe turned to mist.

The Dutchman had taught her to swim like a dog. 'Dog paddling.' On her own she had managed only one length. But he'd encouraged her to keep going, to practise. After a month she could do fifty lengths of the pool. Once, to the amusement of a hotel guest who sat the whole time on a recliner with a cocktail, she swam one hundred lengths to win a bet of ten dollars.

Her shoulders ache, her lips are swollen, her eyes hurt. Her skin wants nothing more to do with her. It has lost the silky touch that guests always liked to comment on. Whenever they stopped to pet her she liked to watch the slow marvel of herself emerge in the eyes and face of a perfect stranger.

Late afternoon she made up her mind to swim. She has a plastic bag with her containing her hotel uniform and the sticking knife made out of the birdcage wire. She will take the buoy with her.

The first task is to get the knife out. Despite the hours spent in the sea, her uniform is still dry. Inside the plastic bag she can make out the fold of a sleeve. The knife is rolled up inside her skirt. She has to pick at the knot with the fingers of one hand. Her other hand holds onto the buoy. More than once she lets go of the rope in order to pick the knot with both hands. Each time there is some progress before the sea parts and she sinks. Once when she thought she nearly had it her head was underwater. But that time failed as well and she surfaced—panicked to think her sinking could happen so quickly, so easily, that it could happen with a lapse in concentration. She remembered once seeing a woman chew an umbilical cord off. When she bites the knot off the top of the plastic bag it releases a puff of domestic air, of laundered air.

She has to get the knife out without getting the uniform wet, and then re-tie the bag, not so tightly this time, or so loosely that the sea would get in.

It took an age to work through the mooring rope, a strand at a time; when she cut through the last one the buoy jumped away from her and she had to swim after it. Her body wouldn't do what she wanted it to. It behaved like a board. Every limb felt stiff. Each time she reached the buoy, it moved away at her touch and she had to dog paddle after it. She thought she had lost the buoy, she thought that was it, she had made it this far, so close to land, when her hand came into contact with the trailing rope. Now, at least, she will not sink. The rest will be up to her. With one hand against the buoy and the other clutching the rope she begins to frog kick for the coast.

She was still kicking as the sun went down. She had the awful feeling of moving away from land not towards it. She kept on though, there was no other option. Then at some point in the night she had the opposite feeling. She could feel herself being drawn towards the shore. There were the lights she'd seen the previous night. It is not as far as she had thought.

As a child she drew pictures of the sea and the world above. Where the two met she used to draw a shelf that rose like a hotel ramp for wheelchairs. This is how Europe arrives too. She finds herself in that vapid ghosted water pissed in by dogs and humans. There, a soggy wad of paper. Here, the sightless eyes of a fish-head turning on a coil of memory. After two nights at sea she lifted her face out of the pissy shallows into a soft murmuring air and a row of sunbathing feet pointing out to sea.

One by one the sunbathers raise themselves off their recliners. They sit up, faces behind sunglasses and under white floppy hats. Pointing, she thought, but perhaps not. She struggles up onto weakened knees holding onto the precious plastic bag, manages a few steps, staggering like a crippled old woman. Because of all those people she feels she has to walk, she has to move. She forces a smile onto her tight face, picks a direction and keeps to the wet shingle. If she smiles any harder her face will split. She doesn't allow herself to look up the beach. At the first hotel she used to experience the same flush of guilt whenever she looked too long at the bowl of fruit put out for guests in the reception area. That flush of guilt was a puzzle to her, because it wasn't as though she had wanted for food at the hotel. It was something to do with abundance—and she knew that abundance lay just back from the beach. So she puts on her hotel face and keeps to the shoreline until she leaves the last of the sunbathers.

It is stony underfoot. The tide rushes around her ankles, dragging scraps and bits of plastic back into the sea. She won't look, not yet. She will not permit herself a glance up the beach. In the same way she used to avoid the unwanted attentions of certain hotel guests. Then the air changes. It smells of the boat, that fishy smell. She has come to a breakwater, a sloping wall of boulders. There is no more shoreline to follow. Now she will risk it. She turns her head away from the sea and the wet shingle to a line of row boats resting on their sides. She walks up to the first one, drops onto the sand beside it and pulls the ribbed hull down on top of her.

three

The inspector

In May the south is the first part of Europe to warm. The birds awaken from the tiny monuments of winter. The first of the super-sized tourist buses arrive. The gypsies begin their shift north. The flotillas from Libya and Tunisia resume their hazardous voyages across the Mediterranean. The surveillance flights increase—and with depressing regularity come reports of Africans in the sea, popping up like corks, Africans clinging to wreckage, arms slung over debris, they cling on, wait. Sometimes a rescue boat turns up, sometimes not.

The cafes around the station provide coffee, ashtrays, snacks. The barmen look like barmen, raised from birth to become barmen. They have the same large faces, lower jawbones that weigh the face down beneath folds of flesh that enclose secrets. They have been trained to listen in such a way that they do not remember what is said. They are like the elected representatives of ghosts.

They accept that she may have passed through, yes, they are quick to accept that possibility but no one appears to remember. Was she tall? So, so? No? Shorter? They can't be sure, they are reluctant to say. Given their uncertainty, to say one thing and not another would be misleading. You know how it is. They do not wish to mislead.

They cannot possibly notice every crab abandoned by the tide.

So where might one look? A hint, please.

They come as far as the door and point to the ramp leading onto the autoroute. That is the way a ghost might disappear into Europe.

At a small truck stop the man behind the cash register inclined his head to one of the corner tables where a large driver, all stomach and round knees, sat open-mouthed and frowning at a newspaper spread between out-held arms. He lost his glasses a few days earlier, and his wife's don't work for him as well as his own. So his eyes burn holes in the newsprint—an obituary of someone important, a shocking sports result, a new tax proposal, his horoscope for the day. He doesn't mind the interruption. He snaps up the newspaper and peeks over the female frames. His gaze was direct, helpful. He rolled his thick tongue. Pushed out his chair. Tugged at his trouser belt, transferred his weight, and then we were at the window. But how did the truck driver get there? Without any discernible movement of his feet. His breath comes in rapid gasps, each word a new gasp. Antonio is the one to ask. His truck comes across on the ferry from Messina. And if he asks for the name of the man who pointed him out? Gatti. You may say Gatti. Who Gatti? Just Gatti. Gatti. Gatti. There, ask Antonio.

Antonio is sitting in his cab, the long mileage visible in his face. His window is down. He was about to light a cigarette, but stopped in order to listen. Then without a word spoken he pointed to the passenger-side door. These trucks are high. It takes effort—how is it that so many truck drivers such as Gatti are fat? Not Antonio though. He is whippet thin. Skin and bone. Shirt sleeves buttoned down to the wrist. One hand resting on the gear stick. Face pale. His eyebrows are dark, so is his hair, not a single grey hair either. Possibly mentally slow. How old? Late thirties, early forties? Forty-one would be a good guess. The skin around his throat is the colour of rash. At different moments the rash makes it up to his cheekbones, at other times it subsides to a full pale face, non-committal. His breath is unsteady, nervous around authority.

He took his hand off the gear stick and pushed the cigarette back in his mouth and lit it. He directed the smoke out the side window and then held the cigarette in front of his face and slowly nodded. There was such a person, he said. She stood up the road away from the prostitutes. Black? Yes, it was her. Because it was clear she was not a prostitute he stopped for her. Why would that be? Why did he stop for her? He's thought about stopping for one of the prostitutes, one of the Albanian or Bulgarian girls. He's thought about it, then afterwards he's felt regretful. By his own admission some of these girls are brazen. They compete with one another. One may pull her top down and shake her tits in his headlights. Another lifts her skirt, and in a passing flash he notes she wasn't wearing panties. Then he might drive off with a memory that might make him regretful, wishful, and so when a woman emerges from the trees further up the road this time he might find himself responding with heart-racing decisiveness to slow down and pull over.

four

The truck driver

She wore a coat. A scarf around her neck. When she climbed up to the cab she unwound the scarf and put it in her coat pocket. I do not remember what colour. It was dark. I asked her where she was headed. At first she did not understand. No lingo. No Italiano. She pointed to the map on the dash. She spoke English. I understand some words. Beckham. Manchester United. Sally. Words to some songs. Yesterday. Summertime. I showed her which road we were on. So I ask her again. Where does she want to go? This time she understands. It is clear. She wants to go north. North, I understand. *Buono!* I don't mind. Sometimes it is good for a driver to have someone to talk to. I have my radio. Whenever there is a football match I listen. I have my mobile. Every night I ring my children. My wife is often too tired to speak. Sometimes she is in bed when I call and from my lonely stretch of road I will sing to her. People tell me I have a fine voice. I like to sing. Sometimes at the other end I will hear my wife sigh and it is like we are young again. So, to pass the time, I sing to the black woman. Everyone understands music. Why? Because in my humble opinion music bypasses the meaning. It addresses the heart.

While I sang she kept her eyes on the road; they did not budge but she smiled. I sang and when I stopped she kept smiling. I always carry chocolate. I offered her some and she put it in her coat pocket. That annoyed me. I felt angry. But why? I offered her chocolate and she accepted. That part did not make me angry. That's what I hoped she would do, that is why I offered it. But why did she put it into her pocket? That's the part that made me feel angry. I don't know why it should. She did not look at me. She look at the road. I wondered if she was late. The way she looked at the road, you see, as if it was in the way, and there is still more road to cover before she will get to where she has to go.

I offer her a cigarette, this time she shakes her head. She is like a zombie woman. She can't take her eyes off the road ahead. Now I wish I didn't pick her up. I turn on the radio. It is not the same as my singing. The music makes it worse, adds to the strain I am feeling in the cab. The silence, the black road rolling away from the window, the night closed all around me and this black woman who does not speak or eat chocolate or say anything about my singing. Which if I may be immodest is unusual. I used to sing for my village choir. We entered competitions. I might have been a singer. My wife who was not my wife just then but a beautiful girl got pregnant. Timing is everything in this world. A rabbit runs across the road and is crushed beneath my tyres. Another runs out and makes it to the other side.

Finally we come to the turn-off. I know she wants to go north, so this is where we part. I begin to slow down, switch lanes. For the first time—no, perhaps it is the second time—since I picked her up she looks at me. She doesn't understand why we are stopping. I show her on the map where I have to go and then I point to the road north. But she refuses to understand. Refuses. She does not understand the divide in the road that we have come to. I find some paper and draw her a picture. I draw a picture of her and one of me. 'North,' she says. I understand. It is clear. I direct her attention to the map. I show her the road I must take. We have pulled over. I am a very safe driver. At this hour there is not a lot of traffic. Mainly trucks, a few cars, not many.

We sit there as the traffic rushes by. Outside, the tall shadows of the roadside trees shift. I wind down the window. It is colder. We have been climbing. It is not a nice feeling to drop a young woman off in the night. It is very late. At that hour things happen that good people asleep in their beds cannot imagine. I don't feel good about it. I think—what if she was my own daughter? Would I drop her off? I offer to take her west. She can come with me, and at first light I will drop her at the railway station. 'North,' she says. 'I must go north. Please,' she asks. So I look at the map. There is a loop road that I can take. But it means driving an extra hundred kilometres. The company will want to know why I went through so much diesel. I will be asked to account for the roads taken. That is a future conversation. For now I don't bother the girl with my concerns. Then I change my mind again. I decide then and there. She must get out. I point outside. I explain to her, here we have to part. I have to get on my way.

Deaf ears. She stays put. Says nothing. She stares at the road ahead, but not as before when she appeared to lean forward seeking north. Now she sits there stubbornly, her arms folded. She is thinking. She takes a deep breath and breathes out. Then she unhooks her belt and she leans across to rest her hand on my thigh, she moves her hand to my crotch, just a little, like bath water rising up the sides, like so, nice, very nice. She smiles but not like before when I was singing, this is a different smile. I wouldn't like to say how but it is, and it is a smile I understand. I have seen it on the faces of the prostitutes talking up to the drivers who have pulled off the road.

'I must go north,' she says. I light a cigarette. Her hand is still on my thigh. Though the feeling is dead now, not like before, just a weight. Three cars go by, a truck, a big one that shakes the cab and blows its horn into the night. A lonesome noise that leaves us alone once more. I feel responsible. She won't get another ride until daybreak. She is someone's daughter. While I'm smoking and having these thoughts she undoes my trouser belt, she unbuttons me. No one is holding a gun to my temple, it's true, but I feel just as helpless. We all have our weaknesses. So I show her on the map where she will have to get out of the cab, just so there is no misunderstanding. She agrees. Fine. It is another hour and twenty minutes. Road works force a detour, a much longer one. Now the company will ask difficult questions. What will I tell them? I have no idea. Still, I keep this matter to myself. She keeps her hand on my crotch. It is a nice feeling. I won't deny it. I don't lie about such things. I understand the nature of the arrangement now. It is late, 2am. While driving I wonder what north means. Ask people in the north and they will direct you to a point further north. I suppose you arrive at some point where north suddenly turns south. The way I see it, we all live with north and south inside of us.

I turn on the radio. The music feels right now. It helps me to relax. I hum and she keeps her hand steady on the rock. The time passes quickly. Too quickly if I am honest. Yes. I am honest. Why not? I am a hardworking truck driver. I don't earn much but enough, and I have my beautiful wife and my beautiful children. And I am a man. I have nothing to hide. Nothing at all.

We reach the junction. It is up ahead, some lights, there's some movement. I slow down. In the lit windows of the truck driver's stop people are up. They sit swaying back from one another, trying to stay awake. I think she will be safe. So I park. As I release the brake she takes her hand away and suddenly sits up. As she reaches for the door I lock it from my side. I am surprised. I did not take her for such a woman. In my part of the world a person's honour rests on their word. I am very disappointed. I have shown good faith. I have gone out of my way. I have done so with a selfless regard. There will be the questions concerning fuel. But she... she has forgotten the nature of our arrangement, I don't need to remind you, that she initiated. I am not really a political person. My wife's family were Communists, every one of them. When the old man asked me for my political affiliations I told him I am a singer. I am not led by belief. I am led by the heart. Goodness has a way of singing that everyone recognises. It is what makes us human. This is sincerely my belief. Honestly. One's word. These are the things that I go by. To some extent the world depends on such understanding and compliance. I have acted in good faith. I have driven out of my way. This is time I will have to make up.

Well, she understands her mistake. She tries the door again, then she understands some more. She must do what she must do. She unbuttons her coat. And she takes me in her mouth. It is a lonely life. A lonely life. But there are moments of happiness. And one must not take them for granted. We can't ever be sure when our luck will shine again. I am happy. I unlock the door. She is free to go. Instead she kicks it open with the back of her heel, like the *Carabinieri* kicking down the door to a criminal's house, she does that in my cab, and at the same time, although it cannot be exactly at the same moment, perhaps I am mixed up, perhaps I am still fuming at her treatment of the door, I am still in that moment as she leans across to say 'Thank you.' Yes, why not? 'Thank you,' she says. It was on this second thank you that she spat my seminal fluid over my trousers, and in my face. It was not an accident. No. Of course not. I'm afraid I lost my temper. It was a spur of the moment thing. I struck her. Then she wrestled with me. She bit my hand. I thought my hand was in the jaws of a dog. She broke the skin. I can show you. There is some discolouration, some damage. For months after I had the tooth marks on my hand.

Two days later I arrive home. I am eating the meal that my beautiful wife has cooked when she notices the tooth marks on my hand. I am the luckiest man in the world, and I wish for nothing ever to disturb that happiness. Do you know what I told her? I told her I was attacked by a dog. When I told her that I did not think for a moment that I was lying.

five

The elderly snail collector

A snail leaves a viscous trail. At a certain hour the rooftops of the traffic blur, turn back into their core element, and melt. I wonder what the hills see, I wonder about centuries-old patience. Why is it the sky cannot be trusted, but hills can? Does it have to do with the quarrelling respective values of stillness and shiftiness? The discreet hills. The same cannot be said about the sky. Whenever I look for the remaining vestiges of 'before'—before the devastation caused by mass transport, the roads, the autoroutes, the trucks roaring into the night, and without any of the delicacy of ships dissolving into the horizon, without the subtlety of the railways, I look to the sedate movement of the snail. I collect snails like others collect vintage model train sets. I am a collector. I collect the Roman snail and the larger *Helix aperta*. They are remarkable. The shell is so delicate. What creature would create its work of art out of the very fragility that condemns it? Look at its whorls. Look at its colour. At first glance you think, Ah, yes, a brown shell. It is brown only because that is what you expected it to be. In fact it is green, but it is unlike any green you have seen. Unlike any. I detest the word 'like', by the way. 'Unlike' is only marginally better. What I mean is this. The shell is its own thing. Unlike any other. Sufficiently alike, or like, but subtly different. Its uniqueness is woven into plain everyday ordinariness.

It was very early in the morning when I saw her, curled up at the base of a tree. Her knees were drawn up, and her hands were pressed between her thighs. *Achatina fulica*—that is the giant African snail. Strange that I should think of that just then, but I did. A plastic bag filled with clothing was her pillow. At that time of year and at this altitude the nights have an edge. She must have drawn a blue coat over herself in the manner of a blanket. In the night she must have kicked it off because it lay beside her, unoccupied, if such a thing can be said of a coat. I have over eleven thousand snail shells in my collection. I collect my snail and then the first thing I must do is to get rid of the occupant. I feed them to the cat. Although some I eat. Certain varieties. Not all. You must be careful, not as careful as with mushrooms, but still careful. I clean the shell. Then I varnish it so it will not break. When I look at my shell I never spare a thought for its previous occupant. If I did I would put myself up before a war crimes tribunal. I cannot afford to be sentimental. At the same time I cannot look at a shell without thinking of it as unoccupied space. I don't know if anyone finds that interesting. I do. Because I ask myself the questions: How is it that those two observations belong to the same thing? How is it that they don't fit, like so, in my head?

Anyway, I saw the woman curled up at the base of the tree, asleep, like a creature from a fairytale. She is African. How did she get here? Here at the base of an oak outside a village of two hundred permanent souls of mainly elderly people. I did not notice her until I was almost upon her. That is because when I walk I am looking for snails. If I was a birder concentrating on the tree tops I might not have seen her. But I walk as though I am afraid of my shoelaces twisting around one another. So another mushroom collector described me once. A silly old man who fancied me and used my distraction as an excuse to follow me because he feared I would walk over a cliff or topple into a hole. Of all the men who have pursued me these past fifty years it is the older ones who are the most inventive. I suspect it is because they no longer expect to be believed no matter what they say, so they might as well stretch the truth. At times I am susceptible to such invention. I suspect it is because in the snail world anything is possible. What other creature is a female in one season, and male in another? I am still waiting to hear a tale to rival that fact.

I stood at a distance looking at her. I stepped closer and stopped, then I moved again. She did not move. So I sat down beside her. I ate a sandwich. I poured tea from a thermos. It was still very early. I had forgotten my giant African snail. I was watching the day find its way through the trees. The light moved to her legs, onto her hip, it moved up to her face and an eyelid fell open. She saw me. She sat up. She snatched her coat to herself. At seventy-eight who expects to give anyone such a fright? I laughed. I reassured her. I tried. It is hard to calm someone when they do not speak your language. I gave her a sandwich. She sniffed at it before eating it. When I passed her my cup she did not sniff its contents. It was hot and I could see she wanted to drink faster than it would allow her to. I showed her my bag of snails. She looked at me differently then—I saw the thought take hold in her face: I was a harmless old woman. I think I preferred it to when she was afraid of me. Then she let go of that look and smiled.

She stayed with me for two days. Of course she was an illegal immigrant. Of course. I didn't need to ask. She was very polite. I would cook the meal, then she would clear away the dishes and wash up. In the morning she made her bed. I have never seen a bed so perfectly made. Maps. She was interested in maps. I don't own a map. I had to borrow a book of maps from my late husband's sister. I woke up one morning to a stillness in the house. I lay there looking across to the window. I knew she was gone. Eventually I got up. I sang my way along the hall to the kitchen. I put on the jug. Then I checked her room. The bed was perfectly made. Normally you'd have said of such a bed it was unslept in. But with her I don't think so. She must have left very early. She had taken the road directory with her.

six

The chess player

It was two or three in the morning the first time I saw her. I had got up for a piss. On my way through the front room I looked out the window. I could see someone asleep on a bench across the road. It's a small park, nothing much. During the day mothers set their toddlers down there. People walk their dogs. There's a fountain that is always breaking down. And there's that bench I mentioned. I thought it was a drunk, then I decided it wasn't, it was none of my business and I went back to bed. The next night I get up. I'm standing over the cistern pissing when I remember the person from the night before. On my way back through the front room I pull back the curtain. There she is, lying on the bench. I think no more about it. Then the next day on my way home from work I detour through the park and sit on the same bench where I've seen the person sleeping. The bench is worn, shiny. I try lying along it but I can't get comfortable. It's too short and it's hard. I don't have enough flesh on my hip bone but I try curling up the way I've seen the person do. My wife is coming home from doing the washing at her sister's—our machine is broken—when she sees me curled up on the bench. She crosses the road to ask what I'm doing. That's one of the harder questions I've had to answer recently. What am I doing? There's only one answer I can give her. I tell her I don't know. She says I must know, otherwise, why would I be lying on the bench? She puts down the washing bag. She asks, 'Did something happen?' Am I experiencing chest pains—again? She insists on taking my pulse. By now I'm sitting up. I tell her I'm fine. She's fussing over nothing. Just because she saw me lying along a bench doesn't mean I am dying. Many people lie on benches. I've seen them myself. 'Who?' she asks. I nearly say black people. Instead I say, 'Members of the public.' She says she can't recall the name of a single person who she's seen lying along a bench like a common drunk. So that's the problem. But she's smart enough to shift tack. She reminds me of my father's death, my uncle's death, the whole motley collection of hearts whose club I have no choice but to accept membership of. In the end she makes me promise to see a doctor.

Well, that night I get up for a piss. I check on my way to the toilet. This time the woman is sitting on the bench, very upright. I decide I won't flush the toilet. I don't want to wake my wife. I put on a dressing gown and slip my feet into a pair of sports trainers. On the landing I have a change of heart. The only people out in dressing gowns and trainers in the middle of the night are nutters. So I go back inside and put on my clothes. I slip out of the apartment. I take the stairs. The lift at that hour can wake the entire building. It is very late. Four am. For some that is an early hour. For me it is both. Possibly more late than early. Depending on chess nights. There's no one else around. As soon as I come out to the street the woman looks up. I have an idea she had been sleeping. An African face. That's a surprise. You don't see many blacks around here. Up north in Rome, yes. On the beaches selling trinkets, those tall, robed guys with skullcaps, and on TV. I used to watch a lot of NBA; that was back in Split. I wander across the road, hands in my jacket pockets. She gets up. I hold up a hand to show that I mean no harm. She's in a smart blue coat. There's a plastic bag of belongings beside her. When she sees me look at it she quickly picks it up. The view from the window was misleading. I can see she's not your usual piece of crap whose life has bottomed out on drugs or bad luck. It's probably why I ask if she would like a cup of coffee. I've never offered a stranger a cup of coffee before in my life. I'm surprised how normal and natural I sound to my own ears. I'm also surprised to hear myself say that I'm an insomniac, which isn't true but could be. She puts her plastic bag down on the bench. In English she explains that she doesn't like coffee. I know some English from the British soldiers stationed in Split. My English wasn't good enough for communications. Socially it was good enough. Funny to think of them still there playing tennis and cricket while we are now in Italy. My wife is Italian, which is why we are here.

A taxi with a single person slumped in the back goes by. I begin to notice the cats. During the day I never notice them, but at this hour the streets are filled with strays. The place I had in mind for a drink is closed. So we set off for another one which I prefer anyway. After ten minutes' walking we discover it is also closed. Our lack of success has made her nervous. She wants to return to the park. We're standing under a street light. For the first time I get a good look at her. She's young. Mid to late twenties. She might be older. It's hard to tell with blacks. I ask her where home is. She doesn't answer—not at first. But because I continue to wait for an answer she says she has no home.

Everyone has a home. They might hate it but it is still home. I pass that thought on but she doesn't reply. Silence would indicate some bad history. I think so. It is none of my business. Still I wonder, as you do. I wonder how she came to this neighbourhood, to this town, and why she sleeps on the bench, and if she has to sleep out why that bench. Is there something special about that bench? We are back there now. I look up at the windows. My wife will be sleeping. I will crawl back to bed and she won't know I have been gone. Just when I think she has swallowed her tongue she answers—Berlin. Berlin. That's where she wants to go. Then she asks me which road she should take. I almost laugh. I tell her there is no arrow at the end of the street pointing to Berlin, Germany. She says she plans to thumb a ride. But she's lost. For the moment at least. Her last ride was angry with her for some reason. He dropped her in an out-of-the-way place. She walked here. She walked until she came to this park. The autoroute is ten k, too far to walk. She has a road guide with her. But our town is too small to have a street directory in it. I offer to drive her to the on ramp. She looks at me as if I might be wanting something in return. But I don't. Just to help if I can. I tell her to wait. The car is parked at my mother-in-law Gina's place up the road. But first I have to climb the stairs back to the apartment to get the keys. In the front room I look out the window. She's standing by the bench looking both ways as if she is expecting someone. Briefly I consider ditching my offer and going back to bed. It would be so much easier.

I'm still thinking that thought as I close the apartment door and run down the stairs. She's ready, all set to go, clutching her plastic bag. We walk up the road to Gina's. Now Gina is an insomniac. A real insomniac. It would be just like her, just my luck, for her to look out the window and see her son-in-law who I feel she tolerates rather than loves walking the street with an unidentified black woman. I look up at Gina's windows half expecting to see her. The garage has a roller door. It makes a low rumbling which I never hear during the day. I finish winding and point to the passenger side of the wagon. When she gets in she closes the door quietly after her. It's a small thing, but I notice it. Closing the door quietly like that. Makes me feel slightly uneasy. But then she clips on her seatbelt and I find that reassuring. At least she is not a criminal or an addict. Once she would have been an explorer and I would have been a Bedouin offering my hospitality to her in the night. You see—you see what's going on here. Already I'm thinking about my story, and how to explain, should my wife wake up in the night to find me gone.

There's little traffic. Some trucks making their way back to the autoroute. I have to stop short of the ramp. I don't want to get onto the autoroute. Otherwise it'll be another thirty minutes before I can get off the thing. So I park and get out of the car. She gets out her side. I point her in the right direction. We can hear the traffic, that low roar overhead. I feel as though I'm about to push her off the side of a mountain. She is young. God only knows what she has in front of her. Berlin. I was there years ago. My wife took the photos. Otherwise I wouldn't have known I was there. I was there for a reunion and drunk three days. There is a photograph of me standing before Brandenburg Gate. I am looking up and smiling at something I have no recollection of, none at all. Before we part I give her all the change I am carrying. Ten euros. Because she is so grateful I tell her, 'Wait, there's more.' A twenty-euro note in my back pocket. She's reluctant to take it. I have to press it into her hand. At least she won't go hungry for a day or two. I walk with her up to the last street light. There, as we shake hands, I see what appears to be clothing and something else, something in her bag that glints once and disappears as she moves off. Something which frankly gives me a chill. I turn and walk back to the car. For a few minutes I sit behind the wheel. I watch her in that cold blue coat rise up to the shoulder of the road. I study her outline against that part of the sky, that plastic bag at her side, those thin legs. Her head turns. Several vehicles flash by. Then it is all dark. And she has gone. I stay there another ten minutes. I half expect to see her. I don't know why. But I do. I stay by the car until the skies lighten. Now I'm worried that my wife will wake and find me gone. Or else Gina will be up watering her balcony plants when her good-for-nothing Croat son-in-law drives into her garage. They will want to know where I was. When I play back the truth it hardly sounds believable. They will think there is more to it. That's when I decide to drive on to the police station. It's the only way I can make sense of or justify what I just did. For the sake of persuading Gina and my wife I will need the police on-side. At the station the night-watch is just about to go home when I appear in the door. He invites me to take a chair by his desk and he takes down everything. The hardest questions come later—from my wife. She wants to know what it was about the woman that aroused my suspicions. After all, she wasn't doing anything. She just happened to be up at a very late hour without a roof over her head. The first and second night she was asleep. The third night she sat there as if she half expected a bus to roll up. Now this is the only thing I made up. I told my wife she was crying. That the black woman was crying. Suddenly it all made sense to her, and without that detail none of what I did or why I did what I did makes sense. A week later a policeman rang me. He asked me to come to the station at my own convenience. He had some photographs he wished to show me.

seven

The alpine hunter and guide

The best way to prepare a partridge—you can take this down if you wish. First, a partridge. Preferably shot early morning under low cloud. That way the bird cannot see the approaching shadows. As far as the partridge is concerned the birdshot has arrived out of the hillsides. There has been no time for it to know fear. I have eaten many partridges. I know by their taste which partridge has experienced a moment's fear and which hasn't. Adrenalin is the flavour of fear and leaves a distinct taste. Next, you need young chestnuts and garlic. To prepare the partridge—pluck the feathers, salt and rub olive oil into its skin, remove its insides and replace with half-roasted chestnuts and garlic. Peel the garlic, of course. Then stitch up the belly. Or you may use a metal clip. I myself don't, my shooting colleagues are less fussy, especially at night around a low fire. This next piece of information is important.

Slowly turn the partridge over a low flame. We bring with us a special contraption for slow-turning the partridge over the embers. When everyone has finished boasting, and exhausted their memories of past women, the partridge is ready to be eaten with rough bread, couscous and a bottle of chianti.

Now to the day in question. We had driven up the day before. Me, Paolo, Leo and Tom, an American food writer who had moved a month ago to our village with his wife, Hester. Hester? No. Sorry, Cynthia. Cynthia. Paolo, Tom, Leo, myself. Tom has come along with our shooting party to experience for himself the beginning and the end of the partridge recipe.

We camp where we usually do, in an abandoned shepherd's hut. Goats used to have the run of the hills. There aren't so many any more. A few wild ones. From the hut we fan out with the dogs and walk through the brush to the foothills and back again. You know what a colander is? We are a human colander through which the country passes. If there is a partridge it will not escape our attention. Leo is grumbling about the light. There is too much of it. Leo owns a restaurant. I've known him and Paolo since school days. Paolo is the footballer. He played second tier in the Italian football league. At the end of his career he came home. He didn't know what to do with himself. At the time Leo was the head chef at another restaurant. Paolo told Leo he would buy him a restaurant and make him a famous chef, more famous a chef than he was a footballer. And that actually happened. Which is how the food writer came to our village in the first place.

The forecast is for overcast skies. Perfect. But they have not arrived. Dark shadows pass over the hillsides. Leo is right. The light is too crisp. But Paolo is impatient. He wants to stretch his legs. He doesn't care so much about the pure taste of partridge. In that respect he is no perfectionist. And that may be why his football career didn't reach the heights that his natural talent promised. But I digress. So, we give in to Paolo's impatience and we comb the hillside. It is nice to be out in the countryside. A gentle breeze blows the worries from your mind. The dogs run with their short excited steps, stick their noses into the underbrush, wagging their tails. The dogs are happy. I am happy.

After an hour we've had no luck. The dogs have barked once or twice. Leo is annoyed. We should have waited like he said. The food writer, Tom, is sweating heavily. He has to keep removing his glasses to wipe the sweat from his eyes. When he bends forward sweat drops from his face. I have never seen that on a man before. A cyclist, yes—but not on a man out on a pleasant hillside walk. Paolo is gazing up at the rocky terrain. The goats are up there. But we have not come prepared. We have only birdshot. On other occasions we have climbed up to the ridge to wait for the cloud cover to arrive. From up there you can look into Switzerland and Austria. It is always a surprise to see how close we are. A slip of the pen and we would be in Switzerland or Austria. And with that slip of the pen we would be eating different foods and reciting different poets. I was pleased when the Azzurri won the World Cup. I drove around with a little Italian flag. I tooted my horn along with all the others. After we beat France I danced with the plainest and fattest woman that night. I believe in good fortune being spread around. After the cup victory I packed away the flag. On the whole, nationalism disgusts me.

While we are thinking what to do the forecasted cloud rolls in. There is no more talk of goats or rabbit. We have to wait another twenty minutes. We sip from Leo's brandy flask. We always do that. It is made of pewter, belonged to his great-grandfather; actually, it was taken off one of Napoleon's soldiers. That's the story Leo tells. It's one of those stories that no one would dare question and that we all want desperately to believe.

We send the dogs ahead and fan out. Very soon there is a commotion. The dogs have banded together. So it is not a partridge. Perhaps it is a rabbit. Leo has a wonderful recipe for rabbit but it requires that someone, Paolo, climb up to the ridge and gather wild herbs. Or else it is a phantom. Dogs are the nerviest of creatures. We are threading our way through the brush when we hear a woman's voice. Paolo runs ahead. We can hear a woman shouting at the dogs. The dogs are barking. Paolo is being quite rough with them, cursing them, kicking them away.

As we come through the brush there is the black woman. She is wearing a blue coat. That's the first thing that strikes me. How odd to be wearing a coat like that up in the hills. No. That is the second surprise. The first surprise is undoubtedly the woman. An African woman. Once, many years ago, we thought we had stumbled on bear shit. We stood around it, photographed it. Another time we saw two parakeets. Probably domestic—escaped. We have seen the odd soul—hikers—on the tracks through the hills leading down into the first valley of Switzerland. But never a black woman. Never an African. She has her arms up in surrender. A plastic bag hangs from her hand.

I have to shout at Paolo before he lowers his shotgun. He wasn't even aware. Later that evening, seated around the camp fire drinking while the partridge we eventually shot that afternoon turns above the coals, he apologises when reminded of how he had trained his gun on the poor woman. In fact he kept apologising to her. To the point where Leo had to tell him, that's enough. The woman looked at Paolo as she might at one of the dogs licking her feet. A glimmer of a smile. She did not speak Italian. We'd found that out much earlier. She spoke English. All of us speak some English—and Tom, the food writer, of course. But it was Leo who asked most of the questions. Leo and myself. She answered as best she could. Tom could have asked some questions but he just sat there listening. Now and then a flame lit his face. Beneath the dried sweat, beneath that was another layer of endeavour (he made me go over the partridge recipe three times, then made me check that what he had written was correct), and beneath that layer I thought I caught a glimpse of another that was pure coldness. That's the moment I decided I might not give him the rabbit recipe or the wild trout with almonds which he had already indicated a strong interest in obtaining.

We asked the obvious questions. Where she was from, and she told us. I forget the country. Somewhere in Africa. We asked her where she was going and she told us. Berlin, Germany. It took a moment for that to sink in. Paolo had spent a season there traded to FC Union Berlin when his career was on the way down. He didn't enjoy it. He said the fans were a bunch of tattooed beer-swilling white supremacists. Leo had also been to Berlin, to visit his daughter Maria, the younger, wilder one. He found her living with twenty-six other young people—Italians, Serbs, Australians, English, Poles, from all over, even a fellow from Vietnam, in an abandoned factory. Leo said the windows were broken. At night they cooked around an open fire. I expected him to say it was appalling and that he was ashamed to find his daughter living in this way. But he didn't. He was accepting, reluctant to criticise. In fact, following that trip, there was a brief period when his marriage went wobbly. Then his daughter returned and things improved at home.

We asked the woman why she wanted to go to Berlin. She stared into the fire. I did not think she was going to tell us. There had been some questions that she pretended not to understand. She could have lied and we would not have known. Instead she pretends not to understand, which is better in my view, more polite. So when we asked her—why Berlin?—this was one of those times I did not expect her to answer. She used the Italian—*bambino. Bambino. Bambino.* Very quickly she became emotional. Leo got up and went and crouched beside her. He rubbed her shoulder. She lay her head against him and cried. Leo managed to settle her down. He gave her some chianti. Tom spoke up then about the partridge. He was right to. Another few minutes would have been a few minutes too long.

She ate with real appetite. But not with any appreciation. She ate to fill herself up. She tore at the partridge, which I admit spoiled the occasion. She did not savour the tastes. Everything went down the same way. She hardly touched the chianti. After a while we forgot her and the conversation turned to the partridge. Tom got out his notebook. He asked many questions. Then he took a photograph. But only of me, Paolo and Leo. Leo had brought some grappa. We poured five glasses—the African woman included. Leo made a toast. We tilted back our glasses and swallowed the fire. The African spat hers out. Her hand went to her throat. Someone handed her the flask of water.

We were back to focusing on her. After the grappa she seemed less familiar, more like how the dogs had found her. I asked her about the baby. Why it was in Berlin. Why she was here. How they had become separated. She pretended not to understand. She sank further inside her coat, stared at the embers. Then Tom said back home she would be considered an illegal, an alien, I think he said—would he have called another human being 'an alien', it doesn't sound likely, even from him, but it is what I remember—'an alien' whom we should report to the authorities. We ignored him. That is, no one said anything. But it did make me wonder—what now? What should we do with her? We asked her more questions. She said a man in a van filled with trays of eggs had dropped her on the mountain road and pointed her in the direction of Switzerland. Then she opened her plastic bag. She brought out a book of maps. She turned to the page showing Italy, Austria, Switzerland and southern Germany.

Paolo has the best eyes. He confirmed for her that we were on the border. She asked him to show her where exactly. But on that map it was hopeless. Too imprecise. Then, Paolo, me and Leo began to discuss among ourselves the best way to get to Berlin from here. That is a conversation I'd never had before. Nor had Paolo or Leo. But we all had opinions. The American sat silently. Switzerland was near. Very close. Two hours if she was a fast walker. It was just a guess. None of us had crossed that border. On the Austrian side we had probably strayed a number of times without ever being aware of having passed from one place into another. Switzerland was nearer, but Leo, backed up by Paolo and me, was of the opinion that Austria would be better. We spoke in Italian and quickly agreed. Paolo volunteered to escort her to the first town. He would put her on a bus or train, whatever he found. Get her to Vienna. From there she could catch a train to Berlin.

We make these plans for her as if we are making them for ourselves. This is the way we would go. For one thing she will avoid running into trouble with the Swiss authorities. They are a bit more lax on the German side, especially on trains. Then the obvious question. This plan comes at a cost. We haven't stopped to ask if she has money. It would be impertinent to ask. So Leo gets us started. He stands up from the fire, reaches into his pocket and pulls out every note on him. Thirty-seven euros. Paolo does the same. He manages to come up with seventy-eight euros. I am surprised to find that I have as much as I do. Three fifties and a twenty. Leo works his way around the fire until he comes to the food writer. The American is staring into the embers. His hands in his pockets. Shoulders up around his ears. Of course he must be aware of Leo standing there. He has seen each one of us dig into our pockets. Finally he speaks up. He says he doesn't think we should 'aid and abet an illegal'. We are breaking the law. Worse. We are willingly breaking the law. We digest that. No one says anything. Then Paolo speaks up. Very calmly he asks Tom if he has any money on him. He doesn't answer. The American. This fucking American. He has swallowed his tongue. Paolo is about to repeat himself when the food writer says he might have. Leo hasn't left his side. The American has sunk even deeper inside of himself. He says he doesn't want to break the law. He doesn't want to get into trouble with the authorities. To give money to an illegal activity might lead to him regretting his foolishness.

Leo looks at me. So does Paolo. As for the woman—we've forgotten her. But she is somewhere in Paolo's shadow, to his right.

I know what I must do. I stand up to make my speech. I tell the food writer that he may think he is in partridge country. But during the war this was partisan country. Partisans broke the law by their very existence. So, his fear of breaking the law is not a persuasive argument. His eyes lower. He picks up a twig and tosses it into the fire. He is like a man pretending that the rain isn't falling on him, only on others. So then I tell him. I have to tell him—and I am sorry it has come to this. I tell him unless he empties his pockets there will be no rabbit or almond trout recipe. The photographs will be erased from his camera, and all the others he's taken of Leo's famous kitchen and of Leo beaming under his white chef's hat, and I will personally throw his notebook with the partridge recipe into the flames. Now it is raining—in the figurative sense. At last he can feel it. Now he wants to get out of it. His face screws up. I see him then just for a fleeting second how he might have looked in the school playground. All the pain is on his inside. Slowly he gets up. His eyes remain half closed. It's as if he does not want to be witness to his own actions. He is like a child. I spit at the ground by his feet. I am disgusted by him.

Luckily he is the only one to have brought his wallet. He pulls out two hundred euros and hands the money to Leo. Leo remains on the spot, his hand out...until another stab of pain behind the closed eyes causes the food writer to retrieve another fifty, which he thought Leo must not have seen. Leo takes that, then he walks around the fire to the African woman and holds out the money. She can't believe that it is for her. Leo has to encourage her. She looks across to Paolo. Maybe she thinks he will shoot her. He nods and so she takes the fifty off the top. Leo laughs and keeps his hand there. She looks at each of our faces. I nod. So does Paolo. The food writer is staring at the ground. She holds out her hand and Leo transfers the collection to her.

In the morning we leave the shepherd's hut nice and early. Leo and the American start off down the hill. I tell them I will catch up. I stay put and watch Paolo and the African woman climb up to and eventually disappear over the white ridge. It is a beautiful morning. Blue skies. Still. No good for partridge. But there is a lightness in my heart. I set off after Leo and the American.

Back in the village I drop the American off at his rental. Then Leo at his house. Then I drive to Paolo's lovely big home outside of town. His wife is younger, from Granada. I explain everything to her. She seems puzzled, unsure. I give her some reassurances.

Next morning I pick her up and we drive up the mountain road. We climb to the shepherd's hut and wait. Around noon we see Paolo come over the ridge. His young wife starts up the scree. I stay back. The figure on the ridge stops. Then he leaps—amazing to see—a man leaping off the side of a mountain. He bounds the rest of the way down the scree. By the time I catch up, Paolo, unshaven and sweaty, has his big arms around his pretty young wife. He is kissing her, panting over her. Then to my surprise I notice he is crying. Paolo 'the strong man in defence'. I turn around and walk back to the car.

part two: *Berlin*

eight

The inspector

On this Sunday afternoon, in a park whose hills and winding paths are built on top of war rubble and the dead, new mothers gaze across lawns dotted with young lovers. There is new sap in the air. The sweet powdery smell is almond blossom. The light is green and filtered. At such moments the world trembles at the thought of itself.

In this park the layers of the world coming into being and departing are more obvious. In the copper mulch of last season's leaves the pigeons grub away. They do not care about anything other than what they may find. A job applicant occupies a bench: he leans forward on his spread knees—look at the way he hangs his head. There is a little too much hope and virtue combed into his hair. Winter is the season when separation is felt hardest. In the hard air the lunch crowds huddle in blankets and wait for the duck pond to freeze, and then for it to thaw. The leaves are not out yet, just the hard buds. The new world is coming.

Feral dogs sniff at the ground where the pigeons were, and years ago in this same place a grieving mother in a coat and bare legs delivered her dead son in a wheelbarrow. With his teenager limbs hanging over the sides of the wheelbarrow she scratched out a grave on her hands and knees. And here too at the edge of the bushes, in more or less the same place, a man spreads himself on top of a woman who also faces the ground. His face is buried in her shoulder. Whereas, she looks up with a foolish bloated smile. She looks like she is being squeezed out of her clothes. With the last of the phantom light hanging in the trees, the paths lead into the dusk. Now the lanterns come on and people spill out of the woods.

Across the road from the park fornicators is a large *kirche* with its administrative heartland of corridors indicating responsibilities for Africa, Asia and Eurasia. Here, the nameless, the unofficial, the windblown and the vermin climb the outside steps. Along corridors reeking of disinfectant they creep, cap in hand, past the doors with the unfamiliar names and allocated territories.

The man in charge of Africa is a pastor of the Ibo order, a portly man used to his desk and the space that divides him from his visitor. Hardly a day passes without a reminder that he is a well-fed man with position. He smiles as the language of calamity and death parts his lips. He smiles endlessly and at times his smile stretches to the brink of hilarity.

nine

A pastor of the Ibo order

If I am laughing it is because you have come here to Berlin to ask a pastor, a black man, about ghosts. Presumably you mean white ghosts. Yes. I am being facetious. I apologise, perhaps just a wee bit. I speak four languages. Besides Ibo, I speak Italian, English, Oirish. I was trained by the Holy Ghost Fathers, an order of sunburnt white men from Dublin. Others like me became the Ibo order 'Sons of the Soil'. I prefer to speak Deutsch since, after all, we are in Berlin. But under the circumstances Italian may be more appropriate.

It is true that I am an expert on some ghosts. For example, there are the ghosts we do not see, the spooky ghosts, the ghosts of the American imagination, creatures appearing in doors dressed in white bed-sheets with the eyes cut out. These are the ones small children worry are lying beneath their beds at night. These ghosts are a puzzle. I like American movies. But what I don't understand about these particular ghosts is that we never see the consequences of the encounter. The ghost remains a spectre, no more than a possibility. Something to be afraid of. A manifestation of fear, such as the opposition parties in each and every undemocratic regime in Africa.

The other ghosts—the real ghosts if I may call them that—are simply those whom we choose not to see.

These people did not start out as ghosts. God put them on Earth as human beings. Here, I will show you on the map. This is where they began life. Around the horn of Africa. Liberia. Sierra Leone. Senegal. Gambia. Ivory Coast. The Western Sahara. Many were fishermen. While they were fishermen they were human beings. But then the multinationals with high-tech trawlers scooped all the fish out of the sea and the fisherman with the net was left in the same state as his brothers gazing across fallow land in the midst of a drought. There is nothing left for the fisherman to do but leave.

This is the way they go. They walk, they catch a bus, a bush bus, hitch a ride. It is slow progress. In some cases I know of, it has taken one of God's souls two years to reach here and here, Tunisia and Libya. And there the human traffickers sit in cafes with their worry beads. By now the process by which a man turns into a ghost is well advanced. A human being is of no more value than a sack of rice. A human being is merchandise. Then, once money passes hands, it is cargo. The cargo sets off in unseaworthy boats. Old fishing boats. Open boats. Over-crowded, poorly resourced. Without sufficient food or water—since when did merchandise have such requirements? And they disappear. They disappear at sea.

A Danish ferry capsizing in the North Sea is a calamity. It is international news. Fifty-one souls lost. A tragedy. Twenty, thirty, fifty thousand black people...Well, it is too big a figure to contemplate. It is apocalyptic. It is a sandstorm blowing across the African continent as fortress Europe nails down its shutters. It pretends. It pretends like the child afraid of the ghost under the bed. And instead it exercises its sympathy and shock and horror for the fifty or so lives lost in the North Sea. I understand. I don't wish to make light of that event. It too is a tragedy. We see on television the grieving families on the shore. We hear them speak of their loved ones who drowned. Before our eyes those fifty souls turn into individuals, faces, trailing lives and families. The blacks continue to spiral down to the seabed of the Mediterranean, where they become food for sharks. The closest Europe will come to them is when Europeans eat the shark.

The biggest human trafficker is Libya. Some blacks make it across to Europe. Lampedusa. If they were to consult a map before setting out they would see that Lampedusa is a tiny place. It is the stone the boot of Italy attempts to kick back across the sea. They step ashore into a detention centre. These ones have the semblance of human beings. They still have names. Soon they will turn into ghosts. There are so many of them that Europe has turned to Gaddafi. The self-proclaimed father of Africa has built a vast detention centre in the middle of the Libyan desert. The Africans who have made it to the shores of Europe now file into the holds of aeroplanes and are flown back to Africa, not whence they came, that would be too expensive, but to the detention centre in the Libyan desert. Here they turn into ghosts, some go mad and wander into the desert to meet their maker.

So, when the authorities come to my office and ask for help to find a particular illegal immigrant I do what Europe does. I pretend these people don't exist. I am not sorry that I cannot be of more help.

There is one more thing. Before I entered the church I studied geology. An oil company made that possible. They hoped I would find oil for them in the future. Instead I became side-tracked by what I found. Did you know there was once a land bridge between Africa and Europe? This was many, many thousands of years ago. Back then, an African could have arrived in Europe simply by following the shoreline.

ten

A man by the name of Millennium Three

I have not eaten since yesterday. That is a fact. Now a declaration. But fear of the inexplicable has not yet impoverished the existence of the individual. No. I don't want any money. Not yet. I believe in the fair exchange of goods. I will accept your money but only as payment. So. What do I have to give? It is all up here in my head. Amazing riches. For example, you may have recognised the words of Rilke a moment ago. Listen again—carefully. . .*But fear of the inexplicable has not yet impoverished the existence of the individual.* And this—from the third stanza. Listen. *We are not prisoners. No traps or snares are set about us, and there is nothing which should intimidate or worry us. We are set down in life as in the element to which we best correspond, and over and above this we have through thousands of years of accommodation become so like this life, that when we hold still we are, through a happy mimicry, scarcely to be distinguished from all that surrounds us.* It is not a very good poem in my view, but it contains some lines which I only have to recite and suddenly the spark they produce warms my insides. Rainer Maria Rilke. He is dead so it does not matter. The language belongs to the entire human race. Rilke is dead. Whereas I am very much alive and when in need of a meal I recite a few lines. *How should we be able to forget those ancient myths about dragons that at the last moment turn into princesses: perhaps all of the dragons of our lives are princesses who are only wanting to see us once beautiful and brave*...Yesterday I recited those lines without attributing their source and a woman wanted to take me to dinner. It was kind of her. But she misunderstood. I was not looking for kindness. I was after payment. She paid ten euros for a different poem, also by my friend and sponsor, Rainer Maria Rilke, this one about a dog.

I choose my customers carefully. Rilke is not for everyone. Some of my customers prefer my flea joke. It is slightly risqué. It is not my joke, that is to say, I did not create it. I lifted it from somewhere, someone, I forget where or who. Jokes are like dandelions. They float across the world lifting away from our outstretched hands. No one remembers where the dandelion is from. No one thinks of its origin. But everyone instinctively reaches out to hold one. That is not Rilke by the way. That is me.

Millennium Three? I changed my name by deed poll before coming to Berlin. You see how easy it is to become the other—to bloom with the same flower when grafted onto a shared stem. Rilke is my stem. But there are others too. My flea joke, for example, it has more universality than many of Rilke's poems. Perhaps I will tell you the short version. The long version you will have to pay for. But let me go back to Rilke. The second stanza of the poem 'Fear of the Inexplicable'. Where he says, *If we think of the existence of the individual as a larger or smaller room, it appears evident that most people only know a corner of the room, a place by the window, a strip of floor on which they walk up and down.* These lines changed my life. These lines struck me with the force of a thunderbolt. My strip of floor was so meagre. It was pitiful. This is what it amounted to—a desk before a class of adolescents who resented my presence and who did not want poetry inflicted on their anorexic souls. In their eyes I saw myself as some kind of oppressor. But I continued. I persevered. At night I planned my lessons. I looked for poems that would break open their hearts and minds. But Rilke's lines would not go away. In the end I tore up the floorboards of small existence. I changed my name to Millennium Three. I drew up a manifesto. From now on, no traps or snares. No fear of the inexplicable.

I left my life in Paris and came to Berlin. It was that easy.

I was in search of other free spirits. I found them late at night on the trains. Artists of one kind or another. Not the kind who puts pen to paper, though some did. Not painters or sculptors or filmmakers. I met a new kind of artist whose medium was not language or paint or film...but their lives. Anarchists. Some. Yes, why not? Late at night on the trains we found one another. We agreed on certain principles. One, borders are inherently evil. They create awareness of difference. We talked long into the night about the kind of difference we would tolerate. On the one hand, you see, we embraced indifference. On the other we abhorred the state-inspired delineations and definitions of difference. Borders. Citizenship. Rich. Poor. Entitlement. We forged political liaisons with other underground groups. The more radical were low-profile. By definition they could not be organised. Their spark was spontaneity. Our movements ignited into magnificent explosions of our ideas and values that showered down upon the sleepy roofs across Berlin. The idea was that the city would wake up feeling changed but not know how.

Well, some were unhappy with this chosen invisibility. These ones exposed themselves by their demands, their cravings. They wanted notoriety. Presence. Headlines. Fame. They wanted to be talked about. The model was the FFF (Fuck the Fucking Fuckers). The FFF, in our view, were not truly anarchistic. They took part in May Day parades. They sold T-shirts and mugs. They marched under banners. In other words, they lived in their narrow strip of floorboard and in their small rooms huddled up to tiny windows dreaming of becoming what they were not. We decided to split. After that we stayed in the east and they went to the train routes in Mitte and pussy areas like Prenzlauer Berg.

When I first saw her I was on a train. Naturally. It was at night, in May. May? If not, early June. No, I think this is incorrect. The evenings were still crisp. I will say May. On the platform people stood by themselves, collars turned up. Occupying their holes in the night air. Is that an expression? I think Rilke would accept it. So. The train sweeps in and gathers up the crowd, and then it is like a sleeping sickness: the train sways, the people sway and nod off like babies in their cribs. Crib. Bassinet. Same thing. It is all the same word. The head of a sleeping man fell against her and she got up and moved to the standing area by the doors. But for that sleeping man's head I might not have noticed her, but for that acorn, that apple...I would not have looked up from my own sleeping sickness and moved my knees for her to get past.

We are drawing into the next station when a ticket inspector enters our carriage. There is, as always, a rise of tension. I get up to make my move, and that's when I see the black woman making her way to the next carriage...and I know. Many get on the train without a ticket, especially late at night. This morning, for example, there was a stampede. I looked up from my stolen newspaper. It was a Chinese woman. She ran down the carriage. She looked like she was fleeing fire or the Japanese. The ticket collector calmly followed. He looked prepared to let her get away. I have seen young girls sitting with their knees pressed together, their heads lowered in shame, some in tears. I've seen so many escorted off the train. Tourists, as well, looking baffled and enraged. I can usually see at a glance who has a ticket. Who does not. But this woman...

She is dressed in a smart blue coat. Very stylish. Italian design. Her face has an earned dignity. I would not have picked her. In the next carriage I find her near the doors, a nervousness twitching in her now. Standing right behind a tall, thin guy with his eyes closed. So, she is not alone. At Alexanderplatz we all dash out. In the crowd and in the rush she drops something. I'm the one following up behind so I pick it up, a plastic bag which I hand to her. She snatched it back. Snatched is a word? Then, realising I am not a thief, she managed a 'thank you'. And with it an ease crosses her face as if to make an adjustment from the moment of accusation just a second ago. I am used to these corrections. My customers always see a thief, an opportunist, before they see the helpful tradesman that I consider myself to be, a fixer of souls, a mood regulator, all of which I achieve with the proper exchange of goods and services.

Now. Why? I don't know. Even now I cannot say why. It just erupts from me. I tell her, My name is Bernard. For eighteen months I have been Millennium Three. I have not used the name Bernard once. Why? Why just then, at that moment? Inexplicable? Yes. I think so. It is a confusing moment. And there we stand, facing one another, as if there should be more, that something else should quite naturally flow from this encounter. The other passengers have pushed past us, the train has left, and now quite naturally we walk together to the top of the escalators. Nothing is said. Yet we are in step. We come out of the station to the plaza. There are a number of wurst stands. I am not hungry. I am rarely hungry. Hunger is just a physical fact. If you cannot move beyond it then you cannot hope to live as we do. But you see, at that moment, the Bernard of Parisian existence has emerged from the rubble of my new being. Bernard knows what to do in a way that Millennium Three has forgotten. He—that is I, of course—he asks if she would like a wurst. To my surprise—Millennium's, that is—she agrees. She ate two. While she is eating I manage to get a proper look at her. It's clear she has nowhere to sleep. No roof or bed. She has just got off a train from somewhere and is new to the city. So the next thing is very obvious really. I take her under my wing. Again, nothing is said or proposed. It just happens, like the weather.

We leave the wurst stand, wait for a tram to crawl by, cross the tracks to the station, climb more escalators. A two-minute wait on the platform during which time nothing is said, nor is there a chance to feel the cold; then the usual carriage smell of coats, beer, ash. We are on the S-Bahn heading to the east of the city. At Warschauer we get off the train and I lead her into my neighbourhood, if I can claim any as my own. Actually, this happens to be an FFF neighbourhood. But those of us who eschew the narrow floorboard have settled a spacious abandoned warehouse. This neighbourhood and the one of cobbles, trees and cafes is connected by a hole in a long wall. I show her where, and lead her through the darkness, past the fires.

I must admit it is nice to have someone's company. Someone to lie beneath the night with. I have a mattress and a pillow. I build a small fire. I still have a bottle of Grand Marnier given to me by a grateful woman who had wept at Rilke's poem 'Loneliness'. She also gave me some euros. As you know I insist on proper exchange of goods and services. The Grand Marnier was a gift.

At last I have a name. Ines.

Ines does not want to drink. She is tired. She just wants to lie down. I make sure she has the good side. I take the lumpy side. I give her the pillow but not before I slip it inside a clean T-shirt that I stole from the Turkish market that morning. It is red and has the Turkish crest.

In the morning I wake to find her still there. Her African face looks beautiful against the Turkish red.

I am surprised. But only for that moment. Then I am surprised that I am surprised. Why not? Why wouldn't she be there? I slip outside for a pee. The fires have burnt down. Across the landscape people are sleeping. A woman wriggles out of a sleeping bag. It is like watching a caterpillar emerge from its cocoon. She is naked, and as she squats her dark pubis spreads. Behind her, sleepy young men stand around peeing carelessly. As I am peeing I realise I'm happy. Which is interesting. Very interesting to me. Because if I am happy at that particular moment, what was I before this woman arrived in my life? Briefly I reconsider my entire philosophy and political liaisons—but only while I am peeing. The crisis soon passes. The moment I do up my trouser buttons all is forgotten, all that questioning, and I return to the inexplicable arrival of this woman into my life and these new inexplicable feelings.

For the next eight days we are together. There is no sex. At night, when we lie down together, she will allow my hand to rest on her hip. Sometimes she will talk in her sleep. I listen carefully. But it is in a language that I don't know. We have to speak in English. She has three French words. *Bonjour* and *merci beaucoup*. She manages them quite naturally, unlike English people, who after uttering these words stand there beaming as if they require a medal to be pinned to their lapel.

For those eight days we are together almost twenty-four hours a day. Except for two hours every afternoon when she leaves me. I don't know where she goes or what she does. Once I tried to come along. She told me—No—she must go alone. She did not explicitly tell me not to follow. And I don't, don't even consider doing so, until she arrives back from these journeys in a state. The first time I can see she has been crying. She refuses to say why. Then, another time when she is late arriving back I find her sitting by the wall and sobbing; her face is in her hands. She refuses to take her hands away. She will not let me into her misery.

So, is her mysterious journey for a liaison? I thought, well, that is her right, in which case I should not be following, but I do. I follow her along the tramlines, down side streets, onto another and another, through the maze of Kreuzberg until we end up at the canal. There is a cycle path, some trees. There's a wurst stand on the corner where the traffic comes off the little bridge.

I stay back on the other side of the canal. I am close enough. I can see perfectly well. Ines is standing beneath the trees gazing up at a third-floor window. Inexplicable? Yes. A mystery. A complete mystery. Of course I want to find out. I must. This is our nature. We do not walk away from mystery. We are drawn to it like moths. Time passes. Half an hour. Five minutes. It is all the same. Then, as I am watching, a man emerges from the building. A black man. Well dressed. A white satiny buttoned-down shirt. Dark trousers. Expensive-looking shoes. He walks briskly across the cobbles to where my Ines is beneath the trees. For the next few minutes they talk. The man is very animated. Well, I would say angry. He towers over her, trying to intimidate her. But at the same time he is not comfortable with the situation because he keeps looking up the street, both ways—he is afraid of being seen.

Ines is also a bit animated. More so than I have ever seen her. She has to talk up to him; he is tall. Now they are both talking. Both of them talking over the top of one another. When she begins to beat her fists against his chest he doesn't move away. If anything he moves a little closer, looks up the street, down the other way. He gives her a shove. The force causes her to step backwards. Then she comes forward beating her fists against him. Now I can hear her, a faint cry above the traffic.

On the third floor a window is raised. Something is shouted down at the street. Then the sash is dropped. That all happens in such a hurry that after I can't recall if I actually saw anyone at that window. When I look back at the two figures under the trees he is hitting her. I don't stop to think. If I did it would have been to remind myself to remove myself from my own narrow board of existence. I am not a fighter. I am a poet. Well, a poet-thief. But there I am running across the bridge, across the traffic. I am running, and then I am flying like a bird, a thin under-fed eagle, and I crash against his shoulder and send him sprawling to the ground with me on top of him. I hit him on the side of his head. He tries to bite my hand. I knee him in the balls. He sticks his thumb in my eye. I grab his ear and twist it until he squeals like a piglet. Then I hit him in his mouth. Again and again. Then he hits me in the temple until, my God, the bells are ringing in my head, all the bells in Paris and across Germany are ringing in my head. Then I remember. I am not in Notre Dame. I am not in the Berliner Dom. I remember to hit him. He tries to get up. This is something which I must prevent. If he is allowed to get up he will hit Ines. So I drag him down to the ground and we roll under the trees over the dirt and the dog shit. We claw at each other. He is trying to press his thumb into my eye again. I punch his nose and his mouth until he removes his thumb. He grabs my hair and pulls and twists. I hit his nose, and knee him in the balls again, and we roll over more dog shit. I am suddenly aware of a cycle wheel and another and another. A party of cyclists has stopped to watch. By now I am out of breath. My enemy is also panting. We hit one another when we remember to, or when one of us has found the extra energy from somewhere.

Then a woman begins yelling. A black woman. Not Ines. The man rolls away from me. This woman is yelling at him and at me, but with me her voice changes pitch. I am a dog she has pulled off her prize pedigree. She would like to shoo me away, chase me off with a stick, that is, until the man, my enemy, holds up a hand to silence her. There is a thin line of blood trickling from one nostril which I am unwholesomely thrilled about. There is dirt on one cheek. His expensive shirt is torn, which I am also very happy about. I wonder what Ines will make of this, what she will say.

I look around, but I cannot see her in that crowd. The cyclists are getting back on their bikes. Two dog walkers continue to stand there. They are smiling, and even the dogs look contented. There is no Ines. I can hear a siren approaching. Although I can hear it I don't think any more of it. I turn my attention back to her attacker. He looks mystified. In Deutsch he asks me, 'Who are you?' Actually, he asks, 'Who the fuck are you?' And I have to stop and think, stop and really think, Who am I? Because just at that moment to reply 'I am Millennium Three' strikes me as silly. It would sound implausible. On the other hand, Bernard is not right either. If Ines was there I might have answered 'Bernard'. But she is not. I can't see her. I don't even know in which direction she took off. I never saw her again.

eleven

The film researcher

She was sitting on the concrete verge. I might not have noticed her any other time or for that matter at another stage in my life. An African woman sitting alone. I might have looked once and forgotten her. As I walked by her eyes tilted up at me. I carried on and near the casino I stopped to turn and look back. That's when I noticed the plastic bag: the way it perched on her knees and how she held onto it with both hands. She didn't look like a beggar because the other thing—and this by startling contrast—was her expensive blue coat. It had seen better days, but its style and cut still shone through. And I would say the same went for the person.

I'd been in Berlin most of the winter, hanging around Alexanderplatz—that's the general area where I saw her—observing the Roma as I might a cage of parakeets. It was John

Buxton of Sun Rise productions who gave me the gig researching the Roma, all of them women, and all beggars, around the station. Just write down your impressions, he said. That is very imprecise. Worryingly imprecise for someone just two years out of the London Film School.

I had been working on a short film in Lambeth on wild-plot gardeners. You know, people who grow cabbages on traffic islands and place beehives on the rooftops of canal barges. Then this came up. Thanks to my Aunt Julia. She used to be in film. Knows everyone. She and JB go a long way back. JB mentioned the project and Julia, who is irrepressible most of the time but particularly when she has my interests at heart, said she had the perfect researcher.

I arrived towards the end of August. A colleague of JB picked me up from the airport and drove me to the apartment in Friedrichshain. Soon the lovely old buildings lay behind us—we were on Karl Marx Allee—and I found myself pining for the wild-gardens project and what a mistake it had been to come here, that when I get back to London I really must sit my aunt down for a chat and gently ask her to stop feeling she has to do these things for me, when we turned into a quiet tree-lined cobbled street and everything was perfect again.

Midway through September it turned autumnal, earlier than in London. October was cold. Until early November, every morning I rode a bike up Karl Marx Allee to Alexanderplatz. In the bike lane I crouched over the bars. I must have given the impression of someone late for work. The Roma who set my daily schedule usually arrived at the platz around 10am and always left before dark.

I never tried to approach them or draw them into conversation. To befriend them—even to imagine I could seems absurd to me now. Observing these tenacious little women over winter hardened me. So that when I saw that black woman I just saw another vagrant that I didn't need to know about. The Roma do that to you. They harden you. They are as sticky as flies. And once they think they have your interest then you are dead meat. So when I made eye contact with the black woman I was quick to look away again. With the Roma, once eye contact is achieved their faces light up, and off they go with small accelerating steps in their thick socks and beach sandals. They are always so pleased to see you.

They moved like crows. Eye and foot movement not always perfectly aligned, as if they didn't want to pass up any opportunity. I came to think of myself and anyone else as a breadcrumb. The way the crows accelerated towards new crumbs spilling out of the station exits. Some people hated to be singled out. It was as though a part of themselves they wished to remain a secret was suddenly exposed. They resented the publicness of it. These ones would switch to a passing lane, first the thought, then their eyes, their legs and bodies follow. Some go by on stilts, their heads in low-hanging cloud. They do not want to know about beggars, not this one, nor beggars in general. I remember a young blonde woman got past a Roma by looking up at the treetops. She had just seen a blue-tailed cockatiel or perhaps a giraffe. Having chosen that fiction she is obliged to stay with it. Before long the high ridge of her cheeks were coloured with shame. It is awful to feel uncharitable. Awful. One woman on tall legs, the tallest legs I have ever seen, raised her chin and set her gaze off somewhere in the direction of Denmark leaving the tiny Roma woman in her hooped skirt in a shadow from the last ice age.

The punks? The beggars never went near them. They huddled cold and drunk or on their way to getting drunk, their faces like mouldy old bread. The black woman? They didn't go near her either. I know, because the next day she is back where I first saw her, on the same bench, and the Roma are moving tidally either side of her, on their way to richer pickings around the station.

After six months I was sick of Berlin. Sick of the reason for being there. Sick of being a crumb. And it wants to rain for the eleventh day in a row. If only it would stop. If only these shitty people would stop shitting up the day. I am sorry, but these are my impressions too.

By now the Roma were used to me. I always knew I had been clocked, a trace of irritability, something like that, tugging down the corners of their mouths. What was I doing there? And, as it must have seemed to them, always turning away from them and at the same time looking—as I had with the black woman. My ideal of invisibility demanded it. One moment I cannot find any of them, not a single Roma, and in the next the women appear from all directions as if spun out of air—thick ropes of black hair, darting white eyes, brown oval faces. It required swiftness on my part, a deft turn, a startled look of annoyance leading to an abrupt stop, as if I have left something behind and must now run to fetch it. So I'd circle around the station and come back to find them in a corner of the platz, their heads pressed together to form a tight gossipy circle. At dusk the crows flew up to the roof of the Berliner Dom and the tiny women in beach sandals disappeared beneath the damp trees. Sometimes I followed, but only as far as the casino, and that's where I saw the black woman.

We recognised each other, and this time she got up and moved away. I thought no more of her that day. But the next day I did. I found myself looking for her, the way I was used to looking for the pamphleteer, the newspaper vendor, the blind accordion player. Anyway what I meant to say is—she joined that loose constituency that hung out around the station. And, in that way, I found myself looking out for her, noting her whereabouts. She preferred the back eddies, the small park beneath the casino where a person can sit without purpose.

She was different from the Roma. She wasn't seeking anything from anyone. Although that's not to say she wouldn't have if she knew how. At a glance you could see she was homeless, hungry too, I imagine. But because she did not carry a sign declaring 'I am hungry' I thought it would be rude and presumptuous of me to offer her anything. That's another funny thing. The very thing the Roma suppressed in me—good will, charity, Christian action, call it what you will—came unstuck with her.

This was around the time of the weather changing. An ice-cream vendor appeared. You suddenly heard the Roma kids laughing—all winter they had got about tucked under their mother's arms like miniature bedrolls. More people filled the platz. More Roma too. New faces. Younger stickier ones. There were other inexplicable events. I arrived outside Galeria Kaufhof one morning to find a long open boat resting on a crest of sand. There was no explanation for it. Its gunwale was buttressed with thick rope. The boards were stopped with black tar. More decoratively, a lifebuoy and an anchor chain lay in the sand. The African woman happened to be standing by the rope. She was staring at the boat. When she saw me she looked like someone caught straying into a forbidden area. She quickly moved away. I called out to her to wait. But she didn't look back.

The dog days piled up. At 8am the streets smelt of warm leftovers. In my neighbourhood I was used to seeing a street person employed to put out the cafe tables and chairs, a man of about sixty. His filthy shirt hung on the back of a chair to dry while he set about his work. His upper body was covered with thick dark animal hair. I had come to admire his professional pride, the way he counted with one finger the number of chairs at each table, that childish method of counting, and the unshaven face. The same dignity did not extend to the drunks whom I passed each morning lying in alcoholic dishevelment over the grass, burnt and trampled down to dirt, on Warschauer Bridge. Their trousers were loosened to halfway down their sunburnt arses. Their red faces appeared to exhort the terrors of alcoholism and the blessings of sleep in equal measure as the full blast of the sun rose over the city. I had stopped cycling—an old hockey knee injury had flared up—so it was the train for me. The heat in the carriages was cruel. People fought with windows that had been jammed or stupidly locked. They stared past one another, stared out the window, watched it all slide by—the hormonal plant growth, weeds that were huge and pointless spreading across wastelands of rubbish and parched land to the edge of the Platen housing whose windows had grown opaque with their own special brand of GDR-inspired unloveliness. At Alexanderplatz I passed out of the heavy air of the carriage into the pizza-oven heat.

When did that attack on the Roma in Naples occur? June, I remember now. I cut my hair. Well, over that same period, in

Berlin, the Roma disappeared. The platz seemed emptier. With all that space the African woman was more noticeable. Each time our eyes met across the platz she moved away. One night, wanting to find out more about the attacks in Naples, I went online and came across an article about a Romanian governor who for sport used to make the Roma climb trees so he could shoot the 'crows'. An awful bilious feeling of shame rose in me. I went through my notebooks. On nearly every page I found a reference to the voracious behaviour of crows, their thick black hair and quick black eyes. I felt very uneasy about these notes of mine. Should I put a line through every instance of the word 'crow', thereby severing the link between my impressionistic language and the Romanian governor's behaviour? On the other hand, would the filmmaker, that anonymous genius, land gleefully on the notion of 'crow'? He might even be grateful—shame on me for thinking as much, but if I am to be honest I had better own up to the thought that the notion of 'crow' might provide me with a leg-up. I didn't know what to do. Or I did, but couldn't quite embrace it.

The next time I show up to the platz I'm without my notebooks. This time I am determined to go and speak to the Roma. If they want money for that privilege that's no problem. But there are no Roma, none at all—just the African woman, and this time I approach her without a second thought.

She looked up as she always did with that slightly fearful roll of her eyes. I sat beside her on the bench. I told her my name. Since she didn't say anything in reply, kindly and calmly I asked her if she spoke English. She nodded. I asked her if she was hungry. She nodded. I asked her if she had a place to stay. This time she averted her eyes. Up close I was surprised to see that she was just a few years younger than myself. Until then she was black, African, other. But now I saw a young woman who looked about the same age as my sister Alison. I could have been looking at Ali, apart from the obvious differences. Now I knew what I must do.

I took her off to one of the cafes. She only wanted orange juice. You have to respect that, I mean under the circumstances, I imagine she was ravenous, but all she chose was a plastic bottle of juice. It gave me the confidence to invite her back to stay with me until she got herself sorted. We caught the S-Bahn across town. At Warschauer we walked past the drunks, by now up and baying at demons. She walked beside me, clutching her plastic bag. We must have gone half an hour before she spoke. It was a sweet voice, surprisingly good English. She said, 'My name is Ines.' Just as quickly the well of words dried up.

Hers was a different kind of presence. She wasn't someone who constantly demands your attention. She didn't talk. She was inwardly focused. All her attention went into not occupying space. I don't know if that makes sense. Let's see if I can explain. At the apartment I had to invite her to sit down. When she did, it was not like someone properly occupying a chair. I'd never thought what 'properly occupying a chair' might involve until then. She sat as if the chair might collapse under her. And so, out of courtesy, as it seemed to me, she mimicked the idea of someone sitting, but it was her knees and thighs and stomach muscles that really supported her. She sat watching me. She was absolutely still, except for her eyes. Soon I was overly conscious of my own movement about the apartment. I felt she was noting every drawer that I opened, every door that closed, each time the tap ran. While she sat—waiting, not quite sitting but hovering over the chair, that plastic bag perched on her knees—I tried to pretend she wasn't there, but it was hopeless. All the air of the apartment was sucked into that room where she sat, as invited, waiting perhaps for invitations to stand, to walk to the window, to look out at the day, to use the bathroom. I remember looking after Ali's baby girl. Whenever I left her alone in a room I couldn't stop thinking if she was all right. That's how it was with Ines. I had to hurry back to make sure she hadn't stopped breathing.

The couch is a fold-out. She slept there for the next six nights. I lay awake for the whole duration. It was the weight of silence coming from the front room. Sometimes I heard a floorboard creak. Then I'd sit up with the duvet wrapped around me and listen. But there was nothing. Just the long willowy silence and my pounding heart.

In the morning I would find her already dressed in the front room holding her plastic bag. The sheets and blankets had been folded. The bed restored to a couch. In the bathroom the towel was wet. I hadn't heard her get up or run the shower. So I must have slept. She stood very still, watching me. She is the gazelle. I am the lion. Her eyes move when I do. I am aware of her eyes following me out of the room. I can hear her listening for my whereabouts. Now I find myself tiptoeing about the apartment.

I tried to get her to talk—but it was hopeless. She would simply trot out what was already self-evident. She had no place to stay. She did not know anyone. So why had she come to Berlin? No one comes to Berlin by accident. Her eyes shifted from mine. She clutched her plastic bag all the harder. She seemed to think that if she just waited the question would go away, like all the other times. This time I said to her, 'Ines, what are you afraid of?' She shook her head, then she turned to look over her shoulder towards the sound of the traffic rising against the window panes. I thought she might sob—but there was no breach of her defences. No sudden outpouring. We remained two strangers, one of us looking over her shoulder to escape the other.

I didn't know what to do with her. I rang London. John Buxton couldn't believe what I had done. 'Are you mad?' he asked. She might have AIDS. She might be scarred from some shitty war that we have never read about. Get her out of there while you can still breathe. I rang Julia. As usual my aunt was full of practical suggestions. So the next morning when I led Ines out of my apartment for the last time I felt shamefully elated. From Alexanderplatz we followed the S-Bahn line up past Hackescher and Friedrichstrasse all the way up to Tiergarten to the African Refugee Centre. With every step taken my heart grew lighter. Soon I would be rid of her. I would be free of my responsibility.

Once in Brighton a few months later I saw a young black woman sitting by herself on a bench above the shingle and I thought of her. Another time it was the newsreader on the telly, what's her name, it was the way she moved her mouth, something about the way she moved her mouth, yes, strange because of course Ines rarely spoke.

When people ask me about the Roma I never include my story about Ines. Although Julia did ask. She was interested to know what had happened to her. I couldn't really tell her. I was able to lead my aunt up to the door of the refugee centre. After that—I don't know.

The following summer I came to Berlin with the cinematographer Harry Porter Lee. I was there to show him the traps, to lead him around Alexanderplatz, to point out the familiar faces. The Roma were back. And without any lead from me I noticed Harry gazing up at the Berliner Dom. The ring of green oxide and the black feathers came briefly into contact and parted. He kept asking me what I was smiling about.

It was hot that day so we wandered through the station to the shade of the trees on the other side. Harry was complaining of sore feet. We ended up at Neptune's fountain, where Harry took off his shoes and socks and gratefully sank his feet into the dirty water. We sat there a while. The floating starfish turned out to be a soggy sticking plaster. A punk lumbered around the fountain with a beer bottle extended from a hand raised in salute. The solemnity of Neptune holding the triton did not suffer a bit.

When Harry's feet had recovered we wandered down to the casino hoping to find somewhere to sit. A number of Roma sat fanned out across old grass. One was breast-feeding. Three more, and a younger one with a baby, arrived. One of them fished a pink baby's garment out of a beaten-looking bush and with the help of the other two fitted the garment over the baby's head. Behind the breast-feeding woman an older Asian man in denim jacket and jeans, a commissar from the glory days of the GDR (I wonder), tugged free a small pink whistle and peed in fits and starts over the grass.

Harry was pointing to a place for us to sit, and that's when I saw Ines; she was sitting with two men, one older, blind—that was immediately clear. But was it her? She didn't have a plastic bag, and without that plastic bag it did not seem possible that it could be her. She seemed to be more still, but in the right way, composed is probably what I mean, less of a hunted look about her. Instead of a plastic bag a large paper bag of cherries sat on her lap. She passed the bag across the blind man. The other man helped himself. Then the blind man returned the bag to her lap.

I could feel Harry's agitation. He was desperate for somewhere to sit. I told him to go inside the station where it was cooler and buy himself a drink. I'd find him. Now a woman in a tartan skirt approached the trio, clasping a baby to her chest. Her hair was reddish brown, her skin light. She might be a child of some other child of a previous generation from Manchester, say, who had journeyed barefoot across Europe in the heady days of make-believe emancipation to find herself drawn to the fires of a gypsy camp on the outskirts of a city in the Levant. She was almost attractive except for her missing some front teeth. The teeth that remained had to bear a greater responsibility and so suggested the vestiges of something once proud. A miniature idol in the jungles of Java. The Roma woman held out her hand, lay her head to one side and produced a gauzy smile. Pigeons by the dozen flocked around their ankles. The blind man kicked at them, unaware of his companion breaking up a bread roll to feed them crumbs. The blind man went on kicking. I don't think he was aware of the young Roma woman hovering. Ines passed the cherries back to the blind man. As his hand dug in he leant his ear to listen to her. He nodded and held out a cherry between his fingers. The young Roma mother took it, dipped her head and thanked him. She stepped aside and stood eating the cherry, her eyes on the Berliner Dom.

The blind man reached in the bag and held up another cherry and the young mother flew to his hand. Now two small girls came running over. The blind man gave each child a cherry. The young mother returned for another. Now one of the women sitting on the grass picked herself up and wandered over; her smiling face shouted something to the other woman. The mother with the cherry in her mouth nodded. The younger man seated to the other side of the blind man stood up. He was white, his sideburns were unfashionably long. He was heavy in the shoulders, a bit plump to be wearing a T-shirt. He wasn't comfortable with all these mouths to feed. He wanted to shoo them away. He couldn't do that while the blind man continued feeding them so he sat down again.

Now Ines was handing out cherries. Six ragged apparitions stood spitting out the stones. The pigeons had withdrawn to the lawn with a sad air of dispossession. Enthralled with their own sense of benevolence the blind man and Ines kept reaching into the paper bag. The Roma showed no sign of leaving. Once more the man with the sideburns stood up, as if to distance himself, though clearly he couldn't leave without the other two. By now the Roma were accepting the cherries with less ceremony. The popping sounds were the spat stones landing on the pavement. *Pop. Pop. Pop.* Some more Roma arrived. Ines took the cherry bag off the blind man's lap and handed it to a heavier woman in a woollen top. She took it from Ines and like a dog with a bone she walked to the grassed area with the other women and small girls dancing at her sides and with their hands held out, which they must have thought in their confusion had worked like a charm just a moment ago.

I wanted to stay. I would have followed them too. I was still thinking about that opportunity when I found Harry in the station. Sure enough he had gotten lost. He was talking to a drunk. I grabbed his wrist and dragged him out of the station. But they were gone. So were the Roma. Harry kept asking me what the hell I was looking at. There on the ground around the bench were red stains and a scattering of cherry stones.

twelve

Hannah

I am not particularly happy to be having this conversation. But, just so you know, may I say this? I never spoke to her. Well, I may have once when I rang the apartment. Usually Ralf was the one to answer. On occasion it was a woman on the other end. When you have been that woman it is odd to hear another picking up the phone, even though Ralf and I have been apart nine years, so there is a brief hesitation at my end. I assumed it was the African woman. Berlin is a large city. But I have found that one's occupancy comes down to a small number of streets, one or two trains, a handful of restaurants, a favourite book shop, cinema and a corner of the Tiergarten or the Volkspark. A pattern emerges. The pattern of our lives, yes, if you follow someone over a period of time you will get to know it.

Of course I am not referring to anything that I did or would approve of. After a forty-year-long marriage I can say with some confidence that I know, even now, where he is, depending on the hour. I have never followed him. To do so would be undignified. That is not a position which Ralf shares. Dignity of that kind requires a process of thought which unfortunately lies outside of his emotional capacity. You will note—I did not say 'intellectual capacity'. No. Ralf is a very clever man. But even intelligence can run into brackish water if it is not carefully steered. My own pattern is known to Ralf and he has never hesitated to contrive an encounter. I have become used to them as one does to a bus turning up at a certain time. So we would bump into one another at Wertheim, at the Dorotheenstrasse *cimitière* where I work. I will turn seventy-one next birthday and I'm proud to say I still have a use in this world. I will continue my work until the day I drop, which I hope is still a way off but not so far as to be obscene.

I never minded seeing him at Wertheim or at Cafe Einstein on Unter den Linden, where we used to like to go for breakfast. You can no longer smoke. So I don't go as often as I once did. Dorotheenstadt was more problematic. With a tour or lecture group I did not have the time to talk to him. Working in a cemetery as I do, wandering around the headstones of geniuses and remarkable people, I am more aware than most, acutely aware, of not outstaying my welcome.

The entire postwar history of the GDR cultural pantheon is buried in that small cemetery. Think about that. Lifelong enemies lie head to toe in the ground. Old lovers, rejected lovers. One's status is always shifting. There they all are, arguing and quarrelling all the way to the grave. So, I would see him through the fog of history seated on the far side, on the bench by the cypress tree, often with the African woman and later with the man as well, I have forgotten his name. I think Ralf called him 'Defoe' but Ralf often likes to give names to people which he thinks more appropriate than their own. Anyway, there they would sit on the edge of my vision, like graveyard ghosts, spectres. Under the circumstances he did not expect me to break away from my group to speak with him. And yet once I had spied him I remained aware of him. He must have known that. Yes. I think so. Think of what a window offers and how often we are distracted by a small fly spot. This is how it was.

After I got over the surprise of him turning up like this I began to look for him. That's when I started to take an interest in his helper. As far as I could tell she never spoke. She sat as one does in the cinema waiting for the main feature, that is to say with a certain obligatory air of boredom. Unlike my former husband, who appeared to sit in a state of rapt concentration, as if he could hear what I was saying. Always at the back of my mind I entertained a preposterous interruption from Ralf, a raised hand, an impertinent question from the far corner of the graveyard. It's true. The graveyard is a favourite place of his. I can hardly object to his visiting it. That he did so when he did is what I objected to, and I said so when I rang his apartment, and it was on one of those occasions that the black woman must have picked up the phone.

Please don't take this the wrong way. But it is funny to think of Ralf with a black woman. I don't mean he was *with* her in that sense. Goodness me, no. She was young. Twenties, I suppose. Ralf turned seventy-three last May. I sent him a card. No, impossible. They are forty or fifty years apart. And besides, my former husband is discreet when it comes to exercising his libido. There are places in Berlin. Doorways that have the discretion of stone.

The task he needed the black woman for is the same one that came between us.

It was after his father died; we were clearing out his possessions. Ralf, at this stage, was not yet legally blind. He could still pick out an aeroplane in the sky, but not a bird in a tree. A word on a billboard but not a word in a book. He would see the car approaching but not the cyclist. His visual world was selective, random, but each day the blind spots grew. Slowly he became a menace to himself. Ultimately he could not be left alone. But before then, when he still had some visual power and independence, we were clearing out Otto's things.

Ralf's father was a lovely man. Ralf used to joke that I had married him but it was his father I was in love with. Perhaps there is some truth in that. He was gentle and attentive. From the time Ralf brought me home his father took a shine to me. I was attractive in those days. In a conventional sense, I mean. Blonde. Bright-eyed. It had its advantages. Do you know something? Ralf and I met on a film set. This is absolutely true. A promotional film on Berlin. I am the big gooey-eyed duckling from the provinces arriving in the city. Ralf is supposedly the city sophisticate. We meet on a tram and he arranges to show me around. *Love in Berlin*. That's what it was called. It was a device, you see—two young people together discover the newly built city of Berlin. There it is, arisen from the rubble and ashes. Anyway that's how we met. I really was from the provinces. It was the May Day holiday. I had nowhere to go so Ralf brought me home. Otto made a great fuss of me. He talked with me, not at me. He asked me questions and he listened carefully, not as his son did with an impatient flicker in his eye as if a meter was running. He listened to my responses. And his questions flowed out of my answers: always a sign. Ralf sat silently. An unwilling student in that regard, staring grimly down at his plate.

After lunch Otto took me to his glass house. He loved his plants, and loved to share his green-fingered passion. He collected woodcuts, folk art, not very good, *naïf* and not what I would call art, but that is beside the point; he delighted in his woodcuts of the forester, the fisherman, the beer drinker. I have barely mentioned Edith, Otto's wife. Edith Grossman. She was more guarded—perhaps like her son. She died of cancer while still in her forties. Then Otto met a widow, a fellow horticulturalist, and they moved to Hamburg. We saw less of him. Then, hardly at all, until he became sick with leukemia. He decided to try and make it to Christmas. He died the day after. We waited until the new year before we returned to pack up his things. I forgot to add—the horticulturalist had also moved on. She happens to be a very good plant artist, very much in demand. A publishing house offered her a contract to paint all the plant holdings in one of the museums. I forget which one. There she fell in love with one of the curators. I met him once and did not take to him. Though he and Ralf got on like a house on fire.

So, back to Hamburg. There is just myself and Ralf who have returned to clear out Otto's things. Old clothes that he couldn't bear to throw out. Shoes he had stopped wearing years ago. Nice shoes, their toes covered in thick dust. Ties. A drawer filled with them. That was a surprise. Neither Ralf nor I could remember when we had last seen him in a tie. Otto was a casual dresser. The only time I saw him in formal shoes was as he lay in his coffin. Shirts. Some still in their plastic. Two very nice shirts I had bought for his sixty-fifth birthday which he had worn when Ralf and I visited, then carefully put back in their packaging after we left. So we packed up all these things along with the pots and pans and crockery, old bowls with rustic scenes, the fish jumping compliantly for the cast fly. I remember those bowls with affection. We were almost finished when I discovered another wardrobe—Ralf, of course, had missed it—where we found his soldier's uniform on a hanger. In another box a very old camera. In a big yellow folder I found the photograph.

When I was a child I saw a dog that had been run over by a car. I heard its bellowing bark and squealing from the house. There on the road it lay, its whole body shaking, its eyes very much alive, and aware. That was the thing that touched me, in fact has stayed with me ever since, its self-awareness. Its sides were split open, and as I stood there watching with horror but also with grim fascination I saw its vital organs seep out. It was a complicated moment. The blood and the gore horrified me and yet I could not move away. I had to look. My need to look was obviously greater than my revulsion. Now its owner came running out of a house. The driver of the vehicle had stopped. He walked quickly up to where the dog lay. Two strangers, yes, and the dog, and me. The two strangers looked at me as if I had seen everything, that I alone could apportion blame, but I had only seen the aftermath.

Now, before Otto's open wardrobe, Ralf and I, who had been more or less happily married for so many years, were about to turn into strangers. The photograph was of a ravine in the Ukraine.

The ravine was filled with bodies, all of them naked, all of them women, some dead, some alive but soon to be dead. The photograph had been taken in a dull winter light. An unremarkable moment: this is what the day wishes the viewer to think. It was like so many photographs that we saw after the war. So. I was not shocked, not as shocked as the first time I saw such things, and possibly not as shocked as I had been to see that dog with its dark bristly fur split open to blood and rib. The shock came of finding this photograph in Otto's wardrobe.

We'd had that conversation that young couples did in those days. We were very interested—some of us, at least—to know how our respective families had been affected by the war. What part they had played, and so on. Ralf was still a boy when the war ended. His memories are confined to summers in Rügen. The beach beneath the white cliffs. The long absences of his father. He said his father had been conscripted and worked in communications. Mine was in the Luftwaffe. There was nothing about Otto's past, as we knew it, or as Ralf had told it, and no doubt had been told by his parents, that would point to that photograph hidden away in the wardrobe.

At first we gaped at it. We looked at it for a very long time, snatching it from one another, peering over each other's shoulders. Then we pondered how it could possibly have ended up in Otto's things. Ralf was determined to believe it was a mistake. That it had somehow found its way into his father's possessions the way a moth will turn up between the pages of an unopened book. He persisted with this line of thought or faith, which it really was, faith or hope, I expect, and I can understand Ralf's wishful thinking. Anyone can. In another folder we found the explanation.

Otto had been a photographer assigned to the killing units employed to round up the Jews in the far east. There, I said, and I stabbed my finger at the irrefutable proof. It was stated in his papers. But why had the old man stowed it among his things? Had he forgotten it? Unlikely. He had only to open up that particular wardrobe in order to see his soldier's uniform and the folders. We wondered if Edith had known about it. Possibly...but it was unlikely she would do anything with it. I mean—destroy it. The horticulturalist? Ralf could have rung her to find out. That was my suggestion. But the moment he said 'Yes, I should...' I knew he wouldn't.

Poor Ralf. I felt sorry for my husband and I felt sorry with him. He must have believed, as I did, that his country's past had not been able to reach out and stain him. So. One after another the mysteries were solved. All but one, I should say. Why would Otto have held onto this unpleasant and implicating evidence? Was it so his son would eventually know? Then why not sit him down and tell him while he had the chance to? Depending on which way you look at it, the matter of the photograph either reflects badly or well upon Otto. He could have chosen to burn it, in which case his involvement would have remained unsuspected. But he kept it, in the sure knowledge it would be found following his death in just the manner I have described. He wanted this to be known about himself but he did not want to have to face the self-righteous indignation and wrath of his son. This is my conclusion.

Now we had to decide what to do with it. I should say—Ralf had to. It had been his father's. Now it was his responsibility. We drove back to Berlin with it on the back seat of the car. What should be done with it? We discussed and argued. The photograph was still in its folder on the seat. We spoke about it as you would a living thing. It was more than a photograph, it was a record of a criminal event. Moreover it contained another capacity—to change my view of Otto, and even of our own lives and our relationship with the deceased, who, as I hope I have made clear, was a dear and gentle man. There was no easy answer. There was no handy program for stepping safely clear of history.

The photograph could not stay in the car. So now we discussed where to put it in the apartment. It was not something you would wish to leave lying around. We agreed on that; it made perfect sense. There. We were in agreement. So if we didn't leave it lying casually around to be discovered by our friends, where might we stow it? That raised another difficult question. Would we not be doing what Otto had done? By placing it out of view we would in effect be hiding it. The scene of that ravine is not something I would wish to see every day in the same way that we live with a vase of flowers or a fish tank. It was very very difficult to know what to do with it.

I suggested the cupboard in the kitchen—and immediately regretted it. I did not want dead bodies near food. My God—that sounds harsh, doesn't it? It's not quite what I meant. Ralf pointed out that a cupboard is no better than a wardrobe. So we wandered the apartment, from room to room, in search of an appropriate place. In the end, one was found. This is how I remember it. First, Ralf's jubilant voice. I found him standing in the door to his office. I didn't need to be told. I saw immediately the rightness of his desk. Its final resting place was even more considered. Ralf placed the photograph in its folder on top of correspondence and bills. It was a master stroke. It would not be hidden. Nor would it be seen or immediately acted upon. Instead it would join a pile of things to respond to in the near future. Perfect.

For a time afterwards we were able to forget about it, the photograph and Otto and the impending sense of mortality that the death of a parent brings forward, especially now that Ralf's blindness had accelerated. There is a window to the right of his desk. It looks out to a tall chestnut growing at the side of the building. One morning he called me from his office. I found him in a state of great agitation. He wanted to know what had happened to the tree. On whose authority had it been cut down? Why hadn't we been told of its fate in advance so we could do something about it? 'My dear Ralf,' I said. 'You are looking at the wall.' It is impossible to know how one will respond to such news. With anger? Astonishment? Followed by a quick decline into a depressed state? Anyone would be forgiven. Ralf chose laughter.

There were other incidents that we classified as 'humour'. Tea was poured onto the floor. Sugar was sprinkled over the salad. I found him naked and wrestling with the doors of the linen cupboard. He was trying to get into the shower. He had been a few years retired from the university. His morale had to be carefully managed. So when we talked about the future it contained the same life we had known and took no account of his condition. To keep up appearances, for my sake, yes, I believe so, he would place things, clothes, books, objects, and measure their proximity so that he could move towards them with the same confidence as a seeing person. I would never describe Ralf as vain, yet it seemed at the time a strange kind of vanity had gotten hold of him.

One morning—wait, I can be more precise, it was April 23, the previous day I had walked through the city marvelling at all the new colour and scents in the air—well on the morning of April 23 I woke to find him sitting on the side of the bed. He heard me stir. He said he couldn't get to sleep. It must be in the middle of the night. He was desperate to get back to sleep. He was sorry if his restlessness had woken me. I told him it was morning. He lifted his head in the direction of the window. At least he managed that much on his own. I have not forgotten his look of grief. Then his pride got the better of him. He smiled—said he had been joking. And I too entered into this make-believe. I pretended it was still night. What is that saying? The blind leading the blind.

Well, after that his deterioration became a private matter. He was careful to avoid making declarations about the state of a world he could not see. His pride demanded more caution from him. And now, it really did become a case of the blind leading the blind. The blind issued orders. I had to bring him this, bring him that. Read this, deliver that. I became his factotum. My limbs and capabilities were turned to his ends. His blindness made me into a slave. I should have felt more sympathetic. Well, I like to think that I was for a while. But it didn't last. Ralf's neediness didn't court sympathy. He didn't allow me that response. Instead, I felt resentful. He claimed still to have a vague sense of the object or the presence of another. I think that might be true. I would catch him looking at his hands, at his face in the mirror. When I asked what he was doing he said he was committing his appearance to memory. This became an urgent task. Before blindness erased his world he was determined to draw up an inventory of things he wished to study, to furnish his blind world with. He was like a traveller packing for a long journey. He had to decide which memories and knowledge of things he wished to take into this new world he was headed for.

There were some sweet moments. For example, my husband looked at me as he had when we first met. He looked at me intently. He was surprised to discover that my eyes were green and not blue as he had once declared. I should have corrected him way back then. I thought perhaps he was colour blind. Then, much later on, I realised he was selective in his looking. Even when he appeared to be looking he might not have been. He was just presenting his eyes to the world. To me. While his thoughts were elsewhere. Now he combed my face with a jeweller's eye. He had to bring himself very close. It was a very intimate experience. It was nice, flattering I suppose, to know that I too was being packed away with his father's woodcuts, which he stood under, gazing at, and the books that he passed by with a finger trailing against their spines.

We went to places he had never shown any interest in before. The flower shop, for example. He wished to see a flower. He peeled back the petals and peered in. We visited places—Schloss Charlottenburg—that were in the film *Love in Berlin*. Ralf and I were filmed walking hand in hand. It didn't make the cut. Alexanderplatz. Tiergarten. We caught trains and trams into the old neighbourhoods in the east, Friedrichshain, Prenzlauer Berg. We visited art galleries, museums. I had to describe the city passing in the tram window. In the Bode I led him around his favourite sculptures. There were times when it felt like one big long farewell. But, as I say, it was quite the opposite. He was packing a lot away.

Which brings us back to the photograph. Although it was in his possession, in the apartment, it could legitimately slip into invisibility because he could no longer see the detail in it. Blindness offered a way out. The thought momentarily cheered him. But then he decided, rightly, I think, that this was a cop-out. And so the photograph was added to the list of things he needed to remember. Of course he could not see the photograph. He needed me. I had to describe it, be tour leader. And this could not be done over one session. There were several hundred bodies in that ravine. I had to look for distinguishing features because his goal was to try to remember them as individuals. He was determined to see the photograph differently from how Otto, the photographer, had intended. Of course, it meant that I had to walk among the dead in order to pass on to him what he couldn't see. It was a horrible experience, horrible many times over and in many ways, to throw oneself headlong into that ravine with its pile of bodies.

Then, I have to say, after days and weeks of wandering in that scene, it was horrible to acquire the kind of mind that I did, a statistical frame of mind. I wish I could state it differently, better, I think I must mean. I no longer saw the bodies for the individuals they were. I no longer wondered about their foreshortened lives. About the minutes and seconds preceding their tumble into the ravine. I even forgot the role of kind, even-tempered Otto in all of this. I had arrived at the same place and the same frame of mind that accommodates the dispassionate eye. The moment I recognised that pitiless place I withdrew. I refused to look at the photograph. I refused to have anything more to do with it. I told Ralf, I told him—no more. I will read to you, fetch things for you, prepare your meals, but this I will not do. He was furious.

He called me names I had never heard from him before. Above all, he said, I was heartless. Why else would I deny him what he needed to see? *Needed*, he said. But what need is that exactly? What was he looking for that I had not already passed on to him? Further to that, as I saw it at that time, where might such a need lead? Pornography? Would I be required to pass on those sordid details as well? His needs, as he put it, were at loggerheads with my own dignity and self-respect. No, I told him. No more. I can't do it. Someone else will have to. I actually said this. In a split second Ralf's fury abated. I could almost see the idea bloom in his mind. It became attractive to him. New eyes would deliver new detail. He would get to see more—better.

So we began to advertise for home help. He wanted foreigners. Young women looking for somewhere to stay in exchange for guide-dog duties. That was our little joke. Possibly in poor taste. So these guide-dogs would visit on a trial basis. The zoo is nearby and that's where he would take them to test their observational skills. It made sense to Ralf. The zoo was an ideal place to test their abilities to tell him something new about those things that were already familiar to him. Anyway, they came and went. Some stayed a week. Later, of course, after I moved out, Ralf would call up with a long harangue about their shortcomings. They were stupid. They couldn't speak English or Deutsch. A Czech girl abandoned him in Tiergarten while she rendezvoused with her boyfriend, a French trick cyclist. A Polish girl smuggled her lover into the apartment. It was a week before he was discovered and Ralf hounded them both out. There were others.

Then the black woman. There was no mention of her until I saw him with her one afternoon. This was at Wertheim. Ralf has a sweet tooth. Wertheim was one of our highlights during those mad weeks of mopping up the city. Well, he was sitting at the table by the Roman fountain. The black woman sat opposite, silent, about as companionable as a vase, I remember thinking, and, poor Ralf. But by now our lives had moved apart. I was seeing another man. And that was the last thing I ever expected to happen, but it did. Ralf got wind of it. Interrogated me over the telephone until I told him there would be no more telephone conversations if he continued in this way. He shut up. So quickly in fact that it made me feel worse. What ray of sunshine I provided by that stage I cannot imagine. But there must have been something for him to shut up so quickly.

Some months passed before I saw him again. He was still with the black woman, and younger man, perhaps in his forties, who on closer inspection looked more like a tourist. I actually thought, *Yes, that's it.* The man is a tourist and Ralf and the black woman are directing him somewhere. But then I saw them again—and they were a threesome. On the Ku'damm, a little gang of three, completely improbable, mysterious in their own way, bobbing along in search of a favourable landfall. I am being grandiloquent. Ralf used to complain to me about these 'flourishes' of mine. He only ever wanted the 'facts'. The description of the thing itself. Not opinions. In this way, my personality was purged, deemed superfluous. It took me a long time, a year perhaps, by which time I had moved to my own flat, before my personality returned, before I became 'me' again—all those parts that host memory and opinion were welcomed back from their exile.

The black woman stayed longer than the others. She must have found a way of living with the photograph. And with Ralf's special request. The constant surprise of a new young woman leading Ralf by the arm had become a thing of the past. Now it was just the black woman. It became impossible for me to imagine them apart. Then when I learnt about the boarder it was different again. The black woman, Ines, Ralf and this new person whose role wasn't clear. Another foreigner. It was possible to see as much at a glance. I have said so. Ralf squeezed and surrounded by foreign borders. I realised how different his domestic life must be now from the one I remembered when he liked nothing more than to be left alone for hours in his study. When the first young women arrived to help Ralf I used to imagine them wandering around the apartment. I used to wonder what they thought in this strange new space. Strange to them, but not to me. It's nine years now, but I imagined I could step inside the apartment and still know where to find everything.

The arrival of Ines changed it—changed the history of the apartment. Now it was a whole new thing I could not see into. And that helped, more than anything, helped to put Ralf's life and mine onto a completely different footing. For the first time we became apart in the real sense. It was as if Ralf had gone to live in a foreign country I knew nothing about.

thirteen

Ralf

Dear Ines. I regret to tell you, I am not much use. I cannot even tell you what Ines looks like. She was with me for two years. I know she is African. Where in Africa? Somewhere like Liechtenstein in Europe, the equivalent thereof, no doubt. She may have said where. Please disregard what I said about Liechtenstein. There was no milk in the fridge this morning for my coffee. It's the little things that irritate and beyond all reason these days.

Ines came into this household one August morning two years ago. Ines Maria Luis. I thought I'd forgotten that. Where does all this information sit? I wish I knew. But August is correct.

I needed a housekeeper. I imagine it isn't an easy job as far as jobs go. She could just as easily have worked in a cafe, but she chose to live here and work for me. I don't know what I can say about her. She was often close to me, in the physical sense, as a matter of inevitability and safety. In public she made a point of staying close by, her arm looped in mine. You would think that to be an easy task, to lead an old man about the city. Not everyone can do it. To guide requires judgment. You don't want to be dragged about like a sack of potatoes. She was a pilot fish to my whale—not very flattering in my case but it gets to the quality of her presence. There, but discreetly apart. Conversation was not her strong point. I would be hard pressed to recall anything of any substance said by her. Ines. That's a Spanish name. Is the rest Italian? Well I asked her once and got no reply. Whenever she did not wish to answer she would go silent, and then it would be as if she were no longer there, present. I'd wonder if I had been talking to myself. That's the thing about blindness. You become overly dependent on your ears. So I would be left to listen to the bird outside the window, the distant crawl of the traffic across the city, then, I'd hear a floorboard at the end of the apartment give up a clue followed by the soft close of the kitchen door.

I gave her money for lessons in Deutsch. After two months I'd say something—*wie geht's*—and the silence would be followed by the trail of footsteps in the direction of the kitchen. Her ability to speak English happened to be one of the reasons for employing her. I enjoy English. Hannah, my wife, has some English. Russian is her other language, and lately, I understand, Italian. Anyway the English Ines had she spoke beautifully. But in quick time I realised she had perfected set-pieces. The way we can all get up and play the one piece on the piano or guitar. Her repertoire was disappointing, but I didn't want to replace her. I'd grown fond of her. I appreciated the quiet way she occupied the apartment. She was no cook, however. I don't know what she did with the housekeeping. I always considered it a generous amount. There was never anything to eat. I'd ask her to buy *apfelkuchen.* The next day she would tell me it was all gone. How did that happen? Well, of course, I asked that very question. Back came the predictable reply—silence, the sounds of the city, the traffic, all of that would fill up the apartment, then I would hear the door to the kitchen open and close, and I'd find myself alone.

I needed someone else, someone with language and conversation, an educated person, and that is how Defoe entered the household. There is a bedsit on the floor below which belongs with this apartment. When Hannah was here we used it as a spare room for guests; her niece from Cologne would sometimes come to stay. In exchange for that bedsit I gained a more able companion than Ines, someone with an eye for detail. Someone competent in English, someone with conversation in him.

Once we got to know each other better—I suppose once we had one another's confidence—I asked Defoe, our new boarder, to describe Ines to me. Naturally I was curious. She had been with me nearly a year by then.

Blindness forces one to become adept at translating the spaces between the words—the pauses, the silences. One pause is not the same as another. As for silence I could compile an encyclopedia on the subject. Taxonomy was my first love. As a boy I remember being entranced when a dragonfly rose above the bulrushes. I reached for it to claim it as my own. I wanted to possess it as a child is wont to do, and, of course, as nature is clever enough to arrange, the dragonfly eluded my clutches and led me on a merry chase through libraries in my teenage years all the way to the lecture halls of Humboldt University after the war.

When I asked Defoe to describe Ines to me there was a silence—a pause, I should say, and then a silence. I told him I don't want to know how much is in her purse. I would just like to know what she looks like. Then he started on his thoughtful description. He didn't use the word *schwartz*. That was interesting because everyone else had. Defoe said she had light skin. He spoke of a 'depleted colour'. I liked that notion of colour being not what it is. 'Like potato peel,' he said. I wasn't expecting that one. And attractive. He said that quickly. Curious. Because we tend to linger before beauty. It's why we look at a painting for as long as we do, or for that matter marvel at the extraordinary construction of a dragonfly. Potato peel, though. That was different. That was original. Never before had I heard a woman's complexion described in such terms. Now he volunteered more. He said she walked with a very straight back. The way he said that I could tell he personally found it very attractive.

In time I became more dependent on Defoe than on Ines. Don't get me wrong. In her own way she was dependable. I am old, officially old, although most days I don't quite feel it in my heart or bones. Dependability is a quality I have come to admire more and more. I can find no fault with Ines in that regard. Some of the helpers I had before Ines you would not trust to look after a goldfish. Defoe became important. He filled in those gaps Ines could not hope to. Nor did I find Defoe to be guarded, unlike Ines. In fact, he was quite the opposite. He spoke freely, alarmingly freely—that's how it struck me, then, but I soon got used to it. His forthrightness. The open-hearted way in which he offered himself up over a range of subjects, his marriage, everything really. I found that refreshing. Very un-European. Not very sophisticated, as my estranged wife would put it. But in light of the person I came to know and respect that kind of sophistication isn't worth much. We touched on the subject once. Sophistication. He wondered what the point of it was. I dare say I made a hash of trying to explain it. 'Well,' I said, 'sophistication is a way of being in the world. One keeps one's emotions in check. One presents a certain fixed view of oneself.' 'Like the prow of an old wooden sailing ship,' he said.

As a child he had boarded a Chilean sailing ship visiting his home town of Wellington. Years later it was revealed that the *Esmeralda* had been used as a prison and a place of torture. It had the most beautiful prow. Wooden, carved, elaborate paintwork. This conversation took place at the zoo, early on. There is a small beach in the corner of the zoo, at the Tiergarten end. That's where we were. Seated together on a bench talking about sophistication while the noises of the zoo—the squawks and squeals, the plaintive roars of the assembled beasts—swirled around us. But where we sat was a gentle and quiet place. There was just enough warmth in the sun. It must have been late August or early September when Defoe first joined us.

There was a pause—not an uncomfortable silence, and that represented a tick in his box. With some of the helpers I've had silence is a threat, something to ward off. There was a girl from Prague. She found it particularly challenging. She would fill up a perfectly lovely silence with chatter and inanity, emptying her impoverished mind into that beautiful silence, which I think she must have viewed as a chasm she might fall in unless she produced a clamour of words to grasp hold of. Silences with Defoe were enjoyable. So after a pause he asked what I would prefer to know about the *Esmeralda*: about her beautifully crafted figure head or her use as a prison ship in the years after Allende was despatched. Which did I prefer—and here he used my own words—how it presented itself to the world or the truth we would come to know about it? I thought it was possible to hold onto both ideas. There followed another silence. Actually, a quite lengthy silence. An erudite silence. At the end of which, he said, 'Yes, I agree.'

We talked about the lungfish. There was his marriage break-up. From time to time he alluded to it. He got the news in the Antarctic. I'll come back to that. On the subject of the lungfish he had interrupted a doctoral thesis to bring up a family. He worked in Fisheries; that's what had taken him down to 'the ice', as he called it. The reason I mention the lungfish is the *Esmeralda*. At the zoo the conversation moved on. He talked admiringly of the capacity of the lungfish to hold two versions of itself. Apparently it can live in and out of water. Now he arrived at the question that interested him. At which point does it become the one thing and cease to be the other? In becoming that new thing how much does it retain of the other?

We moved onto cross-fertilisation. Something I happen to know something about. Genetically modified foods. And racial groups, a mishmash these days, a blend to which we applied the question asked of the lungfish, which brought us back to Ines. Those African features, described by Defoe, planted over a lighter skin. Skin the colour of potato peel. In that way a person carries her history. One of the ways, I should say. With Ines I never got further than that Liechtenstein place in Africa and I've since forgotten that information. One of the indignities of age is also an advantage. Any secret is safe with me because almost certainly it will be forgotten the next day.

Latency, that's what we talked about. And more. Defoe gave me new fields to roam around in. I'd never met anyone who had visited the Antarctic. When he spoke of the trans-Antarctic mountains—that single phrase lifted the idea of Antarctica off that flat grid of ice which up until that moment was all I had imagined there was to it. Defoe's area of expertise happens to be in fish quota management systems. That's why he was down there. But he knew a lot more besides—had seen a great deal. He'd touched with his own hands a fossilised bit of beech. He said it had been part of the great central Antarctic beech forests several millennia ago. Extraordinary, at least I think so, to hold in one's fingertips a remnant of a vanished world. And I said so, until he interrupted me to say it was wrong to think it had disappeared. The spore of the beech lay deep in the ice, beneath blankets of ice containing air breathed at the time of the Vandals and the Picts and long before. Beneath the ice lay a continent with the profile of another Europe: mountains, ridges, even lakes. He saw Antarctica in a form of preservation. For the moment comatose, but in a vigilant state of readiness for that time when mankind had spoiled every last clod of dirt and needed another continent to start over. Latency, you see. So I think I understand his interest in lungfish.

Ines was always within earshot of these conversations. We took her silence for granted. A form of acquiescence, yes, but remember, it was what she preferred. I for one would have been delighted had she waded in with an opinion about Defoe's *Esmeralda*.

I don't know if I have much more to add. I'm getting on. My memory is not the formidable warehouse it once was. It plays tricks on me. I will remember how I felt aged nine waking one morning in Rügen to sunlight spread over the Ostsee but I cannot recall waking up yesterday. Everyone says the same. I'm sorry. I am beginning to sound like an old bore.

For a year they were my closest companions. After they went, first Ines of course, and then Defoe, I was bereft. I felt disabled, helpless. I had been abandoned, stuck to the wall of the apartment, the lights switched off and the doors closed.

I always knew Ines' whereabouts. I could tell where she was in the apartment. I mentioned this to her one day. After that she passed over the floorboards even more like a shadow. She was not completely successful. Then it troubled me that she would try to make such an effort. Why would she want to leave me in the dark as to her whereabouts? A blind man is already diminished, why seek to diminish him more? They were my steadfast companions. Ines and Defoe. I never pretended it to be an equal relationship. They could see me. I could not see them exchange glances, which brings us back to silences, and such moments didn't always escape my attention. I could not tell what the exchange meant. I only knew that it had passed between them.

I remember the terrific explosions of New Year's Eve. Rockets firing over the skies of Berlin. Drunk men toppling about in dresses, according to Defoe. A city bound up in red firework paper. A tide of broken glass around the city, again, according to Defoe. Well it was after that momentous occasion—some time in January, I would say—that I lay in bed listening to the methodical footsteps of Defoe in the room on the floor below progress up the stairs and across the landing. I heard the apartment door open and close. If treachery and betrayal are ever in need of a stock image then look no further than a door opening and closing in such a way. And then I heard Defoe's footsteps trail off in the direction of Ines' bedroom. There is not much more to say.

I felt threatened. I hadn't felt that way in years. What if he took her away? I would be left alone again. I could always find a replacement, a new Ines, but I was comfortable with the Ines I knew. The trust—let's be clear about that—we had in each other. I felt secure, very secure with her at my side as we strolled together through the city. On the other hand, if it came to that, perhaps I would find an even better Ines. So why did I feel this way? I think I was a little bit jealous. Yes. Just a little. Not so big a jealousy for it to be unseemly or grotesque. No. A small feeling that I contained.

From this point on I was aware of a new silence. A suspension of thought, such as the delayed conversation that holds two people in check until the child has been put to bed.

I began to feel in the way. I began to miss my wife. Nineteen ninety-seven is the last time I saw her. My eyes were already in a bad state but something strange and not altogether unpleasant began to happen. As my wife faded from view she grew younger. She liked to hear that. Later, as a matter of course, she moved back into such general terms that she could have been anyone. I could no longer see the small white fish-tail scar beneath her left cheek. She'd had it since childhood after falling off her bike. The scar made her self-conscious and the lengths she went to to conceal it made her all the more attractive. Hannah can be stern at times. The thing about the scar—it made her vulnerable. It was the only thing to have that effect. She was always looking in the eyes of someone she'd just met to see whether they'd noticed the scar. Well, I could not see it any more. I could not find it. With my fingertip I could. Scar tissue is smoother than skin, smooth as a cold pebble to touch, so I could always find her area of vulnerability. I could find it now, if she was to sit here beside me right at this moment I could reach across and find it. A bit like an old and familiar address. You don't ever think about how you got there.

I still miss my wife. I miss the intimacy. I don't mean what happens between the sheets. I am talking about the unspoken part that enfolds one life with another. With Hannah I had the feeling of us looking out the same window at a shared past, seeing the same things, the air of the world touching us at the same moment, so that you felt a coordination of response. I think for periods of our marriage, long periods, we became one person. Then, one day, it is no longer. We are no longer. The specialist warned us it could turn out this way. The catastrophe of my blindness would affect the two of us. She calls me. We talk on the phone. She tells me about her life. But it is not the same. I cannot see it. I cannot see her. I used to think she would come back, just turn up one day, and nothing would need to be said. It would be as if she'd somehow lost her way home or was later than expected, and here she was unloading the shopping and so forth, and of course I'd welcome her in. I used to think we'd manage it to a certain point but not beyond, say, a well-mannered hotelier welcoming back a favoured guest. Things change. The bond shifts. Then you look around for the thing that shaped it, well that's gone too, so there is only memory and no easy fit, nothing to pour yourself back into to make it work.

Back in the days when I could still see we would take the train up to Rügen. She liked Binz. She loved the boardwalk above the beach. We would walk up and down there in the evening. Whenever we stopped my eyes would go automatically to the horizon. There in the distance where all things merge and the boundaries are uncertain, there, I used to think, is a place I'd like to dwell.

Imagine waking up each day and not knowing where everything is—well, that's the place I ended up in. Am I complaining? I hope not. My situation is not a suffering. It is a frustration. You find yourself forever arriving late to the joke. People around you—at the tram stop, say—are laughing. What can they be laughing at? You find your face shifting to join the laughter but you must wait. You must wait for a clue and go from there. You might hear someone say 'I thought she would catch the dog.' So, it involved a dog, whatever it is; it is now a past event. This is how you exist in the world. Playing catch-up.

For how long, I wondered, had this been going on between Defoe and Ines? What had I missed? I felt foolish. I felt as though I had relinquished something. I could not have described what. Perhaps part of it is revealed when I say what happened next. I began to take them to new places. Places which on their own might not mean much but were reliant on me to illuminate. To the cemetery at Dorotheenstadt. This is a world I know intimately. I knew every headstone, the story of every life. That cemetery is an amazing burial ground of old enmities, love affairs and political jealousies. I am surprised that the egos of the dead allow them to lie at rest. I am surprised that personalities indignant about being stripped to mere bones don't erupt from the graves and begin shouting for the world's attention. Of all the personalities buried there we might be prepared to forgive Hegel, but his is one of the quieter ones. So we would visit the cemetery and walk about the headstones.

Bertolt Brecht is buried there. I was amazed. Neither of them had heard of Brecht. In Ines' case I could understand. But Defoe? An educated man, a man who had visited Antarctica. Incredible. I wanted to shout up at the treetops—I am with two nincompoops. *Idioten*. I was so happy! In light of those footsteps I heard almost nightly between the landing and Ines' bedroom, in light of that trespass on my good will, I was all the more derisive. Until the silence I heard was that of a hermit crab recoiling and wriggling deeper into its shell. Then of course I felt bad. I had gone overboard. So, I recalled Defoe's lungfish, its dual capacities, and drew Defoe's attention to the fact that while Brecht was a committed Communist he did not belong to the Party. Silence. Well, perhaps it was a long bow. Or perhaps he chose to punish me by pretending he didn't get it.

I pointed out Helene Weigel's grave. She lies head to toe with her husband, Brecht. Here lies another tale of twin capacities. Their marriage and Brecht's affairs. But no one played the role of mother better than Helene Weigel in *Mother Courage*. I got Defoe and Ines to orient me around to the house at the side of the cemetery. It used to be Brecht's house. After his death in 1936 Helene continued to live there. I haven't been there for years. An old friend, Suzanne Zimmer, used to lead tours of the house. I made them leave me on a bench and told Defoe to take Ines for a tour. I instructed him to ask for Suzanne. They came back thirty minutes later with the news that she had died five years earlier. No one had told me.

The next time Hannah called, as she did in those days fairly regularly, I asked why she hadn't told me about Suzanne Zimmer. I reminded her, I may be blind but I'm not yet dead. We argued, of course. Anything for an argument. But later we remembered a picnic with Suzanne in the Tiergarten. She was seeing a theatre lighting expert, Hans, actually quite famous in his field. We all got a bit drunk on champagne and sunshine and high spirits. Hans ended up wading across Neuer See. Suzanne had to fish him out.

So. Ines didn't have much to say about the tour. I asked her if she had seen the large sunny room at the rear of the house with all the desks. Defoe had to answer for her. Each writing project had its own desk. Brecht would wander from one to the other, from a desk with song lyrics, to one with a draft of a poem, to another with a longer prose work. Each desk, I suppose, representing a different part of the brain. And suddenly we were back with lungfish. It was as if Defoe had been waiting for his opportunity. The desk, different capacities, the muse exacting different forces, even the house with its different air can work on an imagination. Different women have the same effect. Which of course used to be Brecht's defence for his affairs. His grand rationale. He needed to sample new fields, to widen his knowledge of the human condition. Regardless of all the women he had, come their moment on stage they were dressed in Helene's costume, and presented in her voice and personality. The other women were just wheat and maize. This line of argument never failed to ignite my tour groups.

If they had been silent, they were no longer. Husband and wife fought with one another while I slipped away to the next headstone.

Johannes Becher, Heinrich Mann, Herbert Marcuse, Johann Gottlieb Fichte, who made self-consciousness his subject, pegged it down to a social phenomenon. One cannot be self-conscious before a rooster or a tree. It requires another who sets limitations of self. Here Defoe interrupted. He said he had once felt self-conscious in front of a dog. 'Really?' I asked. What on earth had he been doing to make himself feel self-conscious before a dog? He wouldn't say. Then I heard Ines make a sound. A snigger or muffled laugh, and so I knew what Defoe was hinting at, and I laughed. I joined in, and Defoe began to laugh and Ines, who I had never once heard laugh before, began to make a sound like the hiccups. We were laughing so much we had to sit down. What was there to sit down on but tombstones? Defoe sat down on Hegel. Author of *The Phenomenology of Spirit*. Died of cholera.

Well, that set us off again. Tears were rolling down my cheeks. I asked Defoe who he was sitting on now. He answered, Günter Gaus. 'Oh,' I said, 'a very important man.' More laughter. Ines? She had sat down on Anna Seghers. That was the only time I can recall laughter, helpless laughter between the three of us. Suddenly I had to urinate. All that laughter. My prostate is a worn thread. So Defoe led me to the nearest place. I had no idea where. My only concern was that I would not be seen. He gave assurances. Then, unfortunately, I heard a particular striking sound. So I knew immediately I was urinating on a tomb. Of course, I could not stop, not now that I had started, and, as well, I was interested to know whose tomb I was urinating on.

I had to ask Defoe. 'Hanns Eisler,' he said.

He was still laughing. Perhaps I was smiling. If so, it vanished the moment he said Hanns Eisler. He let me urinate on Hanns Eisler, student of Arnold Schönberg. I fell quiet. I heard his footsteps on the landing again, those deliberate footfalls in the direction of Ines' room, and the laughing inside of me, helpless a moment ago, subsided to the resentment of earlier. We pressed on, more solemnly now, in an air of restraint—Ines on my elbow, Defoe hovering over my right shoulder—until the silence built up around me, and soon it was occupied by a wind. I could hear the leaves rustling on the trees. Only leaves rustling and nothing else. We could have been in Tibet.

Then it was Ines who spoke. A conciliatory tone, as I recall. She broke that beautiful silence with 'Please, I would like a *heisse Schokolade*.' A *heisse Schokolade*, she said. That brought us crashing down to reality. After all, what could be more important than a *heisse Schokolade*? I am not being facetious. I mean this. I must confess it hadn't occurred to me until Ines spoke up. I can laugh now. At the time though I felt very differently. I will admit—I felt more alone than ever.

part three: *Defoe*

one at a time, floor by floor. As the crowds pushed out the exit doors they turned into shadows. I looked back and there she was, the African face, smiling confidently up at me. This time I smiled helplessly back. And with that I stepped onto the escalator. She held my eye all the way down. It was as though I had won something. All I had to do was push through the crowd to collect my prize. As I drew near she held up a sign: *Room available in exchange for light domestic duties.*

Whenever I tell people how I came to live in the room beneath Ralf and Ines they can't believe I could have been so naive as to walk into that trap. I can't believe it either. But thirty hours in an airplane will do that to you. It stretches the nerves, puts you beyond care. I'd left my judgment somewhere over the Himalayas. The euphoria of walking out of Tegel Airport into early autumnal sunshine had passed. My clothes were stiff with aeroplane filth. In the short commute from Hauptbahnhof, bobbing along in the carriage, imposing on the localness of others, my skin had begun to ooze sweat, and now all I wanted was a shower and to crawl between clean sheets.

As I finished reading the sign, the black woman reached for the old man's wrist and his great head, white and dim, eyelids lowered into bags of skin, wheeled about. All the movement we associate with curiosity had shifted to the region of his mouth. Now that bivalve opened and closed as if unsure for the moment whether it was asked to give or receive. The woman whispered in his ear. His head rolled back, his face came alive, as if to ask *What have we here? 'Sprechen sie Deutsch? Nein?'* His own English was confident, measured, and very quickly I found myself slipping into his easy cadences, so that to my own ears I began to sound

fourteen

A little push this way or a nudge that way, and I would be writing a different version of my time in Berlin. Or more likely I wouldn't be writing anything at all.

An odd couple at first glance—Ines, young, African, and Ralf, old, white, stooped shoulders of dependency. I was gazing down at them from the top of the escalators at Zoologischer Garten. I don't think I would have noticed either one had they stood apart, but together—the white and black of them—they caught the eye. Ines, I should say, caught my eye.

She glanced up and finding me at the top of the escalators she smiled. She did not smile and look away, which frankly is what I would have expected. She kept smiling. Of course she'd mistaken me for someone else. I imagine now I measured up to whoever they were expecting in a general sort of way—white, male, fortyish. I looked away. Outside the station the city lights were coming on, measured and reasonable. He asked, reasonably enough, what had brought me to Berlin from New Zealand, a place so far away. I mentioned Dr Schreiber and the museum's collection of lungfish fossils. Usually I am more careful of the company before I bring up the topic of lungfish. But just then I was too tired to care. The old man's face lit up. He began pumping my hand. 'Welcome,' he said. 'Welcome to Berlin.' So that in a funny way I did feel expected. I should feel pleased, he said. 'Ines'—and this was the first I had heard her name—'Ines', he said, 'isn't someone easily impressed.' Ines' smile made a brief return. And whatever misgivings I may have had left me. I felt absurdly good to have made a favourable impression.

I picked up my bag and we filed out of the station. I wanted to stop and look up at the neon-lit dusk and breathe the air. I wanted to linger. But the lights turned green and the other two marched across the road. Very quickly the traffic and lights were left behind. We were walking alongside a high wall and I would have said I could smell animal dung when out of the looming night came a roar, and here Ralf paused to announce, 'The zoo, it's one of the places I like to visit.'

I hadn't thought to ask the questions someone more sensible would have. About the blind man's address, and to enquire about the neighbourhood, or learn how far away it was. Those questions came to mind only as we left the street and passed through a cutting. Cobbles and leaves took over. A series of lamps illuminated the dark, and through their white flare and dense clouds of moths I could make out the dark shapes of trees. The black coat in front plodded on. At his side, and slightly ahead, Ines in her white boots. Further on in the dark I heard a man's cough, a branch snapped. I looked behind. The other two walked on. I had to hurry to catch up. At last the path turned back towards the traffic. Headlights glanced off the tree trunks. Finally the road, with its hard lines of direction, the paint glistening up at the night. We crossed. Ines took hold of Ralf's arm to hurry him. His concession was to lean forward although his feet moved at the same pace as before. We passed under a railway bridge as a train roared overhead and the night was left ringing. Soon the traffic noise returned, then it too receded, became sporadic, almost a thing of the past, uninterested in itself, as we turned into a neighbourhood of older buildings with front gardens and lit doorways.

We stopped by an iron gate. First Ines, then Ralf, then myself with my bag over my shoulder, like some articulated creature coming to a complicated halt. Ines handed Ralf the sign while she fished in her coat pockets for the key. I glanced up at my new home. I counted five floors. An untidy fringe of winter ivy framed the entrance. The other two moved forward and waited for me inside the gate. There was the sound of the gate closing. Reunited we shuffled up to the front steps. In the lit ground floor window of the African Refugee Centre I saw piles of clothing and toys on the floor.

Inside the foyer, the two heads in front waited until they heard the door close, then a light came on, a harsh yellow light that scared the spiders down off the walls. A faded rosette struggled to hold its form among the crumbling floor tiles.

In the lift I let the bag down from my shoulder, but then it didn't feel right—abandoned at my feet like that it felt careless, even presumptuous—so I hoisted it back to my shoulder. Ines closed the lift doors and with a jolt we began to move very slowly upwards. Ralf began to whistle tunelessly. I felt myself sink beneath layers of fatigue. As we arrived at the top floor another jolt rocked us onto our toes and the whistling stopped.

We kept the same creaturely form outside the door while Ines unlocked it and as the apartment lights came on different planes came into being—floorboards, some wall areas, paintings, books, a long table shining beneath a chandelier. Ines took off in one direction. Ralf in the other. Ines, he said, would make us some tea. I remained stuck to his shoulder as I had from the time we left the station. At the end of the room there was a high-back chair and a sofa. When I sat down it didn't immediately register. So I coughed, and with a breathless tension I watched him shuffle towards the armchair and grope for threads of proximity. His knees and the chair came into contact and suddenly he knew where he was and the rest was achieved with a swift confidence. He sat down. On the wall behind him was a large painting of a seascape. When he leant back he seemed to enter the painting and my impression of him as a tall and kept-indoors type changed into someone with more nautical qualities. Perhaps my silence gave me away. He leant his head back. He said the painting was a scene from his childhood in Rügen.

Ines joined us. She had shed the blue coat. The housemaid's uniform was a surprise, the white cuffs made her appear blacker; she'd tied her hair back. In her hands she carried a silver tray as a small child does entrusted to the task for the very first time, her eyes silently commanding the cups and saucers to stay put. She set out the teacups and saucers. Ralf with his dead eye-sacks listened and accounted for each sound. Only two teacups and saucers.

After Ines left he talked and talked, and I listened as best

I could, but after two cups of tea and after sliding lower and lower on the sofa a yawn escaped me. The long dissertation from across the way stopped. From the other end of the apartment I could hear the shower running. Ralf hauled himself up to his feet apologising and protesting on my behalf. I must be exhausted. How thoughtless of him. He called out for Ines and she came running in a dressing gown, her wet hair wrapped in a towel. I picked up my bag, shook hands with Ralf and followed Ines out to the landing and down the flight of stairs to my door.

On my first morning in Berlin, in Ralf's household, I woke with the airborne velocity of the past thirty hours to the stillness of the room and the sound of an unidentified bird on the windowsill. The velocity slowed and the room grew around me until I could confidently say to myself, *Yes, here I am, in this room, arrived.* As I lay there the detail of the room emerged with the light through the lemon curtains. A desk and chair were shoved into the corner by the window. On top of an empty bookshelf stood a half-finished packet of cereal and a near-empty bottle of olive oil. Presumably things left by my predecessor. The onions in the plastic rack were sprouting. A coffee cup cracked and lined with ancient sediment stood by the kettle. I got up and opened the fridge, hoping for something to drink. Three eggs—that's all—sat on the egg shelf. Later that morning I would throw them out and buy new eggs—not because I actually desired an egg as much as wanting to fill the egg rack with my own. In this small way my occupation of the room was achieved.

I spent the first week exploring the city. I caught trains and trams and walked in the dying sunshine. Everything felt pleasingly familiar or else just how it should be, which may be the same thing. At times the city was like the set of an old film that I had seen or heard about. I wandered past scarred buildings. Across the Tiergarten the public sculptures bore old bullet wounds. Here and there a patch of cement had been applied to fix the nose on a cherub or mend a shattered arm.

For a few hours every afternoon, in exchange for the room, my eyes were at Ralf's service. We had our beat. A walk through the leafy Tiergarten, the zoo, of course—it provided order in the form of a large number of set scenes arranged by pen and cage. Outside of the zoo the order quickly disintegrated into chaos—grinding traffic, accelerative noises, the whine of a bus and the blinks and beeps of technology replaced the bird shrieks and calls. Without the task of guiding a blind man I would not have noticed these things.

I hadn't been to a zoo in years. I'd forgotten the shock of walking in off a city street to confront an elephant. The surprise of the thing has to take its course. But then you see the Indian rhino with its preposterous head shaped like a boot and wearing layer upon layer of medieval cloaks. Was this of interest? Did 'medieval cloaks' do the trick? This was the problem I never really got on top of—what to pass on to Ralf.

Up to now my eyes had always been in my own service. Right from when I first spied the world through the bars of my crib, and later crawled up onto the arm of the couch to look at the sky and at clouds racing in the window, and saw a tree, perfectly still, like some unexpected visitor who knew everything about me.

Up to now I had selected so much of the world for myself, first without judgment, then with judgment, choosing this face ahead of another's in the crowd—Ines', for example, back in the station—and with the apparent randomness of a fly.

What was useful? What was in poor taste? Once when laughter erupted from an Italian tour group I had to explain it was just a camel shitting. We moved on past the long-haired donkeys, who, as usual, were forlorn stationary figures looking for help—not just out of the zoo, you felt, but out of their wet shaggy manes.

'Ostrich,' I announced and Ralf's ears shifted. The trick was not to overburden him with information. The eye of the ostrich moved back. Something was up—that was the feeling. Something imminent, and that's what kept us there. But as it often turned out, nothing was up. The ostrich was still, that's all.

It was exhausting.

It's not a big zoo. Yet by the time the zebras are darting away on their noisy hoofs the city outside is forgotten. Then, late afternoon, you glance up and there, beyond the pin head of a giraffe looming out of the grey, is the neon-lit logo of Mercedes-Benz. It was time to head home again. Out the gates, down the road to the cutting by the aviaries and across the top of the Tiergarten, into the neighbourhood I was working hard to call my own.

After the zoo it was always a relief to hand Ralf over to Ines. I would head back down to the street to collect myself. Restore my eyes. I needed to get on with my work. I needed to apply myself more seriously to the tasks I'd told everyone about. I needed to get on with my drawings of the lungfish at the museum of natural history. But as I stood there in the street watching Berliners—all strangers, as alien as sea lice, hurrying by on foot or bikes—I would spare a thought for Ralf, detached from his 'eyes' and sloping back to the greyer world of memory. The curtain coming down. Apart from Ines' hotel English there would be no more conversation for him, no words for him to latch onto, words that briefly lit up his world, until tomorrow rolled around. Yet, whenever the time came to part, his handshake was firm, business-like. Then, turning away, he would give the impression of someone who knows his way back to that other life and returns to it the way a dog does to its own backyard and kennel even though it has just discovered richer pickings at a neighbour's house.

I did not try to pass everything on to Ralf. For example, the T-shirt slogan of the young Polish woman who served us coffee at the zoo cafe—*access all areas*—I kept that to myself. There were boundaries, not necessarily declared but nonetheless understood. Dog shit over the pavements—he definitely wanted to know about that. The rush of air that froze a blind man into a state of alarm, I assured him, was just a passing cyclist. But other things that verged on or contributed to a mood, boredom, impatience, frustration of one kind or another, I kept those things to myself. The same with flashes of private fantasy when the cold mist of December and January lifted off the city's canals and turned into horses and chariots and creatures clutching tritons. I also kept to myself the vast number of discarded tissues, repellently white, piled at the base of the trees around Faggot's Meadow on our walks through the Tiergarten.

In the snap cold of February the sound of a trouser zip near the outdoor table-tennis tables where the queers hang out was enough to stop Ralf; his head would crane around, and I'd have to tell him it was just a guy in a black coat pissing against a tree. In the warmer months the sighs of missed shots and those coming from the bushes were indistinguishable and we passed through the area like single-minded pilgrims.

The discrete parts of this new life—me, Ines and Ralf—were hardly a natural association. And yet this is what a household achieves. It planes away difference. It also encourages small intimacies.

From any distance it will seem like an odd life to have drifted into.

fifteen

I was curious about Ines from the start. She said little to me. There was so little of her life to look into. Her door was closed whenever I passed it. As soon as I arrived upstairs to take Ralf out she would meet me at the door in her maid's outfit and smiling in that way of hers which I could not quite place until the day I passed a doorman outside one of the fancier hotels in the city.

Where did she go on her afternoons off? I had no idea. There was nothing about her to suggest the possibility of another life. I could not imagine her out of that housemaid's uniform. I could not imagine her exercising free will. But when she left the building there was an intent about her. She was going somewhere. She wasn't out for a dawdle. She didn't glance up at the trees or stop to look at a squirrel. Ines wasn't ever slowed by a daydream. She walked faster than she did with me and Ralf. She walked as people do when late for work or an appointment.

For that matter, I had no idea about where she and Ralf went when it was her turn to take him out into the world. Which part of the city was she lighting up? What did she see that I failed to?

Whenever Ralf wished to complain about Ines he waited until her footsteps had trailed to the far end of the apartment, then he would lean forward and betray her without a second thought. 'Today in Tiergarten, I asked her what she could see. She said, "Trees." "And?" I asked. "And, Ines?" "Trees. People." It could be China or the Amazon. I don't speak Spanish or whatever it is she professes to speak. Her English is that hotel English you've heard from her. Whole phrases from the hotel lobby flow out of her...'

I used to wonder if he complained to Ines in the same way about me. Sometimes when we were out together I'd get ahead of him. I didn't do it deliberately. I'd find myself stepping out, lengthening my stride and without any awareness, except perhaps feeling frustrated that I couldn't find a way to escape back to my work at the museum. Then I'd remember Ralf, and with a rising heartbeat I'd stop and look back in the pedestrian traffic to find him. As a boy, after placing a driftwood 'boat' in the creek I'd run downstream to wait for it to arrive. This is how it often was with Ralf. Here he comes now—his face alert and on the brink of concern, his hands moving out from his sides, but there is a larger red-faced pleasure too. He could pretend he was out and about in the city under his own steam.

It was hardly ever just the two of us. Ines and me, I mean. There were the dishes—Ralf would remain in his usual post-dinner state of bored contemplation as we raced to clear the table around him—and Friday mornings when she dropped by my room with the flowers Ralf wanted thrown out. It was the scent that interested him, and his preference was for the younger scent. The promise of the thing itself rather than its slow decay.

Anyway I came to look forward to Friday morning. It never escaped my attention when she was late. It affected my concentration, and then I'd realise I'd been waiting for her. So what had happened to her? I'd get up from my notes and pace about the room. Then at last I'd look up at the sound of her light progress down the stairs. As she rounded the lift cage I would be standing by my open door.

In my room she moved about in a housemaidy sort of way, her eyes making contact only with the thing she dusted or replaced or picked up. Hands in pockets, I would find myself following her around. I would look for something to distract her with, to delay her. There was the proud chestnut rising from the courtyard. Ines looked so diminutive in the tall window frame the most natural thing in the world would have been to place my hands on her shoulders. Instead I crouched behind her in order to point out the male bird sitting under the eaves of the far building. Ines leant forward to see and I leant with her, whispering, 'See the straw in its beak. Look. There's the nest in the higher branches.'

Stupidly, I tried to interest her in the lungfish. She picked up a drawing of a fossil and listened with polite interest as I described the creature's remarkable amphibian qualities. There were no questions. I'd gone on too long, as I always do. She set the drawing back on the desk and shifted her attention to the blue broccoli-shaped flowers which she'd already placed in the vase. She shifted the vase an inch, then looked up with a helpless smile.

There was a day in early December when Ralf was kept indoors with a cold and I invited Ines to come to the zoo with me, just the two of us. To my happy surprise she accepted.

Relieved of her usual duties Ines walked more leisurely, her gloved hands shoved down into her coat pockets. She held her face at a more observant angle. At the zoo we watched the wolves tear apart hunks of meat. We laughed at the sparrows pecking and pushing cigarette butts around the heels of people holding up cameras. We stopped to watch a crane lift off the treetops and climb into the city sky. Inside the lion house we stood shoulder to shoulder as a male lion walked to the gate separating him from the lioness and her cubs. He banged his head against the door and when he let go a mighty crowd-pleasing roar we could smell his breath. Ines pushed forward, the lines in her face were set firm. She didn't like the lion being locked up and kept apart from his cubs. It was wrong. 'Cruel,' she said. It was the first time I heard an opinion from her.

That day we ended up at the zoo beach. We pushed through two sets of gates to find ourselves inside an enclosure staring down a strip of trucked-in sand. A small mechanical wave washes up the beach every seven seconds. A number of ducks hovered behind the shore break. A stilt stood ornamentally on one leg and stared with heart-breaking faith towards a make-believe horizon. With Ralf we'd end up here towards the end of the day. As soon as he sat down on the stone bench he would slump forward, hands on knees. I would wonder if he was tired. He would never say. I didn't know what he was used to—or how much walking he could stand, or how much of the passed-on world he could absorb. But I had come to know the signs. The more tired he was the more talkative he became. He talked to delay the moment we would have to get up and walk again.

I thought of him back at the apartment coughing into his bed-sheets. Here at the zoo beach I sat with Ines on the same stone bench. The silence piled up. For a while there it was as though we were waiting for the world to end. I sat forward and began to name the birds down on the sand. And seeing at last I had her interest I made up some species, adding outlandish features and behaviours before she caught on. She laughed and gave my shoulder a playful shove, and in that cold, cold lair we found ourselves smiling at one another, and then quite naturally, well as naturally as it ever feels the first time, I reached behind her and drew her against me. She smiled down to where her gloved hands sat bunched on her lap. I withdrew my arm, again it felt like the most natural thing in the world. She was free to shift back to her former position. Instead she stayed put. On a slight lean towards me. A slight lean. It doesn't sound much, does it? But I felt happy. I remember the moment actually registering with me. *Yes*, I thought. *This is it.* I half expected an official to arrive with a certificate to mark the moment.

A week later we returned to the small zoo beach. But it wasn't the same. I don't know why but we couldn't recover the magic. I'd used up my tricks. The birds had been named, I'd explained away the mechanical wave. It wasn't that Ines appeared to be bored. She simply wasn't there, either in the moment or in body.

I thought she was on the brink of telling me something. I'd felt it coming ever since we left the apartment. Along the way, or in the zoo, perhaps, she must have had a change of heart.

Then later in the park I felt it, this lack of resolution between the moment at hand and what she was actually thinking. Perhaps she was preparing to tell me in the nicest possible way about a boyfriend or husband in another part of the city? I needed to distract myself. I thought of Ralf sitting in a shroud of silence, like some object of marble occupying a corner of a museum at midnight. I thought of his mouth dripping with anticipation whenever we went down in the caged lift. I paused to stare at a pair of women's glossy white panties, snagged on a high branch, exposed by the winter-thin foliage; how wretched they seemed. I looked up to find Ines way ahead. Ines in her blue coat and white boots. Her feet appeared to take separate steps from those taken by her boots, so that at times she seemed to wade. There she was, wading ahead of me.

I had no idea about Ines' life outside of the one where she looked after Ralf. In fact I found it hard to imagine her pursuing any other life than this one.

Not long after that occasion I came around the end of a dry-goods aisle in the local organics supermarket and there she was—a sight as surprising as the deer I saw in the carriage window at the edge of the forest outside Berlin on my way to lunch with Dr Schreiber. She was frowning at the label of a small jar. She looked puzzled. Now she turned her head in the direction of the checkout where the cashier was packing a brown paper bag and talking with a customer. I thought she needed help. I was about to make my move when Ines slid the hand holding the jar to her pocket. It was preserved garlic which we ate that night with pasta.

Later that same day I saw her holding Ralf's coat open for him to move into and I could not place this woman with the one

I had seen shoplifting earlier in the day. I didn't tell Ralf what I had seen. I didn't raise it with Ines either. I didn't give it another thought until the new year.

As the winter drew longer I spent more time in my little room huddled with my notes and drawings of the lungfish fossils. If it was too cold to go out Ines would knock on my door with an invitation from Ralf to come upstairs for a drink.

I wondered about the food she served. Ralf sometimes wondered aloud about the amount of housekeeping money Ines went through. I might have said something then but I didn't.

Two days before Christmas the three of us went ice-skating. A temporary rink had been dropped onto Bebelplatz on Unter den Linden. The cold rose up through the soles of our feet and passed out through our glassy eyes. At the *Markt* Ralf merrily urged more *Glühwein* down our throats and bullied us onto the ice. Despite all the time I have spent down at the Ross Sea I have no talent for ice-skating. At least it's not the foreign substance for me that it was for Ines. She didn't often seem afraid but she did when she looked out across the ice. Ralf turned out to be surprisingly able. For purposes of instruction the creature reassembled. Ralf went to the front. In order to guide him about the rink I stood nervously off his shoulder. Best of all, Ines slapped her hands on my hips. Through layers of coat and gloves I could feel her touch, and once when she laughed with nervous delight at us moving across the ice I felt the trembling of her pass through her fingers. I felt her warm excited breath against my neck, and her slight weight transmitted through her fingers.

The excitement lasted only while we were on the ice. For the trip home I went back to hanging off Ralf's shoulder, my eyes rolling after the white leather boots of Ines as they waded ahead in the dark up Strasse des 17. Juni past the troubled souls gripping the steering wheels of their parked cars. Their eyes rose from dark pits and turned to follow us, or, at least, Ines in her white boots. Behind us we heard doors opening and closing. Voices from the trees. Shadows. Ralf's frozen face and the plodding motion of his shoulders as we passed through a world he could not see.

sixteen

For months on end it was hard to believe in spring, in the very idea of its existence, but then it came without warning. The winter-shaded branches were in sunlight now, and their green was the scum kind, the bog green of the unlit world. There was a preternatural glow about the apartment buildings. Pale faces that had come through the long winter squinted in the white and lime glare. On our way across the city we passed old bodies stuffed into wheelchairs and buried beneath blankets. The big rusting gates of a nearby beach bar were thrown open and a man raked up leaves from last autumn. Across Tiergarten crocuses began to unfurl. On the street more people than ever were out and about, their thin white limbs poking out of T-shirts and summer dresses. Cafe staff rushed to get tables and chairs out to the pavements to catch the passing trade. We stepped around the feet of corpses with tight little smiles leaning back in chairs. Ines had shed her coat. Now she wore her own clothes instead of the housemaid's uniform—a light blue cotton slip and a dark skirt that accentuated her hips and curves—and a new idea of her emerged.

When things started going missing from the apartment...No, let me begin that again. When the blank spaces began to appear on Ralf's apartment walls, although I could spot the absence of something I was at a complete loss to remember what it had been. It was the absence of the thing that caught my eye and, in a way, that had completely eluded the woodcuts and to a lesser degree the painting. I could not recall a single detail of the woodcuts. They'd left a general impression, a line of them like a line of geese. The change of season had had a similar impact. From late April, overnight as it seemed, my coat stayed on the hook by the door. Those bitter afternoons when I wished I'd bought a longer and thicker coat from Strauss were a thing of the past. The line of white spaces along Ralf's walls produced a similar amnesia. I could remember their flat oak frames and a squiggle, the suggestion of something, but nothing else.

I could have asked Ralf. It should have been the most natural thing in the world to ask after the painting and the woodcuts, but I didn't, because of a vague disquiet. Very little happened in that apartment without Ines knowing about it. I could have asked her. Again I felt uncomfortable. I would be lifting a scab on the flesh of another. So I didn't do or say anything.

For a while this seemed to work, and then those telltale blank spaces came between us. I found it impossible to ignore them. The longer I sat on my silence, the more those spaces appeared to glower back at me. And when Ines brought in the tea or schnapps or arrived at my door with Ralf's old flowers I could hardly look at her for thinking she would almost certainly see those spaces reflected in my eyes. Out and about, our creaturely silence had a more distinctive and unpleasant quality. I told myself over and over, I have to tell Ralf even if it means, as I suspected it would, implicating Ines.

One afternoon at the zoo I had started to broach the subject, broadly, in a roundabout fashion, when Ralf was diverted by the crowd building outside the pen of the stone-eating *Trampeltiers* and so mid-flight, as it were, I was forced to break from the transcendent whiteness of the Antarctic plains to describe a long camel-like jaw thoughtfully rolling a stone around in its mouth before spitting it out and licking up another stone from the pile.

We made our way to the zoo beach. We were the only ones there. It was very hot. Ralf was in his yellow Pierre Cardin, which helped to lift him out of his usual undertaker's austerity. The top button on his shirt was left undone as a concession to the heat. The small eyes of the carapace of netting over that beach that had shone with ice crystals all winter now showered his talcum-white face with sunshine. His eyes were closed. He was basking, which is what every other animal in the zoo was doing. His head rested on his shoulders, his mouth open to old caps of mercury and spidery lines of saliva. I urged my gaze back into that intimate space we normally reserve for those asleep, lovers, small children absorbed in play, pets and babies and the dead. I was about bring up the woodcuts when he said, 'God, this feels good, doesn't it, Defoe? I haven't felt this good in a very long time.'

Well, after that, all I could do was mutter agreement and sit on my hands.

I considered the options. It's possible Ralf had sold the woodcuts. He never spoke about them with any affection. The painting was different. Years ago, he had told me, he and Hannah had come across the seascape in a Hamburg gallery. They weren't buyers or particularly interested in art but as soon as Ralf saw it he exclaimed to Hannah, 'That's Rügen!' He had spent the war years there in an orphanage. He said his father was killed in the war and his mother was officially registered as 'missing' after the heavy bombing of Berlin. He said he and the other boys used to listen in bed at night to the hail off the Ostsee striking against the wooden shutters and pretend they were under attack. Anyway, in the Hamburg gallery while Ralf had been unable to move away from the green and black sea battling its way ashore to the white cliffs of Rügen it had been Hannah who insisted they buy it. They went away and returned a few times until, exasperated by Ralf's indecision, she bought it. They brought it back to Berlin on the train. Each time they had moved in Berlin—three times in all—the new apartment was inspected with a view to a likely wall for the painting of the Rügen shore. I could not imagine Ralf casually selling it.

It was late May. The skies were lighter, especially from the roof garden of Wertheim, where I liked to go to read one of the English-language newspapers.

One afternoon I am on the escalators heading down to ground level when I see Ines through the large front department store windows. She is waiting at the lights to cross the road. This was one of those rare moments—Ines, by herself, and outside of the apartment. The lights changed and she bent down to pick up something. When I saw the large bag I knew I was going to follow her. It seemed as obvious and as inevitable as discreetly leaving the supermarket had been the other time. Yet outside Wertheim

I found myself stalling again and the crowd broke around me. I suppose the thing was to walk up alongside her and tap her on the shoulder. A store detective would feel within his rights to do so. But then a store detective has a refined language with which to disarm a shoplifter and win the offender's cooperation.

The lights changed again and I felt the pull of the crowd setting off across the road. And when I saw her disappear around the corner of the building I set off after her. I still hadn't arrived at a plan. It was more a case of wanting to prolong the option of following her. The important thing was to keep her in view.

Up ahead of me now—floating away like a brightly coloured lure spinning and drifting through the late afternoon crowd. I hurried after, running in front of a bus, then chastened by that near miss I decide to wait at the next lights, where some months earlier I had been told off by a woman, a complete stranger, who dressed me down for setting a bad example to children by jay walking. Under such circumstances my natural instinct is always to yell back some abuse, get my own back, because above all what is more important than one's own dignity, and then it sank in. Yes, the woman was right—she was right, I was wrong—I had set a poor example regarding road safety, and good on her as well for speaking her mind and not looking the other way or holding her tongue but for saying what needed to be said. Oh, for an ounce of her courage. What could be worse than the risk of causing offence—a bundle of smiles without a stitch of courage to hold them together? So as I wait at the lights the world slows down. Tourists, hustlers on skateboards. Beggars. A young mother pushed on the pedals of her bike, a tiny boy with a crash helmet behind her in a cart. A man lit a cigarette and inhaled with a tilt of a head that paid homage to the skies and all the days lived so far—marriage, children, affairs, social soccer games, hernia and appendix operations, crowns and stitches—and then that was that, I couldn't wait any longer. I sprang across the road. I thought I heard a mother cry out. No. I heard all the young mothers in Berlin howling at my back. Of course I imagined that part. Nonetheless my cheeks were burning.

This is how I came to follow her up the station escalators onto the S-Bahn and across the city to Warschauer. Here was a part of Berlin I didn't know at all. Broken down, graffiti everywhere, broken glass and hungry ground-sniffing dogs, gypsy men drinking beer at the platform kiosk, drunks sprawled everywhere rattling cans at the legs of passing commuters. As the crowd came off the bridge the neighbourhood softened to glimpses of cobbled side-streets and balconies with hanging flower pots. Traffic noise gave an impression of congestion but there wasn't any. The noise is deposited here from the distant boulevards of Karl Marx and Frankfurter Allee. I mention it because it encouraged me to think of myself as lost in a big city crowd in the event of Ines turning around to find me. But she never did. She didn't once look back.

She turned off the main road with the tramlines into a narrow street of apartment buildings with ground-floor businesses, cafes, *Bäckereien* and newsagents, and as she crossed the road I noted the shop where she disappeared and I popped into a laundrette, where I waited with the washing thumping inside the driers. In the filthy window I saw a reflection I hardly recognised. The long winter had done something to me. Blurred some essential lines to do with self.

I didn't have long to wait, ten minutes or so, before she

reappeared, this time with the bag folded under her arm. I moved to the door of the laundrette. She seemed to take forever to reach the end of the street. It occurred to me it was deliberate, that she was waiting for me to catch her—a crazy idea then and now, and yet look at the way she walked, more erect and more measured than normal as though straining against a leash that neither held her back nor would let her get too far ahead.

I crossed the road and entered the shop. It was jammed with junk of every kind: book cases, accordions, teapots, a very old dentist chair, hammered tin pots, old furniture, card tables, photographs, paintings. Within a minute I saw two beautifully hand-painted vases that I recognised. The funny thing is I hadn't noticed them gone from the apartment. But as soon as I set eyes on them I was able to place them on the long narrow table behind the sofa on which I usually sat. I glanced up at a crowded wall, and there was Ralf's beloved shoreline at Rügen. How she managed to get it out of the apartment and across town I'll never know. The shopkeeper arrived silently at my side. For the moment we both stood there gazing up at the painting. He spoke in German, then, as I opened my mouth, switched to English. It was a fine work, I agreed. However, there in the pile-up of the second-hand shop I could see what was wrong with it. I suppose it's neither here nor there given the more important discovery of Ines' pilfering. But the persistent presence of the shopkeeper forced my eye back into that seascape. The sea was a blue-green stew with chop and spray and yet as far as I could tell the wind had no telling effect elsewhere in the painting. The clouds are too sedate, almost stationary. Most of the painting is given over to sky. One of those skies you see tilting back from a plane window—sea, sky and land all coming at one another. In a more admiring tone this time the shopkeeper said, 'A very fine painting. One hundred euros.' The quickness with which I accepted seemed to surprise him. Already I was planning ahead. I would need a taxi to ferry it across town. I could remount it and Ralf would be none the wiser. Of course there would be Ines to deal with—as soon as she saw the painting there would be the double shock of realising she had been followed. She would feel betrayed. We would have to sit down and find a way through that.

I bought the two vases as well. While the shopkeeper wrapped them I poked around in a back room filled largely with electric guitars. There I found the box with the woodcuts. When I placed it on the counter the shopkeeper looked up. The brown eyes that had so enthusiastically endorsed the painting of Rügen began to look concerned. He put his hands on the counter. 'Is there something wrong? Something I should know?' he asked. 'No,' I told him. There was nothing that he needed to know.

I left the shop feeling pleased. Some of the indignation I had felt on Ralf's behalf was gone. In its place was a quiet ambient state of neutrality as I walked up the street, laden, in search of a taxi.

It is two days later. I've had to wait for Ines to leave the apartment on one of her mysterious errands. In the other room I can hear Ralf's talking book. Without any difficulty I place the painting and the woodcuts back on the wall and the vases on the table behind the sofa and slip out and downstairs to my room. For the next hour I am too restless to sit at my desk. I can't read. My concentration is all over the place. At some point I hear the cage-lift doors open and bang shut, the telltale footsteps of Ines on the landing, then on the floorboards above. The footsteps trail down to Ralf's end of the apartment. I'm waiting for them to stop, but they travel past the wall with the woodcuts and the end wall with the painting. Then they travel back—again without pause—all the way up to the kitchen.

That afternoon it is my turn to take Ralf out to the park. When the time comes I climb the stairs but without any of the earlier excitement. I feel more like a slug returning to its hole in the mud.

I push on the door. It has been left ajar. The floorboards give me away. Ralf calls across from his corner of the room. He hopes I won't mind waiting. But he needs a blast of coffee before we go out. So I sit with him to wait for Ines to appear with the tray. That's when I notice one of the hand-painted vases. Ines has taken it from the table behind the sofa and placed it on the low table between me and Ralf. She means me to see it.

To make space for the tray she carefully moves the vase to the corner of the table near Ralf. She sets out the cups and the coffee plunger. It is always like this, a painful and methodical process. She delights in the meticulous placement of each cup and saucer and the silver teaspoons and sugar bowl. As if we cannot be trusted with the task of doing it for ourselves. We perch forward—Ralf too, with a dropped lower jaw. She pours his first. Then she pours mine. When she passed the cup to me I did not see anything approaching fear or apprehension or anger, if anything it was a look of shared understanding, which irritated me the more.

Now came one of those farcical moments where you see the outcome before it has happened and at the same time remain powerless to prevent it. Ralf reaches for the sugar. It is where it is always placed for his convenience. But, of course, the world has been rearranged. He doesn't know about the vase. When he knocked it the vase pirouetted for a moment—as if it could not make up its mind whether to fall or remain as it was. Then it fell, noisily, smashing over the floor. I saw it happen in slow motion but did nothing to prevent it happening. I remained frozen and perversely committed to the inevitable outcome. Well, Ralf bounced up from his chair. He began to curse himself, his blindness, his clumsiness. Then it dawned. What was the vase doing there on the coffee table? It didn't usually sit there. 'Ines?' he asked. Without any hesitation, much to my surprise, she said it was her fault. She'd put the vase there while she was cleaning the table behind the sofa. She must have forgotten it.

'Oh,' said Ralf, relieved more than anything.

I knelt down on the floor to help Ines with the broken pieces. We picked through them on our hands and knees. We would have looked as though we were taking this job very seriously indeed, but the stillness with which we went about it was really our acute awareness of the other. I hadn't been this close to Ines since ice-skating and that other time in the zoo when the brute cold saw me shift my arm around her. For months on end she had been geographically apart—to Ralf's left side, upstairs, in the kitchen at the other end of the apartment. But here, on the floor, she was close enough for me to smell her, her shop scent. The top two buttons of her housemaid's shirt were undone and I could see the pale of her breasts and the shine of her skin. I could feel her heat. I could hear her breath. These observations were like images passing in a window. A horse in a paddock, a lake, a tree, there goes a patch of sky, a flock of starlings over a field of maize—things which on their own don't amount to much but together contribute to a general feeling of contentment. Well, my itemising of Ines' attributes, her skin, her fast shallow breaths—they will all have to stand for a blooming of desire.

The things that had kept us apart—the ceiling, the floorboards, suspicion, fear—all of that fell away as we knelt shoulder to shoulder and worked around the stubborn feet of our blind benefactor. Our sides touched, we breathed in and out with one another. Best of all, and I was sure of this, at least at the time I was, I recognised in Ines my own attempt to delay finding all the broken pieces, which was a desire for things to carry on as they were. All of this without either one of us having uttered so much as a word.

That night I can't sleep for all the movement in the apartment above. The light is off but I am very awake. I've listened to the shower running. These are the usual last gasps from the world above before silence descends. But then I hear feet trailing along the hall. These are footsteps that don't want to be heard. I hear the door open on the landing. A few moments later there is a knock on my door. She knocked quietly, but not tentatively, no, that would have meant something else; it's a quietly confident tap that I understand and so when I opened it there was no excuse me, or polite preliminaries. I was surprised to see she was wearing her maid's uniform. I hadn't seen it on her for some time. Why she chose to wear it I have no idea. But I've already given that detail more thought than I did at the time. Without a word said she took off her clothes. When I felt her mouth on mine I felt her hunger. I am mindful of Ines as I write this. She won't approve of me unveiling her before a stranger.

But I will say this. At night geography is the first thing to disappear. The Ines I knew, the one tottering across Ralf's apartment with a tea-tray, the Ines with discreet glances, that one was now a stranger. The woman under me arched and fed me into her. She clenched her thighs and she grunted. And where was I in all of this? Part of me was an astonished spectator, pleased and surprised by what I had stumbled upon in the clearing.

Afterwards we lay back in that narrow bed, Ines with her head resting on my arm. Her leg hooked over mine. A few months earlier I was stepping around her in the kitchen, taking care not to intrude. Now I casually moved my hand to her small warm breast. Just at that moment I doubt there was a happier man alive. It was so nice to lie there in the dark and feel fortunate without thinking how this intimacy had been won or arrived at or what would happen next. Actually, what happened next was quite straightforward. Ines announced she was hungry, and just like that we got up and dressed. Ines snuck upstairs to get her coat.

As we left the building I dropped youthfully down the front entrance steps into the waiting night where everything else felt new. The air. The trees. The neighbourhood. Not a word was said about the accident with the vase.

And Ines? When I think back I see a side of her that I didn't dwell on at the time. It was as I pulled out of her. Her face went blank as a sheet. As though any capacity for emotion had been rolled out of her face. She could offer only eye, nose, mouth. Though later as we closed the gate outside Ralf's she did smile up at me. And further along the street she did reach up and kiss me.

We caught the U near the zoo. I noticed our faces caught in the window reflection. Mine and a young black woman's. Who would have thought? Not me, certainly not during the bleak winter months when I had walked the neighour's dog up to the top of the Mt Victoria lookout, and there, under the weathered bust of the arctic explorer Robert Peary, man and dog had leant into the teeth of a filthy gale. Ines waved back at my smile in the window. We ended up at a rotisserie chicken place near the Kreuzberg canal. I thought it was a long way to come. But then I saw its value. That is, I saw it how Ines did. Two euros for half a chicken. I paid for two half-chickens. We stood up at a counter to eat. The skin was crusted with salt. Ines licked at it with a wordless relish. When she caught me watching her, her jaws stopped moving, however, her teeth remained stuck in the white flesh. After that, she nibbled at the chicken pretending it was corn.

On our way home we walked as we had earlier, side by side, completely at ease with each other. There was just us. *Us* was a whole new idea. We found ourselves following the canal. She held my hand. We stopped to admire the white swans gliding out from under the bridges; funnily enough the woodcuts entered my thoughts, but then Ines pressed my hand and the thought departed.

By the time we reached the zoo end of Tiergarten I was nearly falling over with tiredness. It was a relief to turn into Ralf's street. I thumped up the stairs on heavy legs, by now very keen on the idea of bed. Secretly I hoped Ines would carry on up to the next landing. That's how tired I was. Instead she came to my door as if it was the most natural thing in the world, as if this is what we had done every night these past weeks and months. When we undressed and got into bed it was baffling to think that there had been a time when we slept in separate beds, so thoroughly did this new arrangement eclipse the old chaste one. Ines turned on her side. I lay on my back. I thought about telling her how I liked to follow her feet across the ceiling. Instead, something unrehearsed and completely different came out.

I said, 'Ines, why have you been taking Ralf's things?'

She turned over onto her back. I propped myself onto an elbow and stroked her bare shoulder.

'Ines?' I asked.

'For money,' she answered. There she seemed prepared to leave it, as if that explanation was reasonable enough, and surely I understood as much. But I pressed her further.

Why, I asked, did she need money so much that she had to steal?

This time she rolled away from under my stroking hand, onto her side, and shifted closer to the wall.

A few seconds later she sleepily answered. 'To pay a lawyer.' She yawned back at the wall. 'To process my residency application,' she said.

Why not ask Ralf for his help? Ralf knew a lot of people. I also knew how much he depended on Ines.

She sat up, and pulled the sheet to herself. In the dark her eyes were whiter than ever.

'You must not say a word about the lawyer to him. Promise,' she said. And when I didn't answer quickly enough her hand shook my shoulder. 'Promise.'

'Ok,' I said. 'I promise.'

And because my mumbled reply mustn't have convinced there

was a fresh round of promises to agree to. It was her secret and she wished to keep it that way. She did not want the 'authorities' involved. She did not want to worry Ralf. She needed to do this thing on her own. It was complicated. There was a risk she would be deported. I wasn't to say a word to him. It was a private matter. I should respect her. And because I didn't reply straightaway she added that I ought to understand because I had private matters that she knew I wouldn't want discussed with the blind gentleman, and as she said that, in an instant—just as it is said of someone caught in death's spiral where their entire life rushes past their eyes—I saw my life in Berlin flash by, the dissolution of everything, the loss of Ines, and the hard, stinging criticism that would surely come from Ralf. And, as it also seemed, there was not just me standing at the window farewelling that life. Ines was also there, by my side, so that the threat passed silently between us, unsaid but acknowledged. And when the woodcuts disappeared for the second time shortly afterwards I didn't pursue the matter.

For several weeks Ines came to my bed every night. The arrangement wasn't entirely satisfactory. She couldn't sleep for keeping an ear open to upstairs. Ralf was in the habit of waking in the night. He could manage on his own to the bathroom. But further afield, to the kitchen, say, he needed Ines' help.

So we changed the arrangement. At a late hour when I was sure Ralf was asleep I let myself into the apartment and crept along the floorboards to Ines' room.

During the day when the creature assembled, Ines would be frustratingly near, but the old man's crusty chin was in the way, and his pink hanging ear lobe more noticeable than ever, more intrusive, bordering on offensive. I thought I detected an inward change in Ralf. His face was as closed as a paper clip. His silences were drawn out. I wondered what he made of the lighter spirits around him? We didn't quite hold hands, but our shoulders touched. Then I would notice the stillness of Ralf's head. There was awareness. Memory was ticking over, catching up.

Rain has forced us inside the aquarium. Here we stand before the endless varieties. It is like describing carpet. Yet one of the tanks contains an extraordinary creature dredged up from the permanent night that exists at great oceanic depth.

Organs and tissue float and drift on the end of cords attached to a parachute of more tissue. When it pulls down on the cords the parachute propels it upwards. The moment it achieves equilibrium it begins its descent—which is almost a collapse of will—before regathering itself to begin the exercise all over again. The cords are long and spaghetti-like and wrap around one another. Entangled and untangling. It seemed less an organism than a quest to stay aloft and find form.

As I passed this on to Ralf, it might have been a description of our little household as well.

One night I have gotten up for a pee. Outside Ines' room I stop and stare into the dark of the hall. Something is shambling towards me. The light from the far windows caught Ralf's blind face. Perhaps he'd heard noises and was coming to investigate. In his hand he held a pair of long-bladed scissors. We are no more than twenty paces from one another, Ralf in his striped pyjamas, and me, naked as I have never been in his company. In Ralf I am reminded of the ostrich we saw at the zoo at the start of the winter.

That is how Ralf looked, as if he expected the attack to come from behind. I waited and he waited and then at last the old man turned and passed out of the light from the window and into the far shadows at his end of the hall.

I told Ines, which turned out to be a mistake because that night was also the last time I stayed in her room. After that I was reliant on her tiptoeing down the stairs to my door. Whether she turned up or not was entirely up to her. The visits became more sporadic, then dished out in a system of rewards for my silence, my complicity, and later, money.

seventeen

More things disappeared from Ralf's apartment. The silverware—all of it except three sets of knives, forks and spoons—the pewter beer mugs that used to line the cabinet inside the entrance, and that was just the start. I made another trip to the second-hand goods shop intending to buy everything back. But Ines had found another outlet. The shopkeeper who was so welcoming when I first came in looked almost bereft to see me walk out without buying anything.

I told Ines I would give her money, but she had to stop taking the old man's things. It would be my contribution to her residency application. She asked for three hundred euros, then five hundred euros. Two weeks later she knocked on my door to ask for more. I couldn't understand where all the money was going. 'Who is this lawyer?' I asked her one day. 'Would you like me to come along with you to his office? It might help.'

She didn't like that idea at all. She said I didn't understand. It was complex. I told her I didn't have another euro on me. It would have to wait.

That night there was a knock on my door. I welcomed her back into my bed. It was like old times. She was as giving as she had been the first time.

A week later, having parted with another eight hundred euros, I came to my senses. Enough was enough. One night she came downstairs. I met her at the door filled with resolve. Or so I thought. She wore just her maid's shirt, the lavender one, and nothing else. Nothing at all. She pushed me back towards the bed. I told her I had no more money to give, which happened to be partially true.

I needed to be careful. I was spending more than I had budgeted. I had stretched out my stay longer than originally planned. My workmates back home were kind. Kenny Stewart, who had joined Fisheries when I did and who knew all about my 'domestic situation', had written a thoughtful email telling me to take whatever time I needed. This was back in February. I would be on half pay until June and after that it would be considered leave without pay.

Ines took this news well. She acted as if money was the furthest thing from her mind. She walked me back to the bed and we made love with all the old urgency.

Lamp shades, two more paintings, books, silver goblets Ralf said his father had left him—all of it went. Ines behaved like a wronged woman. I began to make lists of things so I would notice the moment they went missing.

Whenever people ask me what it is like down there I think of the great lonely white continent spilling into the Ross Sea, and the tremendous bulge of the Southern Ocean, its massive swells ballooning by the gunwale, and an overhanging sky that appears as a ragged survivor of some unsighted storm in another region. When I returned from my first trip and spoke about my experiences I also heard news about crewmen with knife wounds helicoptered off fishing vessels. So no surprise that my audiences wondered, their eyes lighting up at the thought of the overheated confinement of the cabin, if there had been violence. I learned to direct my smile into neutral space and that ambiguity seemed to satisfy. The fact is I didn't witness a single blow or see a knife used for any other purpose than to fillet a fish. Once the sea ice broke and we nosed our way through the cracks in the white sheet ice there was no time to think or act or do anything other than haul up toothfish and catch snatches of fitful sleep. There is no night at that time of year, and so the days were impossibly long. My more persistent audiences would nod to get that unpleasant fact out the way. There was no disguising their disappointment when told that no one had been cut or hung over the gunwale by their feet. In the few moments I had to myself, I lay in my bunk mentally composing letters so others might see what I saw. But as soon as I began trying to describe this mystical world I would find myself going on about the toothfish. It had become the easy vessel of all that was strange and new.

At night, on our way south, the only noise was the trawler's steady engine. In heavy swell it pitched and seemed to catch its breath before pushing forward. No sooner did we rise over one watery hill than there was another one to scramble over.

Early one morning I woke to a different rhythm of noise, a quiet idling, and I raced up on deck. An oyster-coloured sea spread all the way to a cloud formation I had never seen before. Everything about that world was new and its stark beauty and intrinsic danger could not be told apart.

A few days after I began my inventory of the apartment I was asked to give a talk at the museum of natural history. I took myself off to the park that afternoon to gather my thoughts. It was a hot day, and I stood under the trees feeling miserable, wishing I had never agreed to the invitation from Dr Schreiber. But given his generosity and the access to the museum's lungfish fossil collection he'd kindly arranged, I couldn't decline. So my mind was filled with vistas of the ice plains and the flat slices of clouds that sit like layers of pancakes above the trans-Antarctic mountains when, across that great white sheet, ran an African man trailing a red kite. A small boy ran after him. The kite lifted and the man let the string run through his fingers. The small black kid followed the kite with his hands out from his sides. All his belief in the world moved to the surface of his face as the kite rose to the height of the trees, and then the kite went floppy—its nose came round and it dived back to the earth to land very near to the still and unexcited figure of Ines.

The boy ran first to the kite. Then he looked up and raised his childish hand to point to Ines. The man ignored him and solemnly reeled in the kite. All eyes were on the red plastic contraption sliding and sticking in the grass. Now, from my place under the trees, I saw Ines kneel down and hold out her arms to the small boy. The black guy was heavy in back and shoulders, soft around the belly, receding hairline, well dressed in khaki trousers and a short-sleeved knit shirt. He approached with his chin raised, an uneasy fit of surliness and acceptance. Ines stood up. She reached into her coat pocket and handed the man something. The man quickly pocketed it. So, yes, it was money. He held up his wristwatch and pointed. Ines shook her head. The man rolled his head. They began to argue. The small boy continued to stare at the red kite flapping in the grass.

There was a bit of wind about that day. The kite flapped like something dying. On the back of a gust I could actually hear Ines—her voice was cut up, a high note pitched and drifting. She went to place her hands on the man's shoulders but he stepped to one side. He reached inside his pocket to hand her back the money. Now it was Ines retreating, her hands out in front of her, and nodding to himself the man pocketed the money again. He knelt to whisper something in the boy's ear. The boy nodded. Then the man stood up and walked quickly away. Ines knelt down. The boy picked up the kite and walked towards her. As he got closer she raised her arms to him. The boy stopped, he dropped the kite and ran into his mother's embrace. About their relationship I was in no doubt at all.

For the next hour—I gathered that's how much time she had purchased to be with her child—Ines walked about the park pointing out things. She was interested in ways that she never demonstrated around me and Ralf. There was her outstretched finger, there the little boy gazed up at sculptures of composers and huntsmen. They walked hand in hand, the red kite trailing behind, almost forgotten, until near the path they stopped and they both stared at it flapping on the path thirty metres away. Ines took the string from the boy and hauled it in, hand over hand, until the boy was able to pick up the kite from her feet.

The leaves were shiny and bright. It was a blue sky. And although a wind was blowing it was from the east and very warm. There were a lot of people in the park. Cyclists wove around walkers and joggers on the paths. I wasn't at all concerned about Ines looking behind to find me. I could see just how removed every other part of her world was for her. She was so completely absorbed in the boy and what his eyes saw.

At a fork in the path he yanked Ines in the direction of the path leading around the edge of Neuer See. Near here they disappeared into the bushes. I thought the boy must need to pee. But then I heard laughter and shrieking. They duly emerged, both smiling, the boy first, then Ines. The boy ran off. His mother chased after him.

I know the path. It leads to the boat hirer and the cafe and restaurant on the edge of the pond. I waited until the two of them disappeared around the curve of bushes. I waited for a woman with a pram to overtake me, then I ducked into the bushes they'd come laughing out of. There was the black pond with its tree reflections and just back from the water's edge was a bronze sculpture of a bison. This must have been what all the high squeals had been about. A game of hide-and-seek around the bison. I wonder if they noticed the bullet holes in the bison from a different game of hide-and-seek fifty years earlier. I pulled back a branch. Across the pond I saw the boy licking an ice cream. His mother walked behind with folded arms, the red kite in her right hand. When she came broadside to the wind, which, as I say, was stronger than normal, she had to pull the kite back while her free hand flew up to her hair, and then to the boy, who, even when blown off balance, kept his face in the ice cream.

eighteen

On our way to the museum that night I wanted only for the evening to be over, to be back in the apartment, in bed, waiting for Ines to come to my door. I intended to report back to her everything I had seen that afternoon, from the moment she was left with the boy, and it was smack on the dial an hour later, not a minute more, when they returned to the field to find the black guy waiting, just off to the side of the path, on the grass. When Ines and the boy appeared he glanced down at his watch. Ines released the boy's hand and let him go. The man stuck his hands in his pockets, he stood jiggling, he looked around in the opposite direction, and back, and when the boy drew near he held out his hand. The boy gave it a hard look. The man nodded at Ines, he dropped his hand onto the boy's shoulder, then he turned and left, walking the boy faster than he was used to, or capable of. Ines watched them as far as the trees, then she looked around herself, up at the skies that were so beautiful and warm that afternoon that everyone was to remember, for days after: what a special day it had been.

The talk was to an audience of managers and scientists with an interest in resource management. I wished I'd never told Ralf. But I had wanted him to know—I remember smiling shamefully at my vanity as I told him about the invitation. Of course he insisted on coming along. And that was the price for wanting him to know that elsewhere in the world my life had some standing. As the room filled, I stood in a corner with Dr Schreiber looking long-faced as Ines guided Ralf to a seat near the front.

I spoke in English. Dr Schreiber had given the talk an imaginative but accurate enough title—*A Poacher Turned Gamekeeper's Guide to the Toothfish Stock in the Ross Sea.*

I had brought along images of the ice, which I spiced up with some anecdotal stuff about the early piracy of the fish stock, and the outrageous practice of some who threw sticks of gelignite into the jaws of whales to eliminate the competition. I told of the chef's party trick—usually after he had been smoking dope—of entertaining himself and everyone else on the trawler by shouting up at the cabin ceiling, '*Dissostichus Mawson.*' The toothfish has thick and well-defined lips and round unblinking eyes. The first one I pulled out of the sea looked angry, so did the second and third. These were very old fish. At the time I felt like I was dragging the elderly out to the back lawns of the retirement home and slitting their throats. After one hundred I stopped thinking of them as fish. Collectively they turned into ore which we stowed in the ice hold. On the way home that's what the conversation returned to. 'Ore,' Ralf mused. 'Ore. Yes. I can see that,' he said.

Ines pulled the cage doors back and we went up in the lift. I tried to catch her eye, but she stared dully and resolutely ahead. A face on a lower landing gazed up with evident annoyance as we rose past her floor. At our landing, where we all said goodnight, she gave me a quick smile that just as quickly left her face.

I lay in bed waiting for her to show up. I waited until the building was as quiet as a tomb then got up and climbed the stairs without a stitch on to find the door to the apartment locked.

The next morning, a Friday, there was a knock on the door. I'd left it open on purpose. It would be Ines with Ralf's old flowers. I called out to her to come in, the door's open. There was no reply. I had to get up from the desk. There on the landing she stood as she had on the very first Friday morning in her housemaid's uniform. She held a bunch of irises. She asked with the formality of the old days if she could come in and change the flowers. I stood aside. I followed her from the desk to the bathroom door. She filled the vase with water from the bathroom tap. I followed her to the desk piled with my papers and notebooks. With great care she cleared a small space for the vase. Then she stood back to admire the arrangement. As she folded her arms her right shoulder leant in towards me, and she turned to look up. I thought she was about to smile, only she became self-aware and the whole lovely possibility fell away.

'Ines,' I asked. 'Who was that man I saw you in that park with yesterday? And the little boy? Who is he?'

Her shoulders went still. Her whole person turned rigid.

'You can tell me,' I said. 'You can trust me.'

Instead it was as though she couldn't believe what she'd just heard. Her breath rose as high as her shoulders. Her eyes wouldn't settle.

'No,' she said. 'Whatever you saw in the park is not your business.'

'Yes, but I can help,' I said. 'If you are in some sort of trouble...'

She shook her head.

'And the money, Ines. All that money.'

She turned away towards the window.

'But that was your boy I saw, wasn't it?'

She kept shaking her head.

'And that guy. Who is he?'

I reached for her but she stepped clear of me. She walked to the door. She closed it quietly behind her.

The *kokopu* is a thick-shouldered fish that fancies sink holes, usually on farmland. It wriggles itself into a tight space and feeds until the hole it so gladly wriggled into cannot be wriggled out of. It has trapped itself. It cannot move to escape. This is the position I found myself in.

By the end of the month the heart and soul of Berlin had left for sunnier parts. A light sticky rain wouldn't go away. The trees across Tiergarten sagged under the accumulated damp. Ralf was getting over a cold. This was the first time he'd left the apartment since I gave my talk. Across the park the trees dripped on him. His nose was still red, but, thank God, he was over the fits of explosive sneezing.

As the day progressed the humidity rose and a feeling of

over-heated abandonment stuck to everything. Then the clouds parted and out of a patch of blue came the scorching sun. In a heat-beaten shitless state we wade against the tide down Unter den Linden past the Tomb for Victims of Fascism, where two gypsy girls sit beneath the trees, their dry mouths open, eyes still. I think about giving them each a euro. I am still thinking about it as we walk past.

Halfway across the bridge we stopped for Ralf to catch his breath. We were staring down into the slow-moving Spree when Ralf came up with his plan. He said, 'I feel like smelling sea air. Now I have an idea. It is this. Why don't we go up to Rügen? Ines too. We can walk barefoot in the sand. We can go this weekend. Leave Friday and return Sunday night.'

So that's what we did. We left for Rügen the following weekend. I didn't realise what a relief it would be to get out of the city. The plains of northern Germany flew by. Ralf's head nodded against the window. Ines sat opposite, arms folded, her face closed, without any interest in the landscape we were moving through. At some point I got up to go to the toilet. I opened the louvre window and felt the warm air on my face. Then I happened to catch a glimpse of myself in the cracked mirror. I did not like what I saw.

Whenever I think back to that first night she came to my door I still can't say why it happened, only that it did, inevitably and intensely, and with no other angle that I could discern at the time. But that was also the moment she moved away so that I was left permanently off-balance like a man about to fall. Now I was left with a flirtatious smile across the floorboards of Ralf's apartment. Conversation was back to the banalities of a well-drilled waitress hovering over the table of two loyal customers. And then that day in the park when I glimpsed a whole other world. With some resignation I found myself accepting my place in the scheme of things, a pair of eyes to Ralf, a source of money to Ines. Yes. I went on paying her. I took seriously her threat to tell Ralf. I would have found it embarrassing. Ralf as well, I suspect. It would change things between us. His memory would churn back these past months. Everything would be recast. In his mind I would be transformed into an untrustworthy figure. I was sure of that. Possibly someone to get rid of. So I was desperate to keep my 'thing' with Ines (I don't know what else to call it) a secret. But that secret was not the only thing I was paying for. I continued to listen out for her footsteps on the stairs.

At Stralsund we switched trains and crossed an isthmus to the Rügen headland. The sea briefly appeared on both sides of the train. There in the distance were the white cliffs from the painting. Ralf perched above his seat pathetically trying to see through his blindness the place of his happiest years. Ines trained a steady eye on the open sea. She held that view until the sea was overtaken by farmland.

There was one more change of trains. A small toy-like train delivered us to the final station, a lovely old building behind ghostly GDR-built worker apartments that rose like blunt anvils into the sea air. Within five minutes' walk from the station we had put that blight behind us. There was the sea, stunningly suspended in the trees lining the beach. We leant forward in our eagerness to get there, to be there. I had my overnight bag, Ralf carried his own medical-looking brown bag, and a cane in his other hand which he tapped ahead of himself. Ines walked ceremonially in front, a plastic bag with her white-and-lavender housemaid's uniform swinging from her hand.

A long pier extends from the beach front of Binz. People walk to the end of it and stare out to open sea. Then they turn around and walk back to the shore. The feeling is they have been somewhere refreshing and intoxicatingly new and now they are returning—usually for breakfast or lunch or dinner.

It was at the end of this pier early on the first morning, Ines and Ralf were still in bed, that my mobile unexpectedly rang. It was my older sister calling with the news that our elderly mother had had a stroke. From half a world away I could hear the noise of the hospital and, just as unmistakably, my sister's edginess. She had flown home from Brisbane earlier that day. She thought I should make every effort to get back as soon as possible. I could not bear to tell her just how beautiful a scene I currently found myself in, at the end of a long pier, the Ostsee sliding beneath me, the long beach glowing white in the early-morning sun, the screen of lime trees, the boardwalk, and behind it the rows of old wooden hotels tilting towards the sea. Or that as I listened to her news I happened to be gazing towards a corner of the beach, the FFR stretch reserved for nude bathers, where a fishing boat was coming ashore as a number of early-morning enthusiasts paddled out, their white bodies swollen with purpose. The whole scene was like a postcard, still, framed, as my sister explained how earlier that day our mother had risen, got as far as sitting on the edge of her bed, and then just froze, which is how one of her elderly friends had discovered her several hours later.

I would have to return home. When I met Ralf and Ines in

the breakfast room my smile was the kind doctors reserve for patients still unaware of their terminal condition. I sat down and unfolded my crisp white napkin.

Over breakfast Ralf recalled a hut that used to sell dried fish. It sat further down the beach. He thought we might go and seek it out. He asked Ines if she had eaten dried fish.

'Yes. Of course,' she answered. 'Mackerel.'

'Ha! But not this mackerel…not from the Ostsee.'

This was the first time I had heard him express pride of a tribal nature. Mackerel, of all things. Some weeks earlier the European Cup had kicked off. I watched with Ines, Ralf listened with earplugs to the radio commentary. When Germany scored the opening goal against Poland the television cameras found the Chancellor in the crowd. She rose excitedly to her feet—as any reasonably loyal follower would, and then caught herself, and it was as if all of Germany's history was breathing down her neck; looking very uneasy she sat down again to the knowing mirth of the sympathetic German commentators.

That was one more thing that I failed to pass on to Ralf.

Later that afternoon I returned alone to the end of the pier and rang my sister. It was near midnight her time, she was still at the hospital but in a better mood. The stroke was of the more benign variety. There was no permanent loss of bodily movement. None of that freezing effect you hear about. But my mother's language was a bit scrambled. She had asked for a shower when she meant a cup of tea. With some remedial work she might recover some capacity. In the morning she would be shifted to the stroke ward. 'Good,' I said. 'That's good.' I said goodbye and switched off the mobile. Moving along the pier to claim me were Ines and Ralf.

At the back of my sister's voice, beyond the crash bang of the hospital interior, I had seen the street outside the hospital, the large egg-shaped boulder dragged up from the river and set on its end to commemorate a fracas between Maori and my forebears, a bugler, a boy in uniform, hacked to death on soil now covered with English gardens and tarseal and houses, and a kindergarten I attended pulling a large unshorn sheep behind me on a length of string, and the golf course where I and my childhood friend Megan Rabbit wandered in and out of a lime-lit dream. Well all of that came packaged with my sister's voice, as well as her sun-drowsy vowels acquired after eleven years in Queensland—a part of her life I knew little about—so that, when I rejoined Ines and Ralf, I was not quite the same person they had known at breakfast.

On the beach in the early evening we let Ralf wander confidently ahead, socks and shoes in his hand, guided by the line of the tide. A naked man and woman (a jaunty cock and floppy tits) walked hand in hand across us, and before long we found ourselves in a crowd of naked flesh, and Ines slid her fingers into mine.

I spent that night with her. She slept lightly. She was always very alert to those internal shifts in others. Every so often she would wake and remember where she was and go back to sleep. I spent most of the night listening to the voices from the board-walk, then it was the quiet murmur of the Ostsee pushing up the beach. At a very late hour she stirred beside me, reached for my hand and placed it between her legs.

nineteen

Within a day of our return to Berlin I noticed a pair of silver plates gone from the cabinet and a number of scrimshaw pipes that had belonged to Ralf's grandfather, a seaman who used to sail between Hamburg and British ports. I had decided to tell Ralf. I would not spare myself. I would tell Ralf everything.

I waited a week. Another week spent brooding on how best to proceed. I needed to get Ralf alone. That was the first thing. Again it was as if Ines sensed my intentions. She stayed near. I don't think she went out alone all week. She visited me on three nights and asked for nothing in return. But afterwards, we lay apart in the dark.

It was the weekend of the European Cup final. A Saturday or Sunday—I forget which. Otherwise the details of that day remain deeply etched.

I took my time with everything that day. I was uncharacteristically methodical—the way I showered, the way I made a cup of tea, even the way I ate my muesli.

Late morning I visit the museum of natural history for coffee with Schreiber. I've come to show him my drawings of the lungfish. He puts on his glasses and stares. He likes what he sees. Apart from the lungfish butchered by the museum's taxidermist, which I have faithfully copied—imperfections and all. Schreiber didn't think that drawing resembled a lungfish. I smugly agreed. 'But that's the one on display,' I said. Schreiber wants to talk football. Germany has defied the pundits and the odds to make the final, dishearteningly for some fans, against a flashy and in-form Spain. Schreiber is quietly pleased by the team's progress. He is just a few years younger than Ralf. When I tell him I will be cheering for Germany he is surprised, and then delighted.

That afternoon I follow the colourful crowd up Unter den Linden to Brandenburg Gate, where a massive screen has been erected. The game is still a few hours away. Trumpets sound, whistles blow, drummers pound away, and thousands, tens of thousands, draped in red, yellow and black, swarm through the city to arrive there in larger and larger numbers. Half a million I heard it reported later.

Everything about this day was different. Fading, I would say. A solitary disengaged soul carrying a filthy sack picked up refundable empties. Retracing my footsteps down Unter den Linden I join the tail end of the crowd, late arrivals, girls with their faces painted black, red and yellow, the faces of their boyfriends covered with glee. At Bebelplatz, where on most days tourists stand around groping for the book-burning moment of 1933, a young father crouched by his son encouraging him to kick a miniature soccer ball.

I wandered on enjoying the empty streets in a city whose concentration had been captured and drawn singularly to the one event. The way back through Tiergarten felt countrified. A solitary cyclist passed me, like myself, mysteriously untouched by the business of the hour.

I had changed my mind about watching the game in a bar. I would head back to the apartment and share the moment with Ralf. He'd sent Ines out to buy champagne in the event of Germany winning, all of which would help to lift his spirits before I passed on Ines' shoplifting, her purloining of the apartment's chattels, their sale, and the proceeds. I wasn't sure what to say about the proceeds. Perhaps I would leave it to her to explain the ghastly business of purchasing time with the kid I'd seen her with in Tiergarten.

I turn into Ralf's street. A van is parked up ahead. I kick at a plastic container and then swing my foot through a pile of rusty leaves. I am dreading the moment ahead. Ralf will think differently about me. Whatever he says, he will wonder, as he is entitled to wonder, what took me so long. What prevented me speaking out until now? I still haven't figured out what to say. There is always the truth. It just doesn't sound right. It doesn't sound flattering. This is the moment I glance up. The first thing I notice is the van. It is a police van. And the two guys dropping down the steps of Ralf's building are policemen. With them is Ines. One of them is handcuffed to her. Now another policeman gets out of the van to open the back door. He helps Ines and the handcuffed officer up the step and closes the doors behind. The other officer takes off his gloves and gets in the van. He is followed by the driver. The van moves out from the curb. I watch its ponderous three-point turn. In no hurry it bumped along the cobbles towards me. A drooping willow brushed against the roof. I turned and watched it to the end of the street. There it rolled and bumped in the direction taken by the rubbish trucks.

And then I ran.

I didn't wait for the lift. I ran up the five flights of stairs. I found Ralf in a confused state in the middle of the room. He seemed to think the police were still there. Then he said, 'Defoe? Is that you?' His voice was shaking. I led him to the chair in the corner and tried to compose him. He said, 'The police were here. They've taken Ines. They said it was a routine matter. They need to talk to her at the station.'

The police had left him with a number to call but said he should wait four hours before calling, so that's what we did. We waited. We watched the baby-faced Torres stroke the goal past the German keeper, and in the ecstasy of scoring Spain's first and only and, as it turned out, winning goal, he ran to the corner of the pitch sucking his thumb until mercifully he was enveloped by his jubilant team mates. We sat through the final depressing minutes waiting for the damned thing to end. I poured Ralf a schnapps but he didn't drink it. Then it was time. I brought him the phone and dialled the number.

He spoke in German so of course I have no idea what he said except I noted the shift in tone. He started out with some authority but gradually demurred and by the end was giving cooperative sighs and nods. When he handed me the phone he looked utterly lost. How big and empty the apartment seemed just then. The vast floor area stretching away from the point of the cane held between his knees. How bare the walls looked. In a voice heightened by its own incredulity he said, 'They say she killed someone. In Sicily. A woman. Ines someone. I didn't catch the name. I should have listened more carefully. They say she killed this woman and took her identity.'

She might be a thief. A thief with some justification. Who knew? But a killer? No, no, no. Impossible. With Ralf I found myself vying for greater conviction in her innocence. He didn't know her—couldn't possibly know her in the same way that I did. Who could possibly know her better than I did? But weirdly Ralf felt the same—for days, weeks after, we continued to believe in her innocence. It was a measure of our faith in Ines. That position would change, though it was never openly stated, as more information came to light. And then, as it happens, I realised that neither one of us knew her. We knew a small part of her, one side perhaps, the costumed part on her way across the apartment with the tea-tray, when for a moment the light from the window would capture her, enhance her theatrical effect, and you might think, as I did, and logically enough, *Yes, here she is, here is Ines*. She was what we expected her to be. It never occurred to me that there might be more. Only after it fell to me to pour Ralf's tea did I appreciate the elegance she brought to the task. As much as it was amazing to think now how far that performance had taken her, it was embarrassing to think how willing an audience Ralf and I had been. I wonder if that was the reason we stuck with our agreed notion of Ines, while privately the idea of her as an innocent, a simple housekeeper was left to erode.

On a more mundane note Ralf had to adapt to the loss of a housekeeper. He went through a period of breaking everything he came into contact with, as if to say, *Can't anyone see how hopeless the situation is?*

All of Ines' old chores fell to me to do. I moved into her old room, slept in her old bed and each morning woke to Ralf prodding his cane along the floorboards.

On the second morning I was reaching under the bed to retrieve a shoe when I found the condom wrapper. Ines and I never used condoms. I'd had a vasectomy more than five years before. It was strange. Baffling. After all, there was just me and Ralf.

Over the coming weeks more calls were made. We had the telephone number of the institution in Sicily where she was being held. Ines also attempted to contact us. Once I got up the stairs to Ralf's to find the phone on the floor. There was a stumbling message from Ines. She gave the trial date. Then it was as though her old life reached out to her. Her voice changed. She reminded Ralf where his pills were. She asked me to remember to change the flowers. She hoped we were managing without her. I did not erase the message. I listened to it a few times, hoping to hear more. Perhaps I'd missed a tone that on hearing again I might identify as a trace of this other person, the one who was a mystery to us both. But what I heard each time was a reiteration of the old lines of trust and loyalty. As far as Ines was concerned, that is, from what her tone indicated, nothing had changed. We could still be counted on.

Plans were made to travel down to Catania for what Ralf was convinced would be a 'monkey trial'. He got me to contact likely places to stay. While I dialled he stood over me, an old biscuit crumb wedged into the corner of his dry lips. He wanted assurances that the rooms were non-smoking. He demanded descriptions of the surrounding neighbourhood. In one instance I had to ask the woman at the other end to stand by the window and describe the street below while Ralf bellowed from his corner chair that he wouldn't tolerate noise.

'Ask her about the criminal element!' he shouted.

His questions and his need for reassurances became more and more eccentric. Then, a week before I flew out, I pulled back the drapes from the window by his chair and saw below car tops heaped with leaves. With that fall everything changed. There was a new world to pass on. That afternoon, as we left the apartment the sharp air bit our faces. We were on our way to the cemetery. But halfway to the S-Bahn Ralf had a change of heart. 'I feel like the zoo for a change,' he said, and off we went. Inside the zoo gates he stopped, and held up his face to the fecund smells. Then he took hold of my elbow, and said, 'Let's hear about the elephant.'

twenty

The evenings were dreadful. Ralf sat with his elbows on the armrest, his chin perched on his knitted hands. Every now and then he nodded or growled at a private thought. The only thing to do was drink. My own empty glass was a constant surprise. We sat in bonded silence, me on the sofa, Ralf in his high-back chair, still as a moth in darkness, and as I blurrily glanced up at the bare walls behind him I kept thinking, *I still need to tell him*.

Then I stopped thinking about it. I had a bigger and more urgent problem to think about. I needed to find someone to replace me.

When I asked Ralf for the contact details of his friends he refused to give them to me. He did not wish to be a burden on his friends. I didn't push it. It was a mistake to have asked. The last thing I wanted was all his friends pouring through the apartment and gasping up at the bare walls. I thought about contacting a German social agency. But my German wasn't up to a telephone conversation of that kind. On further reflection, I didn't want to encourage official curiosity. My visa had also expired. There, I was beginning to think like Ines.

Quite by chance, in a kitchen cupboard, I found the cardboard sign advertising 'Room in exchange for light domestic duties.'

I talked it over with Ralf. Something needed to be done. My departure date was fast approaching. He knew about the situation at home and was sympathetic. Of course that sympathy was tempered by the knowledge he would need someone else. He couldn't live by himself.

So one afternoon we set off for Zoologischer Garten. I had wanted to go in the morning, but Ralf, that wily old fisherman, said afternoons were better.

The first time I ever went fishing I could not believe that a fish would be fooled by our dry land preparations. I watched my father assemble the rod and feed the line through shiny hoops, and then attach the tackle, and the lure—this shimmering metal with a tiny tongue of red plastic. I was still doubtful up to the moment he cast, and out to sea I saw the fake bait make its splash. Seconds later there was a strike, the top of the rod bent and delight broke over my father's face, at which point I became a believer.

So when we entered the station with the cardboard sign I had already convinced myself we would attract someone in the crowd. All I needed to do was to copy Ines' example.

We didn't have long to wait, fifteen minutes or so, while I studied the faces coming down the escalator. All the while Ralf stood as still as a cave mystic. Then I saw her. The face had a framed innocence, fresh complexion, light brown hair fell to her shoulders, a woollen jersey with red-and-black koalas crawling across an ample bosom, jeans, sneakers. I smiled up at her. At first it had the scattering effect of a stone thrown into a pond filled with small nervous fish. I kept smiling. I waited—and sure enough—as her face turned back from the exit doors she managed a reluctant smile. I managed to hold her smile down the escalators. She hauled her pack through the crowd and when Ralf heard me speak in English he came to the mouth of his cave and peered out, and said, 'Who have we here then?'

Julia is her name. She'd flown from Sydney to Frankfurt and hopped on the first train up to Berlin. She was pleased to find another from her part of the world. Someone whose trust she could assume as a matter of tribal fidelity.

I'm confident she has the necessary qualities: calm, practical, able to laugh off Ralf's piss-and-miss occasions around the toilet bowl.

I moved Julia into Ines' old room. I walked her to the window. We stared down at the courtyard filled with old chestnut leaves. I pointed out the bird's nest. I showed her the bathroom. I knew all she wanted was for me to leave so she could tear off her clothes and stand in a hot shower.

I moved my things back downstairs. I didn't unpack. I didn't feel like an occupant any more. I didn't feel like I was a part of Ralf's life or the city's. I spent the days standing at the window staring out at the bare branches. I tried to read but couldn't concentrate. I found myself visiting the home news sites, scrolling through the detail of the weather and utterances of politicians and rugby coaches. When I tired of that I got up and stood before the window. I waited for the afternoon to pass. On dusk I left the building and crossed the top end of the Tiergarten and stood in joyless ranks to eat at the wurst stand by the station. I walked back outside the zoo walls and beyond until the noises and shrieks settled into the background of that old abandoned life.

Five days after she moved in Julia stood outside Hauptbahnhof with Ralf, waving up at my face in the airport bus window. She stood as I had seen Ines so many times, with her arm looped through the old man's. As the bus moved out I noticed Ralf's head turned in the wrong direction. He seemed distracted. In the old days it would have been for wondering, *What has happened to Ines?*

part four: *Ines*

twenty-one

The inspector is my only visitor. Every visitors' day there he is. He sits across the long table from me. He places both hands on the table. He sits half turned, as though there might be a fault with the chair. That's what I first thought. Now I realise it is because he wishes to see more. I am used to it now, but in the beginning I felt as though I was a disappointment. He'd come here hoping for more. And now I sit before him, and this is all there is of me. It is there in the way he turns, and then looks again, which makes me believe that there might be more. I have seen people at the zoo with the same expression as the inspector's. The bear is a disappointment. Look at the rhinoceros—it is not doing anything. It is just a rhinoceros. It is just being a rhinoceros. It was like that with Defoe at the zoo beach. He felt he had to compensate for the disappointment of the beach by making things up or telling me stories about another beach from his country on the other side of the world. He used to talk all the time about that country as if it meant something.

But what is more important than one's own child? Countries don't mean anything. Not to me they don't. I can no longer tell countries and zoos apart.

When he visits, the inspector will sit back inside of himself. There are his limbs, his face, his clothes, the outer appearance of the man, but that was just to get him in the door and seated across from me. The other part of him sits deep inside looking out of his kindly eyes, which I have come to believe are his real eyes. The inspector has another set of eyes for professional purposes. These eyes sit further back. These are the eyes that are so easily disappointed with what they find. He was expecting a full tin of biscuits, only to find a few crumbled leftovers. You cannot hide that kind of disappointment. Even in a man who has no eyes. Ralf had no eyes. So his mouth carried the load of disappointment. Whenever he was disappointed his mouth dropped open. It could do so with high expectations of good things such as food or schnapps, in which case his lower lip was lighter and didn't tug on his cheek bones, dragging them down into the pit of disappointment along with his heart and bones. Whenever Ralf's mouth dropped with disappointment it was like his heart was looking for an opening to escape through.

The inspector sits across from me and stares. I am a small animal in its pen. He has information about that animal. And there I am, captured, caged, the living, breathing example of the creature he has read up on.

At the zoo the animals stare back. So I look carefully at his white shirt. It is clean and ironed. The top of the collar is beginning to fray. He has seen me looking and once or twice followed my eyes there, tucked his chin against his chest in order to see what I see. He reacts to such a moment like a truck driver discovering a dead end. He will rub at his eyes, rub away the unsatisfactory aspect of the world. Then he will blink at me. He blinks until I am back in focus. I am back where he first saw me, seated opposite, across the table from him. Now he unbends his legs. He sits up straighter, moves himself into the edge of the table. He is back to wishing there was more of me, more to see.

The inspector's eyes are olive brown. I remember once waking up beneath a canopy of trees and looking up at a pale sky through overhanging brown branches. Sometimes I think I see two yellow flares. It is the harder set of eyes bursting through to settle in the inspector's kinder trusting pair.

His hair is dark. There was a maître d' at the hotel in Tunisia who used to dye his hair black. You felt he was dying of something. Vanity that has lost the ability to see itself. The inspector's hair is dark at the roots but lightens towards the ends. The kelp does the same thing in the sea as it rises towards the light. My pale skin is from my mother. Light is wish fulfilment, she used to say. I was born pale but at night I become the night. During the day my skin lightened—and around white people, to my mother's joy and relief because I would now be saved, my skin became like theirs. When she said her goodbyes she expected me one day to return from the hotel world transformed, as white as the tablecloths. When my baby was born I saw him gifted with my skin. His father looked puzzled. I had to tell him, to put his mind at rest, the baby was still trying out his skin. I laughed at the stupidness of that remark, but Jermayne's face scrunched up.

He looked down at the baby as if it was a problem to fix or solve.

There are high windows in the visitors' room. Whenever the inspector stands to leave, the light from those windows finds his hair. What was dark turns reddish brown, his hand brushes the top of his hair as if he too felt that change, then it turns back to dark as he steps away from the light. There are creatures in the sea who are happiest out of the limelight. Stuck in a crevice of rock or mud they stare back at the floating world. Even at the hotel some guests would refuse a table in the middle of the restaurant. The man would look pained, the woman anxious. She might finger her jewellery. The guests sitting along the wall seemed to have everything in the world they could wish for. If only they could have what those people have, a table by the wall on the edge of the restaurant. I imagine the inspector seated at a table by the wall. I imagine the staff confused. No one knows who seated him there, how he came to occupy that table. This is how I arrive at the visitors' room to find the inspector waiting for me, already seated, his hands arranged with fingertips pointing in and resting on the table top.

After the yellow flares die his eyes moisten. I find myself wishing I could reach across and touch his moustache—to see if it is as soft and warm as it looks. When he smiles lines break out from the corners of his eyes, and then I will feel pleased with whatever it is I have said.

He always comes in the same royal-blue blazer. A darker blue would suit him better. A dark blue would better serve his brass buttons. If he'd shown up to the hotel in that royal-blue blazer we would have taken him for a package tourist.

He wears dark slacks. Whenever he stands to leave I always

look to see the overhead lights reflected in his black shoes. Then the lines break out from the corner of his eyes. He knows I know his vanities. That moustache, the creased line in his slacks and his expensive shoes.

This is also the moment in which he will give me something over and above the cake his wife has made. Yesterday it was writing pads and pens.

The inspector is not my only friend. But he is my only visitor. Sometimes I think I can feel the heat of the outside day coming off him. That is a gift. The inspector has brought that world inside the visitors' room with him. Sometimes I see a bit of ash on his shirt front. When he sees me looking he looks down and brushes the ash away; without realising it he has both given and taken away the moment I imagined where he sat alone in the car waiting for the gates to the women's facility to open.

Yesterday I came into the visitors' room to find him as I usually do, already seated, but this time a pile of paper was set on the table before him. That pile of paper is now in my possession. The inspector explained what it was. Testimonies, he said. Testimonies from people I came into contact with or who claimed to know me on my way to Berlin to get my boy back from the baby thief Jermayne. These testimonies I read in one gulp and I felt the same as I did the first time I saw a worm casting. How did a creature so soft and flexible leave behind, almost in passing, something so set and hard?

It feels like a long time ago now. The day the men in green uniforms came and took me away from the blind gentleman's house. The men in green were polite to start with, and then silent.

Silent as concrete is when used to guard against the wild elements. There was a grille between where I sat in the back of the van and the men in the front. One man sat in the back facing me. But he kept looking away to the small window in the back door. He looked like he would rather be doing something else, boating or playing table tennis. I looked out the same window and saw a patch of grey, a tree. I saw Defoe like some storm-flung thing struggling to hold his feet against a gale. And then I was that same thing I saw, I too was uprooted and now I was being taken in by the authorities. The panic I felt was for my boy. Everything emptied out of me. I felt as light as a husk. I wished I had said something to my boy. The last time I handed him back to Jermayne I said 'goodbye', with a lightness and confidence I would see him again soon. And now I was being torn from him. It was happening all over again.

I often picture him wondering where his mother has gone. Why doesn't she meet him in the park any more? I wonder how much time will pass before I see him again. I worry about that lost time and how I will make it up to him. I worry about the lies his father will tell. I saw my life with my boy drift away out that back window. As we bumped our way through the unseen city I was back in the deep sea pawing around in the dark. And when the doors of the van were flung open there was a flash and I remembered the same blinding light bursting in on the home I had made under the dinghy on the shingle beach. Riddled with sea lice I looked up at the long dark hair hanging down from a face surprised to see me as much as I was to see her. We both cried out, and as the dinghy dropped back the light of the world above raced away from me. I lay curled up on my side, my cheek against the shingle, and waited. Some light crept under the sides of the dinghy, and then a bit more, a bit more and a bit more, until I saw a woman's face turned upside down next to the shingle outside of the hull. She couldn't see me for the dark. She called softly. She could have been calling for her cat. And I couldn't decide whether to creep out of there in the hope of being led to a saucer of milk or to stay put.

The side of the dinghy lifted. The blinding light returned. I made a scuttling movement, such as a crab in panic makes. I reached out. I grabbed some clothing and as I dragged her down to the shingle next to me the hull came crashing down over us. It was instantly dark. How strange it was to feel her dry clothing and her hot well-fed breath so close to mine. How strange to have another crawl under my shell. Now I did things I didn't know I knew how to do. I put my hand over her mouth to stop her shouting. I breathed hotel reception calm into her ear. Slowly her breath came under control. A few minutes is all it took, before I had her trust. Later she would tell me she was relieved when she realised that I was not a man.

On the other hand, I was not the same person who boarded the boat with its human cargo. When I crawled ashore I had shed that skin. I was changed in all sorts of ways by the time that woman raised the lid on my sea-rotted body.

Now and then I peeped out from under the hull. I didn't want to go back out to the world until it was dark. So we had to wait. Some time passed. More than once the woman began to sob. Each time I calmed her with the hotel voice. Soon we could go. But not yet. I am sorry, I am very sorry, but these are the circumstances in which we find ourselves, and so we must show patience. We talked but not much. When she asked me where I was from I replied, 'The Hotel Astrada in Tunis.' I had come ashore in Europe, but where? She was amazed that I did not know. I told her the sea does not recognise countries. It just washes ashore. And that is how I had come to this shingle beach. I had washed ashore with the bits of drift wood and plastics and other debris. You are in Sicily, she said.

I asked her if she had been to Berlin. She hadn't, she said. 'But you know where Berlin is?'

'Yes, of course. Berlin is in the north of Germany.'

'And from here,' I asked her, 'how might I get there?'

'Germany? Airport,' she replied.

'By road?' I asked.

'Yes.'

She said it was possible. But long.

'What is long?'

'And dangerous,' she added, if I did what she suspected I had in mind to do. But what is longer or more dangerous than to be left to float in an ocean? I had made it to land, but none of the danger and fear I'd known in the sea had left me, or would leave me. I was still ocean drift, dependent on currents of helpfulness and luck.

For a long time we lay beneath that dinghy. At some point we heard voices. A man's and a woman's. We heard their feet in the shingle. They sat down at one end of the dinghy. We lay below, our skins crawling with sea lice and sand hoppers, listening to their talk above. In the silences between they were kissing. And then I heard a voice I knew. From a mouth that tries to pick up a peanut off the bar with no hands. A look-at-me look-at-you look-at-us voice. A teasing voice, playful. Jermayne was like that. He had paid me the same attention. I wanted to bang on the hull and warn that woman. She should reach down for a handful of shingle and plug the hole of that sorcery. Or laugh—I had tried that with Jermayne when words failed to work. But it only made things worse. It livened him up. My laughter seemed to encourage him. And then I recalled, while listening to the woman sitting on the upturned dinghy, I seemed to like it. Ridicule does not come easily to me. But with Jermayne I discovered I liked the feeling of power it gave me. If I laughed it made him try all the harder. The more he purred and the more his admiring glances shone on me the more grand I became; at the bar by the hotel pool a bigger me was being wooed out of my staff supervisor's skin. Now I think this must be a trick known universally to men. Because above us I could hear the same thing played out, and even though I didn't understand a single word I knew its sounds.

Eventually we heard them stand up, heard their feet crunch away in the shingle. We waited some more minutes. Then I had a peep out the side. It was dark. I saw pretty lights reflected in the black sea. I heard distant voices that were light and happy. I heard glass tinkling. I wondered if a hotel was nearby. While we were under the boat the woman had submitted herself to my authority. I hope it was no more than I intended: firm but kind in a supervisor's way. From the moment we crawled out from under the dinghy and stood up in the soft night I gave up authority to her.

For hours we'd lain side by side without knowing the creature we clung to. Now in the reflected night we stared at each other.

I looked at her nice dress and her fine wristwatch, while her eyes roamed up and down me. That she appeared as concerned as she did made me worry that I might stick out in some way. Perhaps she hadn't believed me when I told her how long I'd spent in the water, and how I'd come ashore, bitten as a sodden sea cucumber. Her eyes found my plastic bag. I told her it was my hotel supervisor's uniform. She looked freshly surprised. She laughed, she said sorry. She laughed again. Then some books lying in the shingle distracted her. She stopped laughing and bent down to pack them in her beach bag. She took me by the wrist and led me across the shingle. For the first time in days my feet landed on warm tarseal or concrete. We were in a car park. And now we were getting inside a car that smelt of hot plastic; then came the thrill of sitting down, of sitting and driving along streets beneath lights I'd seen from out at sea. I did not want to get out of the car. I wanted to keep moving through the world in this way, looking back at people strolling arm in arm, at other cars diving in and out of narrow lanes. I thought of the Italian engineer with the parrot. Why had he given up this for the lane behind the prostitutes' bar? In the car I saw the woman smile. Seeing that line of pleasure on her face I relaxed all the more. She was not afraid of me. That is also the moment she became my friend. Back at the shore when I stood up out of the shingle was when she saw that everything I'd told her was true. That's when she must have made up her mind to help. She told me her name. She said, 'You can call me Ines.'

She lived in a small flat above a short flight of stone steps. Halfway up those steps I stopped. From another building nearby I could hear music. Someone singing—in Italian. For the first time I felt that beyond staggering ashore I had arrived. I was somewhere.

Under a hot shower I washed the sea off me and out of my hair. She gave me shampoo, and conditioner to take out the knots. She gave me a white bathrobe to wear. She asked why I was laughing. It was because I felt like a hotel guest. I felt like a tourist. I could hear the washing machine spinning my clothes. I smelt the food before I saw it or tasted it. Rich tomato smells. I ate three bowls. I did not want any wine. Then we sat on a small balcony overlooking the dark shapes of buildings. Beyond the rooftops bits of sea shifted beneath a yellow-and-black sky. I wondered how many of the others were still out there. How many of them were hanging on? How many had drowned? I thought about the man with the box on his lap.

Up to now only one other person in the world knew about Jermayne. When I told this woman, my new friend, my account sounded different to my own ears. My friend at the hotel who knew about Jermayne and gave advice freely understood my disappointment at losing a man I had thought of as mine. But that part of the story hardly mattered now. And as I told my new friend I felt like I was telling an older part of a story that couldn't touch or harm me any more. The only part that mattered concerned my boy.

She asked me why I didn't go to the police. The answer is simple. It never occurred to me to do so. It never occurred to me that the authorities would help. Now I wonder. It's hard to think that things could have turned out any worse. If I wanted her to she would telephone a lawyer. She might know what to do. When she said that, I stood up and undid the belt around the bathrobe. I moved towards my clothes on the drying rack. The woman followed me and steered me back to the cane chair. She hadn't meant to startle me.

We talked about other things. I told her about the ride in the truck to the boat. I sat in the back with one other woman, the rest were men, bouncing like pumpkins over unsealed roads until we reached the coast where the boat was to pick us up. She asked me many questions. She kept me talking until I had no words left.

She made a bed up on the sofa. As soon as my head hit the pillow I was asleep. If I dreamt at all I know nothing of those dreams. The night seemed to pass very quickly. When I woke it felt like only minutes ago that I'd stretched out on the sofa bed smiling at the touch of the sheets against my skin. Now I looked up at a white ceiling that I could not remember. Someone was talking. Eventually I realised it was the woman. Though with me she had spoken in English. In her own language she sounded like someone else unknown to me. She was outside. I couldn't hear the other person she was talking to. For the moment, I didn't think any more about it. I lay there discovering aches in my body, in my lower back and shoulders. I lay there thinking, I am dry. I am comfortable. This is what it feels to be safe. Then I came back to the woman. I listened some more. She was on the telephone. As soon as I realised that I sat up. It was early. Early to be on the telephone. My clothes were still on the drying rack. I put on the cotton robe and listened. Why was she talking in that way? In such a way that she didn't want to be overheard. I remembered last night's conversation. Was she speaking to the authorities?

Why else was she on the phone so early? I made my own conclusions. And when I opened the door and saw her look of surprise I knew I was right. It had been dark inside the apartment. Outside the light was hard and bright. I did not recognise anything about the place. I did not remember climbing those particular steps. I saw the little car in the courtyard but that white car held no memory. All of it was strange. Even the woman who I had only seen in the dark. The strong morning light has turned my friend into a stranger, and we don't think of strangers as we do of our friends.

As I reached for the phone she pulled it away from my grasping fingers. I reached again, more determined this time. She lost her balance.

The court decided that I was responsible for her death. I cannot argue with its decision. If I had not washed ashore. If she had not come to the beach that day or at that hour or walked down to that end where the dinghies lay. There is no end to thinking like this. If I had not been born—that is usually where such thinking leads. But I was, and so was my friend Ines and everything that we had experienced of life was moving us towards that moment on the steps where she has something that I want. I am reaching for that stupid phone as she is pulling away from me. And then? Well, it is like in a film. It is as silly as in a film. Her arm flies up. I see a leg, the edge of the stone, the metal handrail her arm bounced against. I hear her head make an awful sound.

When the world settled again she lay at the bottom of the steps, her arm flung out. The phone lay in the dirt near her hand.

It is more shocking now that I am writing these words down.

For the court I had to repeat and describe endlessly each moment. I had to be exact. So that these moments became ends in themselves.

I did not think she was dead. Not that I knew what 'dead' looked like. At the hotel I'd seen heart attacks and others with respiratory problems on the ground slumped against a wall, a stunned look on their faces. That's how she looked too. Not dead, but as though she had fallen down the steps, that's all. Some blood oozed out of her hair. But not enough for me to think, *this is what a dead person looks like*. Her eyes were large and still, like someone who is surprised to have fallen down some steps.

I could hear the voice on the other end of the phone, talking out of the dirt. I picked up the phone and in a calm hotel voice, in English, I told the man on the other end to call an ambulance.

twenty-two

Ramona is the woman I share my space with. When she told me she had killed her husband I assumed it was an accident.

'No,' she said, 'I meant to kill him.' She drove a pair of scissors into his armpit. The point penetrated his heart.

She could no longer stand his lies. Lies about other women. She rang the police and told them what she had done. Then she made herself some coffee. She could hear the siren as she knocked on a neighbour's door for milk. She even left the door open. She was sitting at the table drinking coffee when the first policeman came in the door.

I like Ramona. I like her honesty and her kindness. She has a lot of visitors. Often she shares her food with me. One visitor brings her postcards. The only time she needs the desk we share is when she sits down to write on the back of a postcard. One of her friends is a traveller for a cosmetics company. She collects the postcards from Ramona and sends them off from different parts of the country. The postcards will be read by an elderly woman who believes her granddaughter is visiting all the places on the cards.

My first lie was to the truck driver. I told him my name was Ines. I didn't plan to. It just came out of me. Ines. There it was. The truck driver looked across and when he nodded that is also the moment I began to believe as well. And then I began to like it. Eventually it felt normal, and then more normal than my birth name. And on occasion when I would review it and consider reverting to my old name I would think, no, Ines can live on. She can live on in this new skin. The other name I will leave to crack and dry up in the sun along with the debris on the beach.

When the truck driver the inspector spoke to discovered I wasn't a prostitute he turned on me. He called me a lying whore. I was a whore. Why else would I be on the road at that hour of the night? He hit me with the back of his hand across my mouth. He said he would drop me off outside a police station if I didn't do as I was told. He said I could stay in his truck if I put my hand on his lap. I did so and as he grew hard his mood improved. Then he told me to undo his belt and open his fly. I did that. For an hour we drove like that. I discovered this was something I could do. I was turning into this new person able to do such things. For hours we drove through the night with my hand on his crotch. He reminded me that I was travelling for free. He pointed out at the night. Earlier there had been some scattered lights, but now there was nothing. I might as well fall down a well as be dropped off out here in the night. He would drop me down that well if I didn't do what he asked. He told me to stroke his penis. So I did that. I closed my eyes and thought about the hardness of a table top through a tablecloth. It could have been that—table and cloth. And my hand was a salt-shaker or pepper-pot. It didn't matter. With every kilometre I was that much closer to Berlin. And whatever I had to put up with didn't compare to the woman lying in a pool of blood at the bottom of the steps. The thought of that woman who had shown me kindness was something to flee as much as Berlin was a place to hurry on to.

I tried to concentrate on the road. The driver said I was holding his penis too hard. He said it was a penis not a handrail. He talked about his penis as if it was somebody quite well known to him, an old friend with certain charms. His English was hopeless. But he spoke it anyway. He asked me to think of his penis as a fountain. He laughed when he said it the first time. So that I laughed too. He'd made a joke. He kept smiling at the road. Then he asked me to drink at the fountain and I ignored him. Soon he wasn't asking any more. He was ordering me to drink at the fountain and when I hesitated he lifted his foot and the truck slowed and I saw the night come into detail. Nothing outside looked friendly at all, not the flat fields or the black trees, so I unbuckled my seat belt and moved across and put his penis in my mouth. As soon as I did that a hand came down on my head and held me there.

Ramona says I should have bitten his cock. She would have, and without a second thought. When I told the blind gentleman his response was different. He was not outraged like Ramona. He sat forward, interested. He had questions to do with the man's penis. I am surprised at how little the inspector was able to get out of him.

After a while I forgot about my head in the driver's lap. I forgot about his penis in my mouth. Then I felt my hair tugged and held, and my head was moved up and down under the pressure of his hand. When he came he kept my head down. His penis went soft. I let the goo drip out of my mouth onto his jeans. When he worked out what I'd done, that hand of his pulled my head up and slammed me across the cab. The truck swerved. My head banged against the door. He pulled over. There was no traffic. He told me to get out. He called me a whore. Again he told me to get out. I refused. I had done my part. I had done what he asked. Now he had to keep driving away from and towards. He yelled at me to get the fuck out. I shook my head. He reached over and punched the side of my face. That hurt—for days after it hurt. I wouldn't get out. I wouldn't leave the truck. He had to get out himself. As soon as I heard his feet land on the road I tried to lock the doors but I messed it up. Next thing my door opened and he pulled me out and I landed on the roadside. His boot found my stomach. He went on kicking. When the sun came up I was still lying there, in the roadside grass, and next to me a cigarette packet that someone had thrown out the window.

I don't tell Ramona that story any more. It makes her angry. She starts to pace up and down until I get the feeling she would like to kill her husband all over again.

I've told her I was shown more kindness than abuse.

When I stood up out of the roadside grass a small car pulled over. The driver was an old man. He opened his door and got out to call to me over the rooftop. The passenger door fell open and a small girl's face peered back. It took me a moment to realise that one side of my face was covered with dried blood. I got in the back of the car. The little girl stayed in the front with her grandfather. I didn't speak Italian. They didn't speak English. As we came to the edge of a village I tapped on the window to get the driver's attention. I tried to make him understand I wanted to get out. He shook his head. He said something, and pointed to the side of his face. We drove on, crawled along a lane beside a field until we stopped outside a small cottage. An old woman in a black dress was pegging out washing. He turned off the engine and wound down the window and yelled something. The woman pegging up the washing shifted her attention to the back window. The man turned around and looked at me. The little girl in the front poked her face between the seats and said, 'Come.'

I don't know their names. But they were gentle and kind. My cheek hurt when the old woman touched it with the warm cloth. My ribs hurt. She wiped something from my chin. She had to rub hard to get rid of it. When it came off she looked a little harder at me. They fed me. Then the old man put me back in the car. The woman and the barefoot granddaughter waved from the door. We drove to the village, where a bus sat idling in the square. The driver disappeared inside an office. He came back with a ticket for me. He kissed me on both cheeks. I climbed onto that bus without knowing where I was headed except that it was north.

Two hours later the bus arrived at its destination. Another village, this one surrounded by hills. I watched the passengers get off into waiting cars or be met by friends and relatives. Arm in arm they wandered off.

Outside the bus the driver pointed north out to me. I climbed over a stone wall and crossed a field of dead crops and climbed up to the hills where I could see another village against the sky. That night I slept beneath the trees. The following day the snail woman found me and took me home. Her testimony is the one that makes me feel the saddest. Until I read it I thought all pity had been rinsed out of me. I rediscovered it when I read her statement to the inspector. I wish I had left her a note. I am sorry I stole the road map. I have asked the inspector for her address so that I can write to her. I will thank her for her kindness and for delivering back to me what I had thought I had lost, and in due course I will send her some money and perhaps one of Ramona's drawings of me to pay for the road map.

A baker saw me gazing in at his display window and came out with a bread roll. He wanted nothing in return. I ate a piece of apple nudged along in the dirt by a sparrow. I ate it without a second thought. Thank you, sparrow. I drank from the taps at the backs of cottages. At night I washed in fountains. I stole what I could. A bowlegged man, with some missing front teeth, carrying a digging tool over his shoulder, gave me some cheese and a cigarette. I'd never smoked a cigarette before. A man in an expensive-looking white open-top car stopped to pick me up. He was a gentleman. Well dressed, a white man, tanned, with white teeth and a gold chain that dangled from his wrist. When I asked if he had worked in a hotel he laughed and slapped the steering wheel. We stopped at a village. He bought me lunch. It was fun to feel like a tourist. I ate all the olives and all the bread. He wanted nothing in return. His English was good. I surprised him when I told him I was travelling to Berlin. At first he seemed to think I was joking. Then he asked why. I answered truthfully, my son. But the rest of what I said was lies. The truth tends to frighten people—some are alarmed and want to run away from the natural disaster spilling towards them. Others stare with wonder. The snail woman was like that. Almost frightened to breathe.

We slowed down in the traffic around the station. The conversation dried up. The man hid behind his sunglasses. We were getting ready to say goodbye. My gratitude was waiting there on the tip of my tongue. He dropped me by the steps and at last I thanked him. He took off his sunglasses to smile. I walked up four or five steps. I wanted to look like I was going somewhere. Then when I judged the moment was right I stopped and looked back at the traffic. I waited for the lights to change, then after his white car moved into the traffic I left the station steps and for the next hour I approached different people—a woman with a child, a small boy who took one look at me and ran off, a man with a newspaper, and the baker who gave me some bread—to ask directions to the edge of the town and the road north.

Two days later a chicken farmer dropped me off at the side of the road. He got out of the car and came around to my side to point the way over a pass. He gave me some bread and then because he had trays of eggs in the back he insisted on giving me eggs. He must have known they would be useless. But I took them. Those eggs made me feel more normal, they made me believe that the day might end with me under a roof cooking those eggs. They were the only thing he had to give. Then he remembered he had something else. He opened his car and dug around under his seat. He came up with a screwdriver. I understood what he was trying to say. I showed him my sticking knife and he made admiring noises and took back the screwdriver. The clouds moved and we both glanced up at the sun; that's when he remembered the water bottle in the back of the car. I was so grateful for the water bottle that I forgot the eggs.

As I climbed the path to the ridge pointed out by the egg man it got hotter and hotter. The blue sky turned black with the heat. Birds rose on thermals and then disappeared into the melting sky. I walked and walked. I stayed on the correct path. But the ridge kept growing higher. By now I had a finger of water left. I knew I must not drink it. To hold onto even a little is to still have it. I had to crawl under the brush for shade. I spent the day waiting for the sun to drop. I thought about my boy. Hours later that same thought got me up off the ground. It was cooler now and I set off again, walking through the last of the evening light, towards the ridge and a sky black and shining with stars.

For a time I felt as if I was moving towards something better. I held onto that idea like I held onto the water. At some point it was clear I had left the correct path. The ridge was still where it had been two hours ago. Now I wonder if I was walking around it instead of up. I decided to stop and wait for daybreak. I knelt down and cleared away some small stones and lay down. I shook the plastic bottle and left the water alone. I closed my eyes and thought about my boy. It was the next morning that the dogs found me.

twenty-three

Whenever Ramona rakes back through my story she says she is sorry that I have never known love. In her own mind she has driven Jermayne into the same pen holding the faceless men I had hotel sex with. I don't like to correct her because she has decided who the villains are in my story. Every male is a lighter or darker shade of her womanising husband. So the strangely complex feeling I have for Jermayne must stay unsaid. But there are others. *Were* others? I am not sure of the tense. In the partridge hunter's account Paolo is last seen leading me up to the ridge. I am surprised the inspector didn't try to talk with him. And my Frenchman. I can hardly follow his story; the sentences make no sense. I don't recognise him at all. I never heard him once use the name Millennium Three. I know him as Bernard. Ralf used the name Defoe. I did too, but only after getting the Christopher and Andrew parts of his name mixed up.

I didn't realise how high we had climbed until I stopped for breath and looked and saw the sparkling metal rooftop of the car parked further down the mountainside. That is also the moment my knees began to wobble. I couldn't take another step for fear that I would fall off the side of the mountain, and that is when Paolo, the footballer, took hold of my hand. He told me not to look back, otherwise I would lose my balance. He told me to close my eyes. I could place my trust in him. There was air on all sides of me. Paolo tried to get me to look at how high we were. *Look at where we have climbed to!* The glee in his voice gave him away. I shook my head and told him to carry on, I didn't want to stop, I wanted to keep going. I didn't open my eyes until I felt the path lead down. The terrifying light air at the top of the pass turned heavier and warmer. Air that had only known other air turned to air that knew rock and brush. I changed out of a bird back into a human being. And when at last I opened my eyes I found myself looking out on a different world. Behind me the mountain reared up and blocked everything else.

The path grew wider until we were walking side by side. The stones grew smaller. They were shiny with age and slippery. Whenever I slipped, Paolo's hand shot out from his side to catch me. I let myself be caught. I knew everything that was happening between us. Paolo's hand was the same hand as the one that had supported me in the water and showed me how to float. His hand would grasp my wrist, then rest on my shoulder until he had placed me and I felt placed. Up until that moment I was a salt-shaker falling from a table. Now I stood still as time itself, grateful, patiently waiting for the next event. We came to a stream. Paolo bounded down with our water bottles and filled them. On his return he held the water bottle to my lips and his other hand rested on my shoulder. As he poured the water down my throat I felt the hope of that hand of his. But as I was thirsty I went on gulping down the water and the hand stayed put. I remembered the truck driver pressing down on my head. I took the water bottle away from my mouth. I looked back at the mountain. Cloud was piled up to the ridge, a neat line of cloud. It had run into some kind of superior will and could come no further.

Ramona is mostly a lump in the dark. But then a wail will come from her—not loud, but a woebegone sound that rises out of that still lump on the bed. I wonder if she is looking down at her dead husband with the scissors sticking out of his armpit. The lump then turns into a face peering across at me. 'Was I doing it again?' she asks.

'No,' I always tell her. Because if she isn't aware of what she was dreaming she soon will be.

'Are you ok?' asked Paolo.

'Yes,' I said. 'Yes. A bit of water went down the wrong way.'

Flat land met us off the mountain and we walked for hours without stop. Farm animals raised their heads to look at us. A chained goat sat in the roadside grass chewing and staring. It seemed to know we weren't from its world. It seemed to know everything about me in particular. As it chewed, its eyes followed me.

My knees hurt. They had never been a problem. The same with my back. But now it ached. I told Paolo and immediately I felt his hand exploring the region of my lower back. I lay down on the grass. He knelt beside me moving my legs and arranging my arms until he had tricked and stretched the ache out of my back and I was ready to carry on.

At some point he thought to say we were in Austria. I wasn't aware that we had stepped across a white painted line. But then I saw the rooftops and spires in the distance.

In the village Paolo bought some bread and cheese, and more water. He bought bus tickets. There was a short wait, then we were moving through countryside. I am sure I was the only one on the bus who didn't know their destination. Paolo placed a steadying hand on my knee. Perhaps it was to prevent me toppling into the aisle. In quick time we arrived at a larger town. I thought this was how it would be all the way to Berlin. A succession of towns, each bigger than the previous one. So it was disappointing to arrive at a smaller town. The hand moved to my shoulder to steady my nerves, to reassure. The boat will be by soon. Do not worry. The hand felt like a dead weight now, such as that which rests on the neck of a dog to hold it still.

In this village people looked at me. They didn't look at Paolo. Even the small children. While Paolo was in a travel shop I crossed the road to some public toilets and changed into my hotel maid's uniform. When Paolo came out of the travel place his broad smiling face changed. He seemed puzzled, but no one else in that village was.

He showed me the tickets, waved them in my face. A ticket for another bus and a train ticket. A ticket to Berlin. The ticket was in his name. He'd had to show his passport. He put the tickets in his trouser pocket and wandered off. The dog chased after its master.

I followed him up the street we were on, and down another, across a square, through a series of back alleys. Finally we came to what he had been looking for. In a small lobby I waited just behind his shoulder. After he paid the receptionist I followed him along a hall through a door to a room with one bed. The sheet hadn't been pulled over the lip of the duvet. I rearranged the pillows. Without a word Paolo began to undress. The light from the shuttered windows played over his fine body. When he saw what I was staring at he looked annoyed and moved the tickets to under the small lamp on the bedside vanity. He told me to take off my hotel uniform. He wanted to wash my clothes. I told him I could wash them. I don't like the idea of a man washing my under things. He shrugged and went into the other room. I heard the bath taps running. When he came back and saw I was still in my uniform he said tomorrow I would be going to the city. Tomorrow I will be on the train to Berlin. If I want to avoid suspicion I need to look like I belong on the train.

I told him I needed to be on that train. Need, he said, was another one of those things that makes people suspicious. I should keep that need to myself. I should look like I've been on that same train a dozen times before and there is nothing left to see or experience. 'Here,' he said, patting the chair by the window. I walked over to it and sat down. Then he said, 'Look out the window and tell me what you see.' When I started to describe a balcony, a roof with aerials, a pigeon, he cut me off. He said when I looked out the train window I must appear bored. 'You understand? Pretend to be bored, as if everything flashing by in the window you have seen before on many, many occasions.'

He told me to think of the most boring thing I could think

of. I know what that is. 'Good,' he said. 'Now look out the window.' I was conscious of him moving behind me, checking me from different angles. 'That's very good. Now tell me what you were thinking of.'

I told him. Making beds. He gave a surprised look then burst out laughing. He bent down to kiss my forehead. He said I was from a different planet. But that was all right. He patted my head. The way he did so made me comfortable about getting out of my clothes. He wouldn't do anything. When I undressed I saw that I was wrong. I was no longer a pet. I was back to being a woman. I was back to being a need, an object on a shelf. He reached for that thing. I felt his hand on my breast. There was no pleasure in his face. None at all. I wondered, why is this man touching in this way? I know what a powerful and complicated thing need is. I know what a two-faced monster it is. Ramona never likes to hear me talk about need in this way because then she starts to think differently about her dead husband. She has come this far without feeling sympathy. It is important for her to carry on in the same way. To change now would only bring her back to an unbearable place. She does not want to feel regret over her husband's death.

I can see that. So when I talk to her about need I talk about the goal of seeing my boy, of getting my boy back in my arms. A need such as that obscures everything else. Even physical pain will bend to its will. The need in Paolo was not as simple as mine. His need was mixed up with other feelings to do with guilt. So when he reached out and touched my breast I helped him by laying my hand on top of his. I stroked his fingers until I saw the confusion and disappointment in himself leave his face, and a look replace it, a look that reflected only how my breast felt under his fingertips. That kind of feeling is nothing compared to the need I felt, and so I could satisfy him, just as I have so many hotel guests. Some of those guests have behaved like pigs in a trough. Others just want to feel that it is all right to be who they are, to feel the way they do; I think Paolo was like that.

Afterwards he bathed me, washed me down with soap and cloth. He dried me. He pulled back the duvet and laid me down. I did as he asked and closed my eyes. I listened to my clothes sloshing about in the bath. Then I must have slept. When I woke Paolo was standing beside the bed looking down at my face. My clothes were folded on the chair. He had been to the laundrette. The clothes were dry—and it was time to go.

He put me on the bus which would take me to the place where I would catch the train to Berlin. He handed me the tickets. On the train ticket I saw that he had changed Paolo to Paola. For the duration of the trip he said I was to forget my own name. I was to forget that and if anyone asked I was to say my name was Paola. Well of course I had no trouble following what he said. Paolo would get on a different bus and go back to the first village we had come to earlier in the day. The next morning he would walk back over the mountain pass.

There is not much to say about the next part. Everything went to plan. I got off the bus and found the station, I found the right platform, the right train. I felt clean in my clean clothes. I felt new. In that smart blue coat I felt like I belonged on that train.

I am reluctant to describe what I saw out the window. I don't want to sound like a tourist. I can't say how many beds I made, over and over, but I don't imagine all the beds I made on the train to Berlin is near to the number I have made in my life. For a time the train ran alongside a river. As the hills closed in I began to worry the world was about to play another trick on me. Then, just on dark, but with enough light to see, we left the river, the hills disappeared and we moved onto a broad plain. I felt a pleasing surge beneath me as the train picked up speed. I looked back at the shadows in the window. I was still making beds. A man sitting opposite me smiled. I looked back at the window. There was nothing he could do for me.

twenty-four

Defoe once told me about the journey of eels. He was in one of those moods where his homeland shone like a lamp through the darkest weeks of the Berlin winter. Eels, he said, slithered over grassland and through shingle to the sea. There they changed into sea-going creatures able to swim the length of an ocean. They breed in the depths, then their offspring swim back the way of the parents. When they arrive at the shoreline they change into freshwater eels and crawl through shingle, across grassland, to enter the creek where as a child Defoe sat crouched and ready with a stick and a nail poking out its end. I told him I felt sorry for that eel, and I didn't like the heart of that boy either. He laughed in the way that people do when they think I am joking. He went on to say that his father used to smoke those eels and hang them up to dry. He said they looked like football socks hanging on the clothesline.

I remembered that eel story the first time the inspector asked me what happened when I arrived in Berlin. Berlin is a different stage of my journey. I left 'Paola' on the train. When I stepped onto the platform I was back to Ines. That smart blue coat of hers gave me the same invisibility as my hotel uniform had in that village. I had the money Paolo and all the others had given me. I had my plastic bag with my hotel uniform, toothbrush and sticking knife, and I had the road book I'd stolen from the snail woman.

Unlike the eel I had no idea what to do next or where to go. I hadn't thought about which rock to look under in order to find Jermayne. I didn't want to stick out like the last fish in the sea so I followed the people down the escalators and through the exit doors to the cold air outside the station, and here the crowd broke up and people hurried away from one another. Across a square, a few figures on the edge of the dark walked along followed by dogs with hanging heads.

I took one look up at the cloudy night and turned around and went back inside the station. People sat in plastic chairs outside places offering food. I wanted to sit down, but I didn't want to buy anything. So I joined the end of another crowd walking towards a different set of escalators and found myself on another platform. A train pulled in. The doors opened. I felt the crowd press from behind. It was so much easier to go with it. To turn around would only bring me back to the problem of where to go and what to do. So I entered the carriage. There were plenty of seats. I sat down. No one looked at me. By now I was tired of making beds. I thought this time I will just try to look like everyone else.

The stops came quickly. More people got off than got on. Soon

The carriage was almost empty. At the next stop I got off and walked to the other side of the platform, and within a few minutes a train was pulling in. I got on and travelled back in the direction I had come. This time I knew where I was headed. And there, at Alexanderplatz—where I had first arrived—I arrived again. The escalators had been switched off. This time I climbed up to the level with the shops and kiosks. I bought a bottle of water and some wafers at one of the kiosks and sat down in one of the white plastic chairs. For five or ten minutes I am sure I looked like someone who is meant to be there. But as soon as I stood up from that chair I was back to being lost. I followed another crowd down the escalators to the same platform as before. This time I rode the train to the last stop. I got out and walked to the other side of the platform. The train was already there and, as if it had been expecting me, its doors open. It took forty minutes to deliver me back to Alexanderplatz.

When I left the station police vans sat watching the empty space of the square. I went back inside and found the women's toilets. The receptionist handed me the right change to open the door to a cubicle. The toilet was clean and the tiles were a gleaming white that never sleeps. It was warm and comfortable in there. Every now and then a toilet flushed and my head would snap up from a drowsy sleep. People came and went in the cubicles either side of mine. No one stayed for long. My plan was to spend the night in there but eventually someone banged on the door and said something in a loud and unpleasant voice. It was the receptionist. I came out and left her muttering and shaking her head.

Back in the main area of the station the crowd had thinned out. I headed for the escalators. On the platform I found a waiting train. When I sat down my head fell against the window. The seat wouldn't let me lie on it and I couldn't risk falling asleep. So I went back to making beds. My back hurt and my calves were tight from all the walking with Paolo. If Paolo was with me now I am sure the world would fall into place around his broad smile. The different stations came and went. I'd made my last bed when I woke to someone shaking my shoulder. I opened my eyes to a young man in ordinary clothes. He had some kind of ID in his hand. He knelt in the aisle to bring himself to eye level with me. There was no one else in the carriage, although in the next carriage down I could see another black person looking up the aisle—looking without seeing. The young man crouching by me spoke softly in German, then, getting no response he switched to English. Politely he asked to see my ticket. My answer had a tiring effect on him. He looked into my face. Slowly he stood up. There he remained in the aisle blocking my escape until the train came into the next station. He asked me to follow him. On the platform we waited until the train departed and there was just the two of us. He asked me for my ID. I told him I didn't have any with me. He looked down at my plastic bag, then he looked back into my face. He asked for my name. Ines, I said. He asked me where I was from. Italy. His eyes were still. Where in Italy? I named the beach where I had swum ashore. In Ines' car I'd seen the sign and made a point of remembering it. Then he spoke to me in Italian. The sound of another train arriving drove away the silence. The ticket collector looked over his shoulder. He returned to his softly spoken English. He said I was lucky I had got him and not one of his colleagues. He led me to the ticket machine and showed me how to purchase a ticket and how to validate it. He asked if I had any money. I produced a fifty-euro note Paolo had collected from the partridge hunters. The amount surprised the ticket man. He was regretting his decision to let me off. He looked up the platform at the train coming into the station. He wanted to be on that train. He bought me a ticket, validated it. The train pulled in and we entered different carriages.

I rode the trains for the rest of the night. For each new trip I bought a new ticket. For most of the night the trains were almost empty. I had no idea of time passing. At some point I woke to find someone wedged in beside me, another two bodies sat opposite, eyes and faces poking out the tops of their coats.

At Alexanderplatz I got off and followed the crowd up the escalators and headed for the toilets. A receptionist gave me change and I went through to my cubicle. I hung the plastic bag on the hook behind the door and sat down. I thought, *unless I leave the railway station I will never find my boy.*

This time I went out the other side of the station and followed a path. It led under some young trees to a large fountain where people gathered to take pictures. I tagged onto the end of a group of tourists and followed them through the doors of a nearby church. People took photographs in the dark. A black man, a man of the church, took off his glasses. He rubbed at his eyes, he replaced his glasses and looked off in another direction. I waited for him to look again as I knew he would. Yes, pastor. I am still here where you saw me.

I sat on the end of a pew for much of the day. Eventually a woman came up and spoke softly in my ear.

I walked back to the station. From one of the kiosks I thought

I had bought a cup of hot tea. Instead I was served a glass of beer and a small saucer of nuts. I ate those and after forcing the beer down I went back to the toilets.

I was back in the sea waiting for the promised boat to come by. I thought, *how do I find my boy? Where is Jermayne?* I sat in there for a long time. Toilets flushed either side of me. I didn't mind it in that cubicle. It was easier, because I knew as soon as I left that cubicle with its sleepless tiles I would have to look like I was on my way to somewhere. Just like the other time there was banging on the door and I was turned out. In the main concourse I caught the eye of a black man in a business suit. His confidence reminded me of Jermayne. Another man sitting in one of the white plastic chairs rolled his head back to laugh just as Jermayne had at the cocktail bar by the hotel pool. A man leant forward with a laptop on his knee. Jermayne's intensity had that same tilt about it. I saw a woman pushing a pram. I saw a beggar woman carrying her child on her hip. Jermayne had picked the baby up off my breast. A person deprived of sleep does not know where they are going. They are led by old instinct. Soon I was back on the train.

twenty-five

According to the testimony I dropped my plastic bag on the platform and the little Frenchman picked it up. I don't know why he made that up.

It was the third night of riding trains. By now I knew I was on the U5. I could relax. I could sleep on the train if I so wished. Other people did. Or I could look up at the little television and watch the weather forecast. The highs and lows over Europe. People playing tennis. Men playing football. A plane crash somewhere. Sometimes I looked through newspapers people left behind. I'd fold a newspaper into a pillow and lean my head against it pressed to the window. This is how I slept now.

I woke to someone shaking my shoulder. The plastic bag was still on my lap but another ticket collector stood swaying in the aisle. This one was older, grey, with a moustache, white eyebrows, pale eyes that drown kittens. He showed me his ID. I didn't have a ticket. As I'd come down off the escalators I had seen the train and rushed to catch it; other people were doing the same and we all swept by the ticket machine. I remember rushing as if I too could not afford to miss it. Now I was asked to leave my seat, to stand in the aisle where everyone could see my shame. I followed the ticket collector to the doors. The start of a platform came into view. When another person held up two tickets and spoke to the collector, I saw the back of the collector's head nod. He turned to me and said something I didn't understand, then he moved on leaving me with the stranger who had come to my rescue.

Bernard doesn't stand up very well to close physical description, and I want to be kind so I will concentrate on his finer aspects. Beneath a mop of dark curly hair with bits of grey and red his smile had not left his face. He wore a silver earring. The hair, his smiling eyes, and that earring—that's all there was to him. The rest of him was coat. A long black heavy coat. It hung off his shoulders and reached an old pair of red sneakers. When I thanked him his smile brightened, but I did not see any need or neediness. Instead I saw something glitter from his front teeth. A small diamond, a gift from an aunt, the last diamond from a necklace that had belonged to the aunt's great-grandmother. I would find this out later. In Paris his friend was a dentist. Yes—that and the rest of the story he told the inspector would come out later.

The train slowed down for the station. Faces on the platform rushed by the windows. The doors opened and I followed my new friend out to the station platform and up a flight of steps. At the top step he stopped and introduced himself. I did the same.

'Ines,' he said. 'Would you like to join me for a cup of coffee?' First I had to ask him something. Why did he have two tickets? He smiled—he seemed to warm to me more for having asked that question. He said the collector only looked at the valid one. The other one he picked up from the floor. He told the ticket collector we had got separated in the crowd. There was something else I needed to ask—why me? He shrugged and turned his hands out. He looked away and back again with his diamond-crusted smile, his eyes dancing around me. 'If you must know,' he said, 'it is because I have seen you on the trains.' He raised his eyes but I had no more questions and we moved up to the street above the subway. The sky looked damaged in a way I had not seen before. I wondered if I should start making beds. Then I thought, no. I want to look. I want to see. We stopped at a road for a tram to squeal around a corner. A line of yellow-lit faces turned to watch us waiting at the lights. Then my friend put his arm through mine and led me across the road to a cafe.

It was in that cafe I told my story to Bernard. When I stopped talking I found his hand closed over the top of mine. He dropped his head, closed his eyes, then opened them, but kept his head down. When he saw I hadn't touched the brandy he reached for it and downed it in one gulp. Then he looked up. It was dark in the cafe but I knew he wasn't smiling. I couldn't see the diamond. His black coat hung over the back of his chair. The lamplight caught his blue denim shirt and his flushed cheeks. He asked if I had a place to stay. I told him I have the trains. He gave a nod, looked down at the table. He was still nodding. The diamond flashed briefly in his mouth. 'Ines,' he said. 'I would consider it a great honour if you would stay with me. Tomorrow we will look for your boy.'

Prison has held no surprises for me. Perhaps I am unusual in that respect. Newcomers are usually heard to cry in the night. They call out the names of their loved ones. Then the sun rises and the names are gone. At the hotel I learned how to pass from one world to another. For long periods of the day I shared the foyer and the rooms with the guests. At night I followed the paths to the dormitories where we slept. At the last hotel we were instructed to brush our teeth before speaking to a guest. Our hands had to be scrubbed and our fingernails inspected by the supervisor before we could present ourselves in that other world. In our own world we accepted each other without teeth being brushed or hands scrubbed. We got around in bare feet, which was a sackable offence in the other world. It was hard to believe two more different worlds could sit so close to each another.

I followed Bernard home to another world that night. As we left the cafe I thought I must try to remember the streets in case I need to find my way back to the world of trains. I tried to remember the name of each new street, but they were like the names of hotel guests. They did not stick. Within ten minutes I thought, *I am lost*.

Ramona always asks what made me trust the little Frenchman. I start with his face, its absence of need. She understands that, but not his coat. That huge coat I clung to, stuck like a barnacle to the side of a barge, as we drifted along streets with too much life in them—cafes, bars, people—to be particular in a way that would make them memorable. I decided that, since I was lost, I would trust him.

We crossed a road and arrived at a long wall. There we passed through a gap to another world which at first I could not see. The ground was rough underfoot and apart from the campfires and lit faces it was pitch black. Bernard produced a flashlight from his coat. I followed that beam of light down the side of a huge building to a door. Inside was as dark as out, but here there were small clusters of lights, single lights, fire-fly light, light as tiny as a lit match, but not a light that could be switched on at the wall. I saw sleeping bodies. I saw a naked woman astride a man. The light found a dog sniffing an abandoned mattress. We came into a better lit area. Here a man sat with his back to us facing a computer screen. In a dark corner near the computer man was Bernard's bed. The light landed on a duvet and three pillows. Bernard passed the flashlight to me while he searched for clean sheets through four drawers all different sizes and stacked on top of one another. I took off my clothes. When he looked up from fixing the bed his eyes went blank. He showed me my side of the bed. He gave me two pillows, and kept the small one for himself. After I lay down he switched off the light. Bernard did not get into bed. He lay on top, on the other side, in his coat. When I woke the next morning I was able to see that he had taken off his sneakers. His eyes were closed. He slept without seeming to breathe. I looked up at the pigeons roosting in the rafters. I saw a white dove, and then another. I counted three children's party balloons caught against the rafters. I listened to babies and small children waking. I heard tiny feet and the complaints of tired parents. A small face appeared next to mine and then ran off.

twenty-six

Thanks to the man with the computer it turned out to be easy to find Jermayne John Hass. John was his father's name. His father was an American soldier. Jermayne took his mother's maiden name for his own after John returned to Detroit. I told this to Bernard as we crossed the bridge into Jermayne's neighbourhood. He replied with something in French. I asked him what it meant and he said it didn't matter; it was something mean and I didn't need to know. He was letting out the viper that lived inside him. 'Now,' he said, 'I will be perfectly behaved.'

Bernard's head turned to follow a green van moving slowly along the street. He asked me if I had a passport.

'No.'

'Do you have any ID?'

He stopped walking then to ask me where I was from. I told him I was from the Four Seasons Hotel. I waited for the next question. But he didn't bother. We carried on, and then the questions arrived. Did I have a photograph of the boy? 'No.' Would Jermayne recognise me? I wasn't sure. What about his wife?

'What wife?' I asked.

I had waited a long time for this moment, yet why was I dragging my feet? Why did I feel so unhappy? I'd spent every waking moment thinking about what might lie around the next corner. Why the tears? I don't know. 'Why?' That is the little Frenchman asking. 'What is this? Look at you.' Through blurry eyes I saw the diamond. I told him I was sorry. 'Sorry for what?' he asked.

'For everything.' I was thinking about the woman lying at the bottom of the steps. In the here and now of the grey-misted traffic in Berlin, a stranger with a diamond in his tooth was smiling and cooing at me as strangers once had at the parrot through the bars of the birdcage.

We came to a canal. As we started to cross a small bridge Bernard put his arm around my shoulder. He held me close to him, as if we might be lovers, and that was the point. Trees. Cobbles. Buildings with ancient bearing. We were in the right street. We walked quickly, faster than before. Bernard told me to look straight ahead. Think of France, he said. I thought of France. I'd once had hotel sex with a man from Tours. A vain little man who liked to slap his cock in his hand. Bernard looked up the street—to France, except for a brief moment when I was aware of him staring into my face. I hoped the man from Tours didn't show up there. He walked me a little faster. At the corner he stopped. He said we'd just walked by Jermayne's building. Now what? What did I want to do?

We walked on down to the next bridge, crossed the canal and

walked back the other way under the trees. Near the first bridge Bernard put his arm around my shoulder again. He pointed out the door of the building. I counted up five floors. I looked in every window. Bernard led me to the cafe on the corner. We chose a table by the window so I could look back at the building that held my boy. He ordered hot chocolate for me. He asked if I was cold. He said I looked cold. I did not possess the kind of feeling that registers cold or hot. I had lost that capacity. I was two eyes and a beating heart. He told me to stop staring. 'Just look like a normal person,' he said.

We were two hours in that cafe. That afternoon the door to the building on the other side of the canal opened just the once, and when it did my heart rose to my mouth and dropped back into place—all in the space of a second—as a white man got his bike out the door and pedalled off under the trees.

Before we left the cafe Bernard produced a woollen hat from his coat pocket. He told me to put it on. I pulled the hat down to my eyes while we sat on a bench above the canal under the trees. Swans glided by on the dark water. Joggers ran past. Cyclist after cyclist. Once I heard a child cry out. Bernard got up to walk his feet back into feeling. He asked if I was hungry. I shrugged. I didn't want to leave the bench. We saw the man with the bike return to the building. We looked up as a light came on in one of the third-floor windows.

We went back to the cafe. Two women were sitting at our table. They looked up at me. Bernard apologised and led me to another one. We sat there until all the lights had come on in the building. Bernard left the cafe to cross the bridge on his own. I watched him return, head down, hands in his pockets. He nodded and I got to leave. This time we walked over the bridge, we crossed the cobbles and walked up to the door. Bernard pointed to the names above the intercom.

I pressed Number 14 and waited. I pressed again. This time a male voice answered. 'Hello?' I saw Jermayne as clear as day. I saw him more clearly than I'd ever been able to remember. I saw him and heard again that same lazy put-at-ease tone of voice as he told me he was just taking the baby out for a walk. I was back at the hotel bar. I was beneath him. I felt his hand holding me afloat. I saw his white teeth and laughing eyes. I saw the confident manner in which he moved across the lobby. I heard him say he wouldn't be long. When I heard him say hello I said nothing. In the end the little Frenchman pulled me away from the intercom. He put his arm around my shoulder and led me up the street.

He did not touch me that night. I lay in the dark waiting but it did not happen. I had to lift my head off the pillow to see if he was still alive. There he lay on the far side of the bed, in his black coat and socks.

We rose early. We didn't make a sound as we crept past people asleep, small children. The pigeons in the rafters blinked down at us. Outside we walked past other people huddled in blankets and sleeping bags by the fires. We went through that hole in the wall back into the world of early risers. A tall truck wobbled up a narrow gullet, its sides brushing the trees. A woman waiting to cross the road held the hand of a child. We walked back to the canal and waited in the mist rising from it. Out of that mist came a woman pushing a pram. Then there was the same young man with the bike we'd seen the day before. Bernard wanted a hot drink so we went to the cafe and sat at the table by the window. We were drinking hot chocolate when Jermayne came over the bridge walking with that slightly bow-legged walk of his; his shoulders lifted as he blew warm air into his cupped hands. A few minutes later he came by with bread and a newspaper. I watched him rise again over the bridge. Then we left the cafe to sit under the trees. It was the same grey day as before and everything about it followed the same pattern. I began to wonder if my boy lived in the building at all.

The next day Bernard has a firm hold of my arm as I inch my way across the icy path on the bridge. I have on his woollen cap and I'm looking down at the ice. When Bernard's fingers clench my arm I look up and he nods behind us. And that's when I see my boy walking beside Jermayne. We'd passed each other on the bridge. Three years and two weeks. That's how long has passed since Jermayne picked the baby up off my breast. We stopped there on the bridge. I studied his back view. Ski jacket, woollen hat, miniature legs in jeans. For the second time Bernard's fingers dug into my bicep—this time to hold me still. He held me there until Jermayne and the boy disappeared around the corner of the cafe.

The boy looked happy enough. Look at the way he walked, his hand in his father's—and in a city I didn't know, towards a future that excluded me. I did not exist in his mind. There was no reason for me to exist in that child's head. Jermayne had seen to that. I often wonder if this was the moment I was meant to walk away. The first time I shared that thought Ramona sat up on her bunk and thumped her pillow. I wasn't sure if it was

Jermayne or my silly head she was thumping. When I say I often wonder, I don't really mean it. No. And it didn't enter my head either as I stood on the bridge staring after my child.

I remembered that my mother's brother made pots and he could recognise another man's pots by the grooves in the clay. That boy would know who I was as soon as he set eyes on me. A blind dog knows which are its pups. Ralf's physical world didn't change just because he couldn't see it any more.

That night my little Frenchman shifted onto his side. He was still in his coat and on top of the duvet. I felt his hand stroke my cheek, stroke my neck, stroke my shoulder, and my neck and cheek again. In a far corner of that dark building a child was whimpering. From the fires outside I could hear someone singing. And close by the little Frenchman whispered his urgent songs in my ear.

Here is the part Ramona likes best.

The next day I press the buzzer. Jermayne answers.

'Hello?'

I say, 'It's me.'

There is silence. I can sense Jermayne mustering all his authority. He replies in Deutsch. He waits, and then I hear the line go dead.

I check behind me. Bernard is under the trees where I left him. He gives an encouraging nod, so I press the buzzer again. This time before Jermayne has the chance to speak I say again, 'It's me.' I can picture his face drawn into calculation, aware of whoever else is in the background in his apartment.

In English this time he asks, 'Who is it?'

'It's me,' I reply.

And the silence returns, though this time the intercom does not go dead. When he next speaks his voice is almost breathless. 'How the hell did you get here?'

'I swam.'

There is another silence.

'What do you want?'

'I want to see my child.'

'Wait down there,' he says and the intercom goes dead.

By this point Ramona is rolling in her bunk, beside herself with joy, picturing bad Jermayne thumping down the stairs and across the landings. I have never told her the truth about that particular moment. About how terrified I was standing outside his building.

The door swung back and there he stood in his slippers.

'Fuck,' he said. 'Fuck.'

He looked back over his shoulder. He levelled his eyes into the dark behind me. He pulled on the collar of his black leather coat. He grabbed my arm and walked me quickly up the street. I managed to turn my head without Jermayne noticing and across the canal I saw Bernard move out from under the trees. We walked to the end of the block without so much as a word exchanged. Then he led me across the cobbles to the shadows beneath the trees.

I'd given him time to think, to consider his strategy, because now I heard the old charming Jermayne of the hotel bar. He wished me to understand that the boy was happy. That his life was here in this city. He said things were fragile at home. My turning up the way I had was like a rock thrown against the window. I had to understand that he had only the child's interests at heart. When people are panicked they talk just like Jermayne did. Words, thoughts. The doors swing wide open on their hearts and minds. They let everything out and hope that something they say finds the mark. Not once did I hear him say sorry. But then Jermayne is smarter than that. He wouldn't want to concede that much. As he spoke I looked at the face I thought I knew and I saw something I did not recognise at all. His mouth was swollen. Not from anyone hitting him—no, it had come from within. I couldn't take my eyes off his mouth. If I had seen the same mouth three years ago I would not have slept with him. I would not have ended up in Berlin or in prison; the woman would still be alive, and most likely I would still be supervisor, smiling my hotel smile and sympathising with the guests' sunburn.

I said to Jermayne, 'I want to see my child.'

'Jesus,' he said. 'Have you not heard anything I just said?'

'I want to see my child,' I said again.

He told me to shut up. He had to think. 'If I let you see the child,' he asked, 'what then?'

'I don't know,' I replied.

'Will you leave us in peace?'

I told him I had no wish to cause trouble. That wasn't why I was there.

'No,' he said. 'I need better than that. You must promise never to speak to Abebi.'

'Who is Abebi?'

'My wife.'

'It's the boy I want to see.'

'Do you understand? You are not to speak to her. Ever.'

He took a step back. Under the streetlamp I saw how angry and scared he looked.

'I'm going through a very difficult time at present,' he said.

'I just want to see the boy.'

'Yes. Yes. You're like a fucking parrot. You have no idea.' He glanced back up at the building.

'When can I see my boy?'

'All right. All right,' he said. 'You can see him. But I advise you not to tell him you are his mother. Because you're not. Promise,' he said, and when I didn't answer he said, 'Those are the conditions. Take them or leave them.' Still I didn't say anything and he added, 'You've forgotten something that is important and not entirely irrelevant. You signed the adoption papers. Abebi is the boy's mother. His legal mother.'

'Tomorrow,' I said, 'I want to see my boy.'

'And if I don't allow it?'

'I will still see him. Only,' I told him, 'it will be a time and place of my own choosing. And you can forget any promise I have made.'

Jermayne's eyes widened. I thought he would hit me.

'I don't remember you being like this,' he said. He turned his head slightly to view me from side on. 'Are you here alone?'

'Yes.'

His eyes shifted. 'Are you sure?'

'Yes,' I said. 'Quite sure.'

Then his face softened in a familiar way. 'You are still pretty,' he said.

He reached to touch my cheek and I slapped his hand away.

'The paw of the lioness,' he said, and he laughed quietly.

'Everything has changed, hasn't it. Very well,' he said. 'There is a playground further along the canal. Twenty minutes' walk along the bike path you will see it. Tomorrow at four o'clock. There are some things you need to know. His name is Daniel. He speaks only Deutsch. So. How should I introduce you, as my friend?'

I said, he can call me Ines.

twenty-seven

The next day I sat on a bench next to a red plastic slide and waited. Bernard had written down some words in Deutsch to say to the boy. He didn't know about my promise to Jermayne and had put down 'mother' as well as *How are you? Are you happy? Do you know a song?* Bernard had written down what he said was a nursery rhyme.

Little boy. Little boy
Look at the trees
What moves the leaves
What moves the leaves
It is the wind
It is the wind.

On our way to the playground Bernard stopped to buy some chocolate and on the paper added the phrase *Would you like some chocolate?* We walked to the far side of the canal. Outside Jermayne's building I imagined him getting the boy ready for his outing. His wife was at work.

I sat on a bench looking down at Bernard's list of words and phrases. When I heard the gate open I looked up. There was Jermayne in his black leather coat. Bundled up in the ski jacket I'd seen the day before was the boy. The boy saw the slide and ran towards it. Jermayne put his hands in his pockets and walked over and sat down beside me. He may have said hello, that would have been normal, I don't know. I was watching the boy climb the steps on the slide. The steps were too far apart for his little legs but he managed each one. He came down the slide with his hands raised. As he dropped off the end Jermayne called him over.

I couldn't take my eyes off the little brown face hiding in the hood of the ski jacket. I heard Jermayne say my name. The little face peered up at me. I held out my hands. He looked back at his father. Jermayne gave a nod and he stepped closer—half hidden in that hood, but wary. I put my hand around the back of his hood and drew him closer until his cheek touched mine. I had to sniff him, taste his skin to see if he was really mine, but the boy drew back and went and stood by his father's knees.

I looked down at my phrases. I asked if he would like some chocolate. Jermayne laughed out loud and went on shaking his head. What I had attempted to say he said quickly to the boy and then answered for him. He said, 'The boy does not eat chocolate. His mother is careful about what she feeds him.' The boy spoke up to his father. Jermayne gave a nod and the boy ran off to the swings.

Jermayne stood up. He gazed off towards the bike path and sat down again. As I watched the boy swing higher and higher Jermayne crossed one long leg over the other. I thought, that boy does not need me. He did not even need to know me.

Jermayne's long legs unfolded, I felt his weight come forward. He said, 'You know the time will come when you will have to walk away.' He looked down and wriggled the toe of his shoe. Then he looked up. 'Where did you get that name Ines from? It almost sounds real.'

'I hope so,' I said.

'Anyway, what you need to understand...'

But I'd stopped listening. I told him I still wanted to see the boy again.

He said I was being selfish.

'Yes,' I said.

Later, when Bernard asked me which words and phrases I had used I told him I hadn't used any. His words didn't work in my mouth. The boy kept swinging higher and higher away from my eyes. My words had sounded ridiculous to Jermayne. He had laughed out loud.

When we stepped through the hole in the wall I felt my anger rise. I said, 'Look at these stupid people. They don't have homes.' Bernard stopped and turned around. He looked at me evenly. Without anger, with patience. The people I had denounced, he said, were not stupid. They were brave. Brave where it counts. I asked if there was another kind of brave. 'Look at them. They live like dogs.'

Bernard turned away and walked on. For the rest of the

afternoon until early evening I lay on his bed. Bernard left to go and do his work. The computer man fed me some soup. I looked carefully into his face. He didn't appear to want anything, so I accepted the soup. On dark Bernard returned. There he stood, with his diamond smile and a football under his arm.

Now the boy engaged with me. That is, he engaged with the ball. He kicked the ball to me, his keen eyes looking up as it left his foot. He waited to see if I would stop it with my own outstretched foot. The ball made me more interesting—more useful, more relevant to the moment. He would look up to see where I was, wait for me to nod, then kick the ball. Then I would do the same—look up for his signal, a nod, sometimes a raised hand. I would kick the ball over to where he stood on his little island, me on my little island. This is how a ball forces you to think. Over by the slide Jermayne sat on a bench, one leg crossed over the other, smoking, watching us carefully just in case I picked up the boy in my arms and ran towards the boat waiting on the canal. He always wanted assurances that I was alone. I don't think he ever quite believed me, and the fact is I was never alone. Bernard was always there, on the far side of the canal, beneath the trees, reading his book.

That afternoon Jermayne gets up from the bench and comes over to where we are playing with the ball. He says something to the boy. The boy glumly picks up the ball and hands it to me. Jermayne said something else and the boy walked to the gate, where he waited. Jermayne said I wouldn't be able to see him next week. He had some business in Hamburg.

For a week I worried that he had taken the boy. I worried that he and his wife had moved. I returned to the bench under the trees and watched the windows of the apartment.

There was no sign of him on the first day. Nor on the second. I was sure now. Jermayne had stolen him again. On the third day I happened to be standing on the bridge staring down at the canal when I heard feet and a mother's voice—not any woman's voice but a mother's voice. By the time I looked up they were coming off the bridge. The boy was holding the woman's hand. While they waited for a van to pass the boy looked back over his shoulder. He didn't quite smile at me. But there was intent in his eyes. He recognised me. And there was a knowingness that should never be seen in someone so young. He'd seen me and he knew that I was someone—his mother, well, he didn't know that part yet—I was someone he had to keep secret from the woman holding his hand. The van passed, and the woman, Abebi, led him across the road around the corner of the cafe.

The rest of the week dragged by. To kill time I went with Bernard to his work. We caught the train, just like the other people setting off to work. We hurried from the station so Bernard could catch the lunch crowd leaving the museums. He told me to leave him alone for fifteen minutes; he needed to get into character. He was right. I found a different Bernard when I returned. A circle of people had gathered around him. People laughed—they applauded. He shouted out his poems, then he passed around the black hat he wore for such occasions. People put money in the hat and after the last of them had drifted away he looked around for me.

At night I slept with my little Frenchman's face snuggled into my neck. He'd stopped wearing his coat to bed, but he still lay on top of the duvet. 'Bernard,' I said one night. 'Do you not want to touch me? What kind of man are you?'

'Yes,' he said. 'But I am more afraid of you leaving me.'

I told him I would never leave him. Why would I want to leave him? I had never trusted anyone as much as I did him. At the same time I didn't know the man he turned into for his performances. The man who spoke to the inspector, the man of that testimony, is a stranger to me.

Jermayne returned from Hamburg, and the meetings in the playground with the boy resumed. One afternoon I was a few minutes late. Jermayne and the boy were sitting on the bench near the red slide. When I came in the gate the boy looked up and slipped off the bench. In that same moment I saw my worth to him. The ball had just turned up. I asked Jermayne if I could be left alone with the boy. He winced and looked down. Then he began to shake his head. He said it couldn't go on like this. At this rate Abebi would find out. He'd already done more than any reasonable person could expect. And in any case my request was ridiculous. How would he know I wouldn't run off with the boy?

I told him I wouldn't. I promised. But that wasn't good enough. I was taking him for a fool. What would he tell Abebi if I ran off with the boy? He looked away and breathed out slowly. He shook his head. He said I'd asked too much this time.

'People always did—they pushed things to the point of no return.'

We'd forgotten about the boy. He stood staring down at the ground between us waiting for the talk to end so he could have someone to kick the ball to.

I dug in my coat pockets and brought out all the money I had. Jermayne looked surprised, but not entirely so. That's the thing about Jermayne. His mind travels in the lower circles. His surprise was at seeing where my own mind had sunk to. But I also saw how quickly he swept the surprise from his face. He looked at the money as if it was of no interest at all. He put his hands in his coat, wriggled down into his shoes. He looked off in the direction of the slide. 'And your coat,' he said. 'You won't get far without a coat.'

I took off my coat and placed it on the bench. His face was still calculating. 'I'll need your boots too,' he said. 'And your socks.' I sat down on the bench and took off each boot, then I peeled off each sock. He had a good look at those. The socks belonged to Bernard and in the end he couldn't decide what to say about them. He stuffed the socks in the boots and wrapped them in the coat. He looked at his watch. He said we'd already used up fifteen minutes. He'd be back in another forty minutes.

It was cold that day. At first the cold seemed to sit on my skin like a coat of paint. Then it discovered my bones and it settled in them. The ground hurt my feet. Each time I kicked the ball back to the boy I thought my toes would snap. Soon I had to switch from kicking with my right foot to my left foot, and when that one turned raw I switched back to the other.

Another woman with a child came in the gate. She looked at my bare feet, at my coatless state. She looked at my face and finding no answer there she herded her child out of this playground of fools and mad women.

When I couldn't stand it any longer I picked up the ball and walked the boy to the slide. I picked him up under his arms and placed him at the top. He slid down and ran around to the steps for more. Each time I picked him up I rubbed his cheek against mine. I wanted him to get to know my skin, its taste and its feel. With Jermayne out of the way I was freer to put myself inside the boy's head.

He didn't seem to notice my bare feet. He ran off to the swings and I picked and hobbled my way after him.

He sat on the swing waiting for me to get there. I pushed him and he swung his arms. I pushed him higher and higher...until I caught him and held him against me. He thought it was a game—his panting little body waited excitedly to be released.

We were back to kicking the ball between us when Jermayne came in the gate with my coat and boots. I ran to get them back. He held them out of reach and laughed as I jumped like a dog. Then he must have noticed the boy looking on and so he let go of my things like they were something he had just caught in the wind. The boots hit the ground and my coat floated down after them. I pulled on the socks. There was no feeling left in my feet. Even after I pulled on the boots, I had no feeling. I got into the coat and did up the buttons. Jermayne called to the boy but the boy stayed put. He held onto the ball. He couldn't take his eyes off me. Probably he had never seen an adult sitting on the ground zipping up their boots. Jermayne spoke to him and he came forward on his little legs. He handed me the ball. He was very careful about it. He made sure I had hold of it before he released it. Now Jermayne took the boy's hand and pulled him away. When the boy looked back over his shoulder I shouted after Jermayne, I called out to him, 'Tomorrow.'

'No,' he said.

'The next day,' I said.

He shook his bald head so I named another day. This time he left the boy and came back inside the gate. He told me from now on I could only see the boy once a week. Even that he thought was generous and might change in the future.

twenty-eight

The following week at the appointed time we met at the playground. The weather had improved and there were more people on bikes and on the paths by the canal. While I sat in the playground waiting for Jermayne and the boy I could feel the sun against my face. It was hard to believe that things could change so quickly. Jermayne could demand my coat and boots and today it wouldn't matter. My coat sat folded over my lap.

But he didn't want my coat. He didn't ask for my boots either. But he took all the money for security. While I swung the boy and kicked the ball to him I saw Jermayne's tall figure under the trees on the far side of the canal. He was easy to pick out in his denim jacket and black beret.

Once I might have worried about him bumping into Bernard. But Bernard had stopped delivering me to Jermayne's neighbourhood. I knew the way well enough myself.

This was the first time I had seen the boy out of his ski jacket and pants. There seemed to be less of him. Thinner—perhaps that was me I was seeing in his shoulders and arms, although there was a hint of what was to come in his father's frame. His face was larger. For the first time he wasn't wearing gloves. I kept reaching for him, feeling his little hand in mine. I still had the words and phrases that Bernard had written down for me. Abebi might not allow him chocolate, but I would. Just a little bit, it was harmless. He nodded unsurely when I asked him if he wanted some chocolate. He didn't know what he was agreeing to—only that it was new and came wrapped in silver foil which peeled back to dark chocolate. I broke off a square. He popped it in his mouth. He ate that and held out his hand for more. I broke off another corner. While he ate it I did not exist. The playground did not exist. He wanted another piece. I returned his hand to his side. 'No,' I said. 'No more.' It was the first time I had denied him and I saw his eyes move. Jermayne was approaching the playground. I saw chocolate on the boy's finger so I put the finger in my mouth. Chocolate marked the sides of his mouth. I licked that off.

The lovely weather hadn't had any effect on Jermayne. He was as agitated as he was when he dropped the boy off. I remember in Italy a man driving me to the motorway in the middle of the night looking the same way as Jermayne did now, wanting something but unsure of what, or if he could ask.

By now the boy was familiar with the handing-over routine. Any moment he would use both his hands to pass the ball up to me—that's what he was waiting to do. Jermayne began to count out the money. I told him I wasn't worried about him stealing any but he didn't hear me. He went on placing each note in my hand as if I was a paying customer. Then there was just one note left. Fifty euros. He folded his hand over it and placed it in his back pocket. He drew himself up to full size, seeking to diminish me or any complaint. 'That's for my time.'

Part of me was left swaying. Another part responded to the new rules as if they had been in place all along.

When I asked Jermayne if I could see the boy again that week he didn't object.

I paid Jermayne another three times. Each time it was fifty euros. I hadn't seen where this would lead.

One afternoon on the swings the boy's face lit up and I pushed higher to make his face light up more and when I least expected it he let go of the swing ropes and flew through the air. I thought I had killed him. I picked him up off the dirt and praying to a god I did not believe in I asked for one more favour as I carried his whimpering little body over to the bench. His head pressed against me. I kept rubbing his knee. I could tell it wasn't hurting any more. But he didn't ask me to stop either.

The next time I met Jermayne I handed him my last thirty euros and he looked at me like I had spat in his hand. What was I trying to prove? I knew the rate. Fifty euros. We had established the price. So why was I giving him thirty?

I bent down and whispered to the boy to wait on the bench near the slide. Jermayne told him something else. The boy looked up to check with me. Jermayne saw that and swore at the boy. He swung the gate open and closed it with a bang. I told him I only had thirty euros. He said thirty euros did not come close to properly valuing his time. I was setting out to humiliate him. Did

I think he was a common labourer? Why was I intent on insulting him? Why did I treat him this way? He had done everything that was humanly possible to make himself available, to make the boy available, to behave honourably. 'I knew this would happen,' he said. 'Something told me you would try to take advantage of me.' I told him I'd bring more next time. Next time I would bring seventy euros—an extra twenty to make up for this afternoon.

After he left, the boy and I kicked the ball to each other. I tried out one of the phrases Bernard had written down. I asked the boy if he was happy. I had to repeat the phrase. He listened with his eyes and his mouth. In the end he nodded. I had managed to ask him something which he had understood and answered! I had imagined it would bring us closer; instead, it felt mechanical, as mechanical as hotel smiles. The language I shared with the boy ran deeper. It had started out with kicking a ball to each other and over the space of a few weeks our islands had moved closer together.

Now those islands were about to move apart again. I had no more money. When I told Jermayne I would bring seventy euros the next time I hadn't thought about where I would find that money. The need to see the boy was as strong as ever. I walked along streets that meant nothing to me. Past faces that held no interest. When I entered that hole in the wall to the little Frenchman's world I didn't feel anything other than a need to see the boy.

The days were longer. The little Frenchman called them his 'earning days'. This was his other self evaluating the world.

I told him I needed some of that good earning weather to shower down on me. He asked me what I could do, and I told

him. I knew all about the world of hotels. I knew h
in and out of a room without a guest noticing me. I k
smile pleasantly. I could make beds, clean toilets and
of the toilet paper. I could arrange fruit. I knew vario
first aid. And because at one hotel I had risen to superv
how to look out for the tricks of lazy staff. At the en
my skills the little Frenchman took my toilet-bowl clea
and kissed it. He said I didn't need to make any mor
time being. I should use this time to think about r
Learning Deutsch would be a good idea if I planned
and he assumed I would do so, because of my effo
here, and because he knew how important it was for
near the boy.

That's when I told him, 'I need money to see the bo

Almost right away the two selves of the little Frenchm
to war with each other. He wanted to help me. He w
criticise me. He said he loved me. He said I was stupid. Ho
I have got myself into this situation? And because it was l
people were sleeping around us, he couldn't stand it any
he had to get up and go outside and shake his fist at the
and at my stupidity. In the middle of his outburst he be
recite a poem that moved him more than it did me, because
seconds of finishing the poem he was kissing my eyelic
cheering me with his words of kindness. He would do every
within his power to help. As he made these promises, the
promises seemed to deflate him. I left him muttering and p
my way back through the dark and the sleeping bodies to th
we shared.

The first time I ever had hotel sex I did not charge eno

did not know what I was worth and I did not understand the value of the different currencies I was paid in. The first time Jermayne took fifty euros it could have been one hundred or five euros. Paolo had paid for things, then Bernard. I soon realised how hard it was to earn fifty euros.

For a month Bernard wore himself out on my behalf. Some days were better than others. Rain meant bad earning days. I wished there was something I could have done. I would have gladly worked through the night to earn the money Jermayne demanded in order for me to see my boy. I had to see him. And that need turned me into someone with no heart or conscience. I didn't care how the money was earnt.

Every Wednesday afternoon we met in the playground. As soon as we parted I would set my mind to when I would see the boy next. The intervening period meant nothing to me.

Then Bernard stopped earning as much as he had, even on good days when the city was filled with tourists. He couldn't explain it. What had worked for him all winter suddenly stopped. They didn't want to pay money for his poems. Then he got beaten up by the Serbian jazz trombonist. He should have seen that coming. The Serb had complained before. Certain soft notes played on his trombone could not be heard above Bernard's ranting. They started pushing and shoving one another. Out of that came Bernard's black eye. Maybe it was that black eye that made tourists wary of him.

One Wednesday afternoon I showed up to the playground with the football. Jermayne was slumped on a bench, his head hanging between his knees. It was a beautiful day but Jermayne didn't appear to know it. There were people laughing but

Jermayne did not hear them. The boy stood some distance away watching the other children on the slides and the swings. When he heard the gate swing back Jermayne's unshaven face looked up through smoke-ringed eyes.

When I told him I had no money to give him today he became angry. He wasn't interested in my promises to bring more the next time. I found myself wanting to explain so that he would understand that it wasn't all my fault, it was the trombonist's, but I didn't. It was better I take the blame and the criticism than for Jermayne to hear about the little Frenchman. He didn't want to know about anyone else in my life. He didn't want the story of our arrangement going beyond the two of us. I was the bird which flew down to the playground once a week and then flew back to its roost on top of a dead tree stump.

Now Jermayne was very angry. I had wasted his time. I had abused his trust. He went on listing all the abuses and insults then he stopped mid-rant—he saw me looking at the boy. He must have realised I was getting something for nothing. He said something sharp to the boy. The boy approached us, his eyes on the ball in my arms to start with. But then his eyes found mine. I saw some light there, and quickly it was gone. His father dropped a hand onto his shoulder and steered him out of the playground gate.

On my way home I saw men collecting refundable bottles. I saw tramps selling newspapers. These were things that I could do. I mentioned this to Bernard. I could sell things. I had sold myself before. I could do that again. When he heard that the little Frenchman sat up and looked stunned. 'No. No. *No*,' he said. 'You cannot do that.' He looked distressed just thinking about it. He hurried over to the broken mirror hanging on the wall near computer man. There was still bruising around his eye. It was no good. Tourists wouldn't go near a man who looked like he had just picked himself up from the gutter. Those are Bernard's words, not mine. But as he looked at his black eye a different thought led him back to the bed. He got down on his knees and dragged out carton after carton of books. I had never seen so many books. I often saw him with a single book, but not this many books. It was hard to believe they were worth anything—hard to believe it of anything that had sat in cartons under a bed for so long.

He borrowed a broken-down pram from the Polish mime artist woman. She didn't have real babies; she had two plastic ones. But people still paid money to see her craned over the pram with her face and hands frozen with alarm. We stacked the books in the pram. Bernard carried another carton of books in his arms. We set off for the second-hand bookshop with me pushing the pram.

There a thin young man, who did not once look directly at me or Bernard but only at the books in the pram, bought half of them for one hundred and twenty euros, of which Bernard gave me a hundred.

For the rest of the week I worried that Jermayne would not show after the disappointment of last time. He would want to put me in my place. But the next Wednesday at the appointed time I saw him hurrying the boy along the bike path.

I took the boy out of the playground. We walked down to the canal. I had brought some stale bread. I broke it into pieces for the boy to feed the ducks. *Ente.* That's the word for duck. The boy taught me that word. *Ente. Ente.* As he repeated it something unpleasant grew in his face. It was his father's understanding of the power of transaction. By the time Jermayne returned we were in the playground kicking the ball.

I could not wait another week before seeing the boy again. I told Jermayne I would give him another fifty euros on Friday. When he picked up the boy on Friday I told him I'd see him next Wednesday, even though there was no more money.

This time Bernard sold his black coat to one of the young musicians. There was time for him to buy a new coat before next winter. The coat was worth thirty euros.

I spent the next few days wondering where I could find that extra twenty euros. Bernard wouldn't let me out of his sight. He followed me around like a lost dog.

On Monday we visited a pawnbroker. Bernard took out his diamond-inlaid tooth and placed it on top of a glass counter. He didn't want to sell it. He couldn't do that. But if he'd asked me I would not have stopped him.

The man in the shop put a glass to his eye and held up Bernard's tooth. He looked at it for a long time. He looked at it from every angle. Then he put it down on the glass top and frowned at it with a naked eye. He and Bernard finally agreed on two hundred euros. The shopkeeper had wanted to give more in the hope that the little Frenchman would fail to pay back the full amount.

Before handing me the money Bernard led me to a cafe. There we sat, him with the cash in his pocket, a coffee set before him, a hot chocolate before me, and the matter of the money hanging over us like a cloud. He told me this was the last money he was prepared to give me. He had nothing left. I had to talk to Jermayne. I should try to find a way to appeal to his better instincts. Jermayne had kindness in him. I'd known that kindness. But something else inside of him had seeded down and overtaken it. Bernard was right about that. I saw it in Jermayne's face when he dropped the boy off at the playground. A strange wild beast looked out of his eyes.

Now, after every visit, Bernard would ask me if I'd had that conversation with Jermayne. Each time I said no he became downcast and he'd go back to following me around, in and out of the building, to the hole in the wall where I sometimes went to look out at the world.

He didn't want me out of his sight. He made me come with him to the places where he recited his poems to tourists. Each time I saw how hard it was to earn fifty euros. I realised that Jermayne had put a high price on his time. But whenever Ramona asks what price would be too high for me to spend time with my boy I never have the answer. I can't imagine what that price would be. I would have to be a different person from the one I am because I cannot come up with a figure.

I had spent the two hundred euros but I still turned up the following Wednesday afternoon to see the boy. There was just time to pass him the ball. After Jermayne discovered I had no money he grabbed the ball out of the boy's hands and he booted it into the canal. Then he grabbed the boy by the hand and hauled him out the gate. I ran after the ball. I didn't care about the other mothers or the old faces that occupied the benches. What did they know about anything? What could they possibly know about a ball that contained language? I had to run for ten minutes along the banks before I overtook the ball. I broke off a branch from a tree and, standing on the stone steps cut into the canal, I dragged the ball in from the slow-moving brown water.

Without a date to look forward to I felt the boy once more move out of my life. I must have made Bernard anxious because again he insisted I accompany him to work. He said he needed me to watch out for the mad Serbian trombonist. We both knew what he was more afraid of and I could not give him a guarantee that if a man offered me fifty euros I wouldn't give myself to him.

I spent the nights sitting on the bench across the canal watching the windows of Jermayne's apartment. Sometimes I saw life in the windows, which was reason enough for me to return the following night.

One night Jermayne came out of the building. He stood on the cobbles smoking a cigarette. I stood up from the bench. When he saw me he took the cigarette out of his mouth and stared the way you do at a dog that has fouled your patch. I started across the bridge. Jermayne stepped further out onto the cobbles. He looked up at the windows. Then he flung his hand at me as if he was throwing a stone. I walked on pretending I hadn't seen him.

I had found Jermayne's weakness. I had made him afraid. This was good, Bernard said.

twenty-nine

It had rained overnight. Thick gluey clouds hung over the city. It was a bad earning day and Bernard decided to do something else. He said he had some business to attend to. I took that to mean he was off to the pawnbroker to pay back some of the loan. He was missing his tooth. He said it affected the delivery of his poems. The gap in his teeth made a hissing sound. In other words, no money could be spared for me to see the boy. Even so, I set off for Jermayne's neighbourhood by myself.

Shortly after midday I arrived at Jermayne's building. As soon as he heard my voice the intercom went dead. Abebi must have been at home. So I waited. Sure enough, I heard someone flying down the stairs. Jermayne didn't so much open the door as come bounding through it. Next moment his hands were on my shoulders and I was being pushed backwards across the cobbles. In the shadows beneath the trees he hung onto me. Called me all kinds of names. If he ever saw me here again he would ring the police and I would be deported. I would be flung across the sea back to where I'd come from like the stinking dead fish I'd turned into.

I told him I was here to see my boy. I told him I would pay. Not that day, but soon, as soon as I could. My promises didn't interest him. I was a liar. My heart was rotten. I would say whatever it took. A person like me could not be trusted. Besides, the boy didn't need me. He had a mother. A good mother who read to him at night, who bathed him, and who the boy loved. Who the fuck did I think I was to turn up the way I had, like something scraped off the dirt by a gust of wind?

Jermayne wouldn't shut up. I banged my fists against his chest to make him listen and he slapped me hard across the face. The next thing Jermayne is falling away from me, his eyes wide, as the little Frenchman jumps on top of him. Bernard is beating him with his fists. He is screaming in Jermayne's face. Jermayne yells back. The two men roll in the dirt under the trees. A crowd has gathered. Men on bicycles. Walkers. One old man, with a thick newspaper held under his arm, hunched his shoulders forward so that they became part of his smile.

Then I hear a woman's voice and I know who that is. I don't need to look. The voice is coming across the cobbles as I slip away towards the bike path and I run.

Past the second bridge I stop and look back. There is just a jogger and a black dog with its nose in some old plastic.

Bernard was hours coming home. I waited by the hole in the wall. When I grew sick of that I went inside the warehouse and sat on

Bernard's bed. Computer man kept turning to look. I was making him nervous. So I went back to the hole in the wall. The Polish mime artist brought me a bread roll. She laid it at my feet and smiled. The young musician who had bought Bernard's coat passed me his bottle of beer.

I sat out there until dark then I walked back to Jermayne's neighbourhood. There I found Bernard beneath the trees. Someone must have sat him up. He was leaning against the trunk, his rag-doll legs splayed out in front. His eyes were glazed, his mouth all caked with dried blood. I bent down and I held his head in my lap. He let me do that but he didn't speak. One of his shoes had come off. His shirt was torn. An eye was closed—the same eye the trombonist hit. The greater hurt was inside of him. I lay his head back against the trunk and I crouched before him so he could see me. His eyes shifted—and when I looked behind there was Jermayne.

One of his eyes was closed. He'd changed out of his earlier shirt. In his hand he held a broomstick. He spoke quietly, calling me a Judas bitch that leads the lambs to the butcher. Now look at what I had done. Judas bitch. He poked Bernard in the ribs. He spoke in Deutsch and slowly Bernard began to get to his feet. He groaned with the effort it took. In English Jermayne told me to leave him alone. He said it was only fair that he find out where we lived. And so we walked back to Bernard's neighbourhood. I carried his shoe. I had tried to give it to him but he stared straight ahead. He walked lopsided, like a man with a limp. Jermayne followed with his stick.

We reached the hole in the wall. Bernard went through first. As I went to follow the stick came between me and the wall. 'Not you,' he said. Bernard turned round. His miserable face peered out at us. Jermayne said something for Bernard's ears only and the little Frenchman turned and wandered away.

Now Jermayne steered me with the broomstick. He drove me along the wall towards the station. I asked where we were going. He said the Judas bitch would find out soon enough. If I stopped or tried to look back over my shoulder he poked me with the stick. We had to wait at the lights. Again I asked him where we were going. This time he said we were walking to find out. 'We are walking away from your old home and that stupid fucker of a boyfriend. If I ever see you with him again you will never see the boy. That is my promise to you,' he said. 'I don't think it is such a difficult choice. You think you can come into my life and destroy everything, well, think again. It works both ways. If Abebi ever sees you there will be trouble. If I ever see you and the boyfriend together there will be trouble.'

The lights changed. We crossed the road and walked beside the tramlines and the early-evening traffic. Whenever I came to an intersection Jermayne said 'left' or 'right'. Soon we came to the busy road where I had surfaced with the Frenchman all those weeks ago. He pointed to the television tower in the distance. 'That's where we are headed,' he said.

We walked for half an hour, in the same formation. Jermayne didn't say another word until we reached the square around Alexanderplatz. There he stopped me and told me to turn around and to listen to what he had to say. His face was covered with sweat and his eyes were calm. But there was bitterness on his breath. He repeated some of what he'd said earlier. What had happened that afternoon could never happen again. If it did he would not hesitate to telephone the police. If he ever saw me with the Frenchman I would never see the boy again. He asked if I understood and I nodded. Then he surprised me. Did I have any money? I shook my head. 'You haven't thought about anything, have you?' he said. 'Look at what you gave up. A perfectly safe and respectable life in the hotel. Now look where you are. Do you think this is better?'

'It's the boy I wanted to see,' I said.

Jermayne didn't reply—unless silence counts as a reply. The silence went on a while. I wondered if he might be reconsidering everything so I did not dare interrupt that silence. When at last I thought to look behind me he had gone.

I walked across the square to the station. With my last euros I got change from the receptionist in the toilets. I found my old cubicle. I sat down and stared back at the white tiles. Soon after that the banging on the door started.

thirty

I had no idea about the steps you might take in order to give up. If someone had pointed out a door with the instruction 'Go through there,' I might have been tempted. I might have drifted towards that door and taken a peep to see what lay on the other side. But pulling me back from that door was the idea of seeing the boy again—and Bernard. I had two people to think about now. Two people in the world who I cared about enough to go on sitting in those toilets and wandering in circles around the railway station.

I noticed the changes since I was last there. The warmer weather had brought out more people. Some of them were strange-looking young men with yellow-and-purple hair. There were men and women with winter in their faces. Dogs who kept their heads down. The dogs I noticed always seemed to know what they were doing and where they were headed. Once I found myself walking behind a man with a large trombone strapped to his back and when he turned round it was not the Serb.

I kept the last of my money to pay for the cubicle in the station toilets. I washed there. I brushed my teeth with my finger. I'd left the plastic bag under Bernard's bed. I was confident of finding my way back, but I kept thinking, *What if Jermayne sees me?* Although I never saw him during the day, the feeling that he was there haunted me. He was about to poke his head between the clouds and wave that stick at me.

I was back on the trains at night, travelling up and down the same line, half hoping I would run into Bernard, half hoping I wouldn't in case a sleeping passenger suddenly pulled a hat back off his face to reveal Jermayne.

Whenever Ramona gets me back to thinking about what I would do and wouldn't do under certain circumstances—hunger or love—I tell her I have known hunger. I have watched people eat at the station kiosks the way tourists line up to watch sunsets, and yet I have never found it in myself to beg.

Instead I stole fruit. I ate leftovers off the kiosk tables. I swooped on crusts ahead of sparrows.

One morning I was sitting on a bench on the park side of the station. An old white labrador I'd seen hanging about, ownerless, came and sat on the ground by my feet. The dog paid me no attention. It just wanted that patch of ground in front of me. People walked by. I sat unnoticed, whereas the dog drew glances and smiles. Those who missed it the first time slowed down to look back over their shoulders. Some stopped to pat it. One woman fed it a sweet. She had to unwrap it and the dog gulped at it, then the sweet seemed to become lost in its mouth. It chomped and chomped, and in the end spat it out so I bent down and picked the sweet up and ate it myself. The dog lay down with its head on its paws and its eyes floated up in the direction of someone approaching. I tried the same—only with women though. I didn't want any of the other business.

Within two days I had attracted the help of the Englishwoman the inspector spoke to. Her testimony is filled with stuff about gypsies. It says nothing of the money I stole from her. The stealing didn't start at her place. It started when I risked Jermayne's face suddenly appearing in the moonlight on the night I snuck back to Bernard's neighbourhood. I was hoping to see the little Frenchman and hug him. I slipped through the hole in the wall. I kept to the shadows and avoiding the light from the fires crept into the warehouse. Bernard wasn't there, but my plastic bag with my hotel uniform, toothbrush and sticking knife was still under his bed. I felt under the mattress where I had seen Bernard stick his own plastic bag with money. I took half the money—I hoped he had paid off the loan and got his tooth back—and I slipped out of there. I didn't breathe until I left the hole in the wall. I walked up the same block where Jermayne had driven me with his stick. Under a streetlamp I counted twenty euros. Another thirty and I could see my boy.

When someone picks up a stray there is no telling where it has come from. From the point of view of the dog and its saviour this is good. There is no history to speak of. Without any history there is nothing to worry about, no dark shadows to fear. Dog and saviour start out as new.

So I did not tell the Englishwoman anything of my past—

Jermayne, the boy, Bernard, the Four Seasons Hotel and the whole story of how I had come to Berlin—all of that had to stay unsaid. I did not want to be somebody's problem to solve any more. I preferred to be a stray dog.

The Englishwoman made me up a bed on her couch. She fed me. I took hot showers. I used her soap and her shampoo and her toothpaste. I stole two pairs of her underwear. I stole the ten-euro note I saw sitting under a glass on the kitchen table. The next morning there was another ten euros—in the same place—and I took that too. On the third morning there was a twenty-euro note. I took that and made my way to Jermayne's building.

When he heard my voice the very air itself seemed to be sucked out of the intercom. So I got in quickly. I told him I had fifty euros.

We sat under the trees above the canal. 'Look. *Ente. Ente*,' I said. The boy's eyes stared at his feet. We went to the playground. I put him up on the slide and in the swing. His weight felt dead between my hands. He went down the slide without his hands in the air. He sat on the swing with his little body collapsed in on itself. I wished I had some chocolate. I wished I still had Bernard's list of things to say. We needed to start over, and to do that we would need the football.

I was planning to visit Bernard the next night. That same morning, the Englishwoman said she had some people she wanted me to meet. She didn't mention the African Refugee Centre.

The pastor was a black man. He sat me down in his office. He asked if I was hungry. I wasn't. Did I need something to drink?

'No,' I said. I kept looking around to see where the Englishwoman had got to.

The pastor asked me what I knew best in the world. I told him I knew how to be a hotel maid.

He sat back in his chair and folded his hands beneath his chin. His eyes were warm, though, and I didn't mind them peering at me.

'I'd be interested to learn,' he said, 'what a hotel maid knows.'

So I listed the things—how to clean, how to fold sheets properly so that they don't get a crease, knowing when to look the other way rather than cause a guest embarrassment. I told him a guest lives their life more openly than the rest of us. We make the same filth, but no one else gets to see it.

The pastor listened and thought about what I had said, then he asked me if I had God in my life. I said I like to think He is there but He hasn't been paying me much attention lately. The pastor laughed and shifted in his chair and became round-faced and kindly again.

He wanted to know what had brought me to Berlin. I didn't mention the boy. When I told him I had drifted here on the tide his smile slipped from his eyes and teeth. The pastor had a willing laugh but he didn't want to be taken for a fool. Then as he thought more he began to nod his head.

He asked me if I had any experience working with blind people.

'Just myself,' I said.

Again the pastor laughed. He picked up the phone and began dialling. The person at the other end answered and as the pastor talked his eyes didn't leave mine. He was like an old concierge showing off that he could talk to the white people. After a few minutes he put the phone down.

He looked at his watch, then back at me. Very politely he asked me if I had time to meet a blind gentleman. He sat with his arms fanned out from his sides, half out of his chair as he waited on my say-so.

I thought we would go off in a car or walk up the road to catch a train. But we didn't leave the building. We went out to the foyer, where we got in an old lift and rose to the top floor. As we came out of the lift the old gentleman was standing by the door to his apartment.

The pastor introduced us and the old gentleman shook my hand. He was tall and sagged down through his shoulders. It was as if he had been looking forward to meeting me for some time and here at last we were. I have known hotel guests like him. They are so polite it is as if they need to prove that the pecking order that exists in the world does not apply to the moment at hand.

Some chairs at the far end of a long room were waiting for us. The pastor and I stood back to watch the blind gentleman make his way. The floorboards were like a tightrope. At any moment he might make a mistake. But he found his chair and when he dropped into it I noticed small beads of sweat over the pastor's forehead. They hadn't been there back in his office.

The pastor talked me up. He talked up my success and hotel experience. He told the blind gentleman I had risen to 'the trusted position of supervisor'.

The blind gentleman directed the conversation back to me. He wanted to know what I was interested in. Did I like to read?

Did I have hobbies, interests? How many languages did I possess? After that he and the pastor talked between themselves. They talked about Tunisia. Years ago, the old gentleman said, he'd looked into a holiday there. He had a skin condition that only the sun made better. Psoriasis. Instead of going to Tunis he went to a spa in Turkey where he sat in a hot pool with other skin sufferers and tiny fish nibbled the dead skin.

The pastor talked about the therapeutic properties of salt water. He said a soul ready for baptism ought ideally to wade into the sea. A pond wasn't the same. And a bowl of water was just a gimmick. The talk returned to Tunisia. And on to Yemen. Yemen interested the blind gentleman and for a while they discussed mud buildings, Yemenite Jews, the Islamists. For a longer while still they talked about Iraq. The blind gentleman held out his palms to the pastor and asked, 'But why would they lie?' The Americans, I think he meant. They went on talking until the pastor glanced down at his watch. The time gave him a surprise. He stood up. I went to follow but he put out a hand. I should stay put. Now he spoke in Deutsch. Then, in English I heard the pastor say, 'So it is agreed. Excellent.' That rounded smile entered his face, eyes and teeth.

'Our friend wishes to know when you can start.'

'Now,' I said. The blind gentleman's cheeks rose as he smiled. The line of pleasure stopped just beneath his sightless eyes.

Before the pastor left the old gentleman showed me my room. My own room. I sat on the bed. I walked to the window. The two men stood in the door watching me, well, the pastor did at least. It's hard to see what the old gentleman did with his eyes. That part of him just seemed to droop from his face, but it drooped with kindness and the lived-in quality of old fruit.

I walked the pastor out to the lift. I thanked him briefly, but not nearly enough, no more so than you do someone who has picked up something you've dropped.

I saw the pastor only a few times after that. Each time I thought I must go and thank him again, thank him from my heart. I saw his face through the ground-floor windows. Another time I saw him getting into a car.

A week went by and I decided to go downstairs to thank the pastor properly. In the same office where I had sat watching the pastor on the phone a black woman looked up at me with unfriendly eyes. I asked her what had happened to the pastor. She said he had just been filling in for her. Now he was back with his parish on the other side of the city. After that I never went back to the refugee centre.

thirty-one

To lie down flat and sleep will sound like an ordinary privilege. I only mention it out of respect for the decision I made never ever to take it for granted. To lie down between clean sheets and with a pillow for my head. Apart from the cubicle in the station toilets I could at last be alone without anyone to see me and wonder what I was doing in their neighbourhood or how I had come to be. When I was alone in that room it was as though the world had forgotten me. The world could not cause me any more trouble. All I had to do was to stay in that room.

That is how I tell Ramona to think about prison. I tell her not to think about the world not letting her out to join it. I tell her it is better to think of the world being kept away in case it tempts her back into trouble. Knowing Ramona, she will meet a man and within a week will want to stab him through his armpit. The only way to get through where we are from one day to the next is to think of where we are as a better place.

For a time the world didn't spring any nasty surprises. I put on my hotel uniform and went to work. I made the old gentleman his meals, I made him his tea and coffee, it was up to me to go out into the world to buy the food and take him out for walks. He gave me money which he said was to pay for my housekeeping duties. On top of that money he gave me more for food. At the money machine I had to steer his blind fingers onto the right keys for him to draw money out of his account. He relied on me to count out the money. I never took more than what he wanted withdrawn. I discovered I could take from the money meant for food, but I couldn't go into his account and fill a sack with money. Three hundred euros a week went on food and the alcohol he said he needed. I made sure he was never out of alcohol, but I could be stingy with food.

Jermayne was suspicious. Just a few weeks earlier I had no money and I was begging him to see the boy. Now I had money and I was as calm as a face in a passing tram window. What had happened? I told him I had a position at a hotel. Jermayne seemed happy with that explanation. It made sense. What else would I do? The world was back to working order. 'What about your ridiculous friend?' he asked. I told him I hadn't seen him. I'd taken Jermayne at his word and not gone back to Bernard's hole-in-the-wall neighbourhood.

'Good,' he said. 'Maybe you're not as stupid as you look.'

I continued to visit my little Frenchman, but never during the day, always at night, and at an hour when the lights were out at Jermayne's. I know because I always checked before continuing on over the bridge into Bernard's neighbourhood. No matter how comfortable my life was, it didn't give me what Bernard did, which was a devotion. I felt it in his hands and in his breath when I lay down next to him in the dark. When it was time to go he wouldn't come further than the hole in the wall just in case Jermayne was waiting to pounce on him outside. He wasn't afraid of Jermayne, but he took his threats seriously, as I did. Bernard did not want to see me lose the chance to see my boy. He liked to say I had turned myself into a shooting star. He would look up in the dark and there I was. The next night he'd look up and in the same dark space between his head and the rafters he couldn't find a trace of me.

The other reason for sneaking back to Bernard's neighbourhood was so I could get the football.

And now, in the warm afternoons of early summer, we kicked the ball back and forth as we'd done when we were still two unknown islands seeking connection.

There was another change. Abebi was working different hours. So these days we met by the bronze lions at the bottom of the Tiergarten. Jermayne was feeling more secure because now he left us alone. I could do whatever I pleased with the boy, but always it had to involve the ball. Even when we went for a walk we had to do so kicking the ball back and forth to each other, until I came to think of it as a ball and chain like I'd seen in a film starring George Clooney on television at the Four Seasons. They break the chain, I forget how, and end up singing songs at a radio station.

One afternoon in Tiergarten some barefoot white minstrels wandered across the grass blowing flutes. The boy trapped the ball. He looked up, then he picked up the ball and placed his hand in mine. I don't know what it was about those barefoot minstrels that made him afraid, but I am glad they came along when they did. For the rest of the hour, hand in hand, we walked the paths and beneath the trees and across the grass. I bought the boy an ice cream. I saw other mothers with children floating plastic boats on the ponds and thought, *that's how we must look too*, like the most natural thing in the world.

Whenever I need to persuade myself that there was once a time when I belonged in the world this is the afternoon I return to. The boats on the ponds. The boy's hand in mind. His other hand gripped the cone, his happy eyes looking up over that white hill of ice cream.

My life as a normal person continued throughout the summer. I could notice a green police van without turning away and looking for a place to hide. On my time off I looked in the shop windows and saw clothes I would like to buy for the boy. Shoes and shirts. But, I thought, I would hate the day to come when I had no money to buy time to see the boy and at the same time know that I had wasted fifty euros on clothes he didn't need. As far as I could tell he did not go without. In any case it was a stupid fantasy. Jermayne would need to support it and tell Abebi that he had bought the clothes and then the boy would have to be sworn to silence.

Bernard was curious to know about the old gentleman, what he looked like. He wanted to hear about the conversations, what the gentleman said and what I said. Well, I did not have much to say. Since the old gentleman had opinions on everything. He knew about everything. When we walked out in the world with his arm through mine we walked no faster than what allowed him to talk. He did ask me questions about myself. Where I was born. How

I came to live in Italy. Once he asked me if I had ever been on an airplane. I replied honestly, 'No.' Just then I pointed to a squirrel that ran across our path. For a few minutes he talked about squirrels and how the squirrel population had suffered during the war. Then I pointed up at the white vapour trail of a plane. He raised his face, out of habit I suppose, and looked lost. He talked about a cruise ship he'd been on, and the strangeness of swimming in pools of water far out to sea. He asked if I had ever been on a ship. 'No,' I said. I had replied honestly and without seeing how talk and words could lay down snares. Snare is a word Bernard taught me. The next ten minutes were uncomfortable. The old gentleman stopped talking. The conversation we just had still rung in our ears as we walked on. His arm looped through mine and yet I had the feeling the more nothing was said the more we seemed to be walking apart from one another.

I had been caught out. Now the story told by the pastor had a crack in it. So did his trust in me. On our walks he did not speak so freely as he had. When we visited the zoo he asked to be led to the birdcages, and there he would ask me to describe a bird. It was a game he'd invented. He had to guess the name of the bird from my description. But my description was the problem. My English was not as good as the gentleman's. When I said a bird had a red chest he would ask me to refine red. Red came in many varieties, he said. As many varieties as there are birds. And so I would have to rack my brain to come up with something else that captured perfectly the red of the feathers. I was no good at this game and soon we stopped playing it. Then we stopped going to the zoo. We walked in the park and we sat down on the bench without anything to say. We needed a football. We needed something.

That something turned out to be the feel of my skin under the gentleman's blind eye.

We are back to Ramona's preoccupation—of finding out how far I would go in order to carry on seeing my boy.

One night after I had cleared the dishes away I sat with the gentleman. I asked him what it was like to be around someone he couldn't see. 'Like being round ghosts,' he said. 'You hear the voice, but don't see the body. Take yourself,' he said. 'I have no idea what you look like.'

So, hearing that, I drew up the chair next to his at the table. I reached for his hand and I laid it against my face. His fingers began to walk softly across my skin. He stroked the bridge of my nose with his finger. He brushed my lips with his finger. He rose in his chair and eased down again and made a sigh, a croaking to life or a dying, I couldn't decide. I had beautiful skin, he said. 'Good God,' he said. Good God. His fingers wandered up to my eyes. The tip of a finger drew a circle around one eye, then the other. Bit by bit of me fell to his wandering fingers. I undid my uniform. I undid the bra I'd stolen from the Englishwoman. His fingers wandered and here and there they paused to catch their breath the way tourists do on a walk to take in the view. I wanted to be a special view that he could not do without. I wanted to keep my room. I needed the housekeeping money and what he paid me to pay to see the boy. So I had to be a beautiful view. The gentleman was standing up now, craning over me.

That night I left the blind gentleman fast asleep. I went back to my room. I sat on the edge of the bed. I thought, I could steal the boy and keep him in the room with me. The blind gentleman would never know. I will teach the boy to turn himself into a ghost.

The next night I am in bed when I hear the blind gentleman at the door. As the old man came in the idea of the ghost boy went out.

The following night I heard him clawing at the door, and the night after, and then I began to lie there awake and expect him. And when he didn't turn up I was angry I had stayed awake for nothing.

One night he knelt by the bed and licked me from head to toe. Then he turned me over and licked me from my neck down my back between my legs, the backs of my legs, then he turned me over and licked again, went on licking me like a cat. For the third time he rolled me over onto my back. This time he moved my knees apart and entered me. And I wanted him to.

Now the days were easier. When we went out for a walk the blind gentleman put his arm through mine and held me close. When we sat in the park the silences were no longer a problem. The blind gentleman was like a child with its favourite soft toy.

Towards the end of summer those bad old silences returned. He would talk about his wife. He would talk about the things they used to do together, he could recall entire conversations, and what interesting conversations they were, on things which I knew nothing about. I began to worry again. Every child grows out of his soft toy.

I didn't know there was a room on the next landing until he asked me if I would object to another live-in companion. The person wouldn't be on top of us. He or she, he said, would live in the room on the next landing. For a few afternoons a week the new live-in companion would give me a break. What did I think about that? When I didn't answer quickly he said that, of course, I would have to choose the person on his behalf. It would be my choice, but he didn't want any young men. It would be inappropriate. Young men, he said, were generally untrustworthy. An older man, yes, perhaps, why not? Another younger woman? Yes, possibly. But it would need to be someone around whom I felt comfortable.

thirty-two

The man the blind gentleman called Defoe irritated me. He thought of the world as a child does—as a place to play. He was like a tourist. He was always searching for something new to stare at.

I don't know anything about the world he comes from. He would drink all night with the blind gentleman. Sometimes he would try to help in the kitchen. Often he ate in a rush, then he'd sit there, his arms folded, while he waited for me and the blind gentleman to finish our plates. When he ate like that he would be wanting to get back downstairs to his fossils.

The first time we all went to the zoo they forgot I was there. They forgot the flamingos and the seals. A giraffe could have come and sat down beside them and they would not have noticed because they were too busy talking about other animals—not the ones in the zoo—but lungfish and, in the blind gentleman's case, butterflies. I don't know why they felt they had to go to the zoo to have that conversation. In their talk I saw my own shortcomings. In Defoe's company the blind gentleman talked in a way that he never did with me.

For a few weeks I felt threatened. If I lost my position I would have to go back to the railway station.

Bernard talked some calm into me. He made me see myself the way the blind gentleman might see me, and then straightaway I saw my uses. I kept the apartment clean. Defoe couldn't do that. His own room was a mess. I made coffee and tea for the gentleman, I brought him schnapps. I cooked for him until he got sick of what I made and after that came into the kitchen to talk me through the cooking of the things he wanted to eat—meals that required certain ingredients which, if I couldn't steal them, we could not really afford because money spent on a special ingredient could have been money spent on seeing my boy. What else? I was company. I didn't tell Bernard what kind of company I was. Nor did I tell him—or Defoe—about the photograph.

We had to wait until Defoe had left for the museum, then the gentleman would ask me to bring him the photograph. It was kept in a special place. Of course I knew where. In the gentleman's office I would sit down and describe the photograph.

The first time I thought I was looking at white slugs. But then I saw what those white slugs were. Some of the women are dead. But not all of them. Some of the women are curled up as they wait for the bullet that will end their lives. One woman lay on her front. I cannot forget her. She is raised onto her elbows like a sunbather at the beach, as her executioners approach from the rear, one man with a pistol, the other with a rifle.

The gentleman asked the same questions as he did at the zoo. What did the women look like? And I would have to look carefully to find the birthmarks, the hair, and the heaviness or thinness of the torso. He had given each woman a name. The ones that were still alive, that is. That way, he said, they could not be mistaken for the garden slugs that I had seen the first time. The one he liked described the most was the sunbather. He wanted to hear about her flesh. How firm it was, and I told him until, to my ears, it sounded like I was describing meat in a shop window.

Since reading Hannah's testimony so much more is clear to me. Now I think I understand his questions in a way that I didn't before. He liked to ask me, and he never tired of asking, what I thought of the person who had taken this photograph. What kind of man might he be? He leant forward, concentrating, and his face still as death itself as it had been when he asked for the truck driver's details.

I looked at the photo, and I thought there could only be one answer. 'A bad man,' I said, and he eased back in his chair. He turned away.

'Yes,' he said. 'But I cannot afford to think that.'

He would disappear in one of his silences so that all I was aware of was the dimness of the office, the closed blinds, the stillness of everything. He shook his head, and when he stopped shaking his head he would sigh heavily. Then he would lean forward and then ease back, and then maybe shake his head one more time. 'What are we supposed to see? What is it we are supposed to think?'

So with my eyes he got to see what he didn't when in the company of Defoe, though when the three of us went out it was always Defoe's eyes that reported the world back to the blind gentleman. Defoe's were the trusted eyes. I was just an armrest or handrail on those outings. It was up to Defoe to decide what was of interest.

When it was just me and the blind gentleman we went to the cemetery. Defoe came twice, the first time so he could be shown the headstones. When it was just the two of us the blind gentleman hardly paid the headstones any attention. All he was interested in was his wife, Hannah.

She led parties of tourists around the dead. The blind gentleman knew all about them. He could talk about the dead as if they were relatives. But none of them interested him in quite the same way as she did. He never said why she didn't live with him and I didn't like to ask. But after reading her testimony I think I know because some of the impatience the blind gentleman showed with her carried over to me.

She is a small woman with the quick movements of a small dog. I think blindness has made the gentleman slow. Everything he did looked thoughtful. As he stood up from a bench in the cemetery he rose as if he was thinking about the movement of doing so every inch of the way until he achieved his full height.

'Is she here today?'

That's the question he always asked. It was our reason for coming to the cemetery. And he never tired of asking it.

Sometimes she would come and speak with him. Afterwards he would ask me how she looked. 'Good,' I might say. She looked good. Then he'd snap at me, 'What does "good" mean?'

'I don't know, sir. She just looks like she did the last time.'

'And?'

'Well she looks good, sir.'

'Is she wearing clothes?'

'Of course, sir.'

'And?'

So I would have to dress her before his eyes

One afternoon she left the tourists photographing each other around the headstones. She came flying across to where we stood. She hardly gave me a look before she started shouting at the blind gentleman. I don't know what that was about. Afterwards he wouldn't say.

One afternoon the trains aren't working and we are late. The tourists are already moving out the gates of the cemetery to the street. I see Hannah and I am about to alert the blind gentleman when I pause. A car is parked across the road. The driver is an older man. He has wound down the side window and he is smiling up at the blind gentleman's wife. His eyes follow her around the front of the car. She gets in and through the window I see her lean across and kiss the driver on the cheek.

'Well?' he asked.

I told him we were late. We'd missed her. Slowly he breathes out through his mouth. A minute ago he was high with excitement. Now his body has turned into a sack that can barely hold him upright.

What will we do now? What interest does the day have left? I often experienced the same thing after handing the boy back to his father. The highlights had been experienced; now there was all the rest of the day to get through, and the night, maybe two or three days, longer when the money was hard to come by, before I would see the boy again.

In the blind gentleman's case the day still held another possibility.

First I would lead him to Wertheim for cake. He would give me money for two cakes. I'd buy just the one *apfelkuchen* and it was for him. The money meant for my cake went towards the money I needed to see the boy. Then I'd sit opposite the blind gentleman and make eating noises. I became good at pretending to eat cake. Your teeth must click and the sigh of contentment must come from a closed mouth. The small fork must bang against the plate, then at last there is the sound of the fork laid to rest. The scratching noise is the chair leg moving back to move a full stomach out from the edge of the table.

After eating cake at Wertheim I'd lead the blind gentleman to the cafe across the road from Hannah's building. We always took one of the tables at the window. And there we waited—with coffee and hot chocolate—for Hannah to appear. She usually did between five and six in the afternoon. Whenever she failed to turn up the blind gentleman grew silent. He sat shrunken inside his coat, his hands slumped down in their pockets.

The only way to bring him back to life was to describe a woman who hadn't passed the window yet, but she might as well have, because the blind gentleman didn't know the difference between her passing and my description of her doing the same.

Did he need to know that I had not eaten any cake? No. I don't think so. If I was blind and had to be led to the park in order to see my boy I'd rather my minder provide me with a picture of him. That's how I had come to think. A lie had to be better than disappointment.

And, when I consider it, isn't this what Defoe was doing when he spent his mornings looking at the outline of something in rock? Wasn't he trying to make up the whole out of a few details? I did exactly the same when I wasn't with the boy. I drew him up in my head from an impression put together from all the other times we'd spent together. Often, on our way home across the park when we fell into one of those long silences, it was almost as if I was walking with the boy; the boy was at my side, not the blind gentleman. Now I am in prison I am left with the fossil remains of all those times together. I don't have to try hard to conjure him up.

That winter was a long one. According to the blind gentleman it wasn't so cold, not by his standards. By any other reasonable human being's it was freezing. I didn't care for the cold, it was the lack of light that got to me. Up to now I'd never thought of light as a living thing. It disappeared in November and December and everything in the city died a little. People bundled up so that their faces were the only part of their body visible. In January the ponds in the park iced over. One afternoon I saw a reflection of the boy with me in the ice. I told him to look carefully. There's the two of us. Just like in a photo. Now stick that photo in your pocket. I hope he still has it.

Over that winter, late at night, I tiptoed barefoot or in socks out of the apartment and down the stairs so the blind gentleman and Defoe would not hear me. On the bottom stair I sat to pull on my boots. Then I went out into the aching cold to catch a train across the city. First I went to Jermayne's and stood outside his building to make sure his lights were out. Then I crossed the bridge into the little Frenchman's neighbourhood.

Bernard was back to sleeping in his new coat. He had paid off the pawnbroker and the tooth was back in his mouth. I brought him leftovers from the meal I'd prepared for Defoe and the blind gentleman. I always left a bit behind. Bernard would eat it cold. Afterwards I didn't mind his dog breath. I liked the smell of his new old coat around me. Inside the warehouse at that hour I felt like I was in a huge litter of warm bodies and smells.

The blind gentleman had given me money for lessons in Deutsch. I almost enrolled, but when I worked out the hours it would buy me with the boy I decided I could not waste it on language. Ramona says she would have taken the lessons in order to talk to the boy. Well, I tell her, it wasn't quite one thing or the other. I didn't enrol but I did keep learning. I never left Bernard without a new sheet of words and phrases. *Do you want to climb a tree? Do you want an ice cream? Are you tired? Do you miss me?* The last phrase was the first one I learnt off by heart. Bernard said my pronunciation was near perfect. I never did get to ask it.

thirty-three

Some time in the new year the blind gentleman asked me to sit with him. He said he had some unpleasant news. It had been brought to his attention—that's what he said, brought to his attention—that he didn't have as much money in his savings as he had thought. He said the whole world economy was teetering. Once upon a time, he said, it took a week for the mail boat to reach Hamburg from New York. Now time raced at the speed of a finger to a computer key. Everyone was affected, including our household. It meant I wouldn't be getting the same amount that I had been receiving. It wasn't that I wasn't worth it. He just didn't have it to give. He said he would understand if I felt the position was no longer worthwhile, but he hoped I would stay on. He hoped the circumstances would change for the better. They usually did, he said.

The weather had certainly changed for the better. Bernard

was making money again. I asked him if he would take his tooth back to the pawnbroker. He winced, he screwed up his eyes. I wished I hadn't asked. I apologised. I told him the tooth must never leave his mouth again, no matter what. I'd find another way. Now a different look entered his face—that old look of fear. In his panic he dug his hands in his coat pockets and brought up handfuls of euros and pressed them into my hands. I took the money, and I took more out of housekeeping. I stole money off Defoe's desk and out of his trousers that hung off the back of his chair. I still had only enough money for one visit.

One afternoon we're in the cafe behind Wertheim waiting for the blind gentleman's wife to show. A truck is parked outside her entrance. I didn't pass that on, and a few minutes later I'm pleased I didn't. Around the side of the truck comes Hannah with two removal men. The three of them gaze up into the back of the truck. A third man joins them. I recognise him. It's the man in the car I'd seen outside the cemetery.

'Any sign of her?' asks the blind gentleman.

'No,' I tell him. 'Not yet.'

He orders another coffee, then after he's drunk that he orders schnapps. He has two glasses. Over the same time there is a procession of household stuff from the building out to the street, where it is loaded into the truck.

Across the road, the entrance to Hannah's building looks emptier than ever.

'Well?' he asks.

'No sign of her.'

He wonders if she is sick. He wonders if I should cross the

road and hit her buzzer. She may have had a fall. She might be lying there. So I go across the road and pretend to hit her buzzer. Then I come back and give him the first honest information all day.

'She isn't home.'

'No?'

'No, sir.'

We kept going back to the cemetery and on to Wertheim for the one piece of cake and then to the cafe opposite Hannah's old address. For a week we did this. In the end it was easier to make her up.

I didn't need to look so hard, in the way he had insisted of me at the zoo. All it took were a few things—a hat, flowers, new shoes, no umbrella if it was raining, details which I pinched off the crowd in the window and he would make the rest of her up.

All winter I watched a large bird build its nest in the chestnut tree outside my window. That nest looked to be a solid thing, but it was made out of the flimsiest of materials, straws which if they weren't in the bird's beak would have been blowing up the street.

Out of scraps the blind gentleman created a picture of his estranged wife.

Here are some of the scraps I passed on.

She is in a hurry.

She appears to be in a daydream.

She looks preoccupied.

Here in each instance is what he said.

'She is in a hurry? Really? Interesting. No, that is interesting. She must have forgotten something. Perhaps she is late for an appointment. She usually has that nice leather briefcase my father gave to her before he died. He adored her. And she adored him. She did. Sometimes I think she adored him more than she did me, and in my case perhaps the word "adore" is a bit strong. After all, do wives adore their husbands? Ever? Beyond a year or two? Before the general absenteeism of the husband takes over and all that remains is the flawed replica of the object once adored?'

'She is in a daydream? Well it wouldn't be Hannah otherwise. Comes as no surprise. Really, I am amazed she hasn't been run over. Have you noticed the way she crosses the road? Have you any idea of the faith it requires to wander across the traffic, to believe that they will actually stop? Well, I have never believed they would for me, and at such times I could feel her draw away from me and the abyss grow between us.'

'Preoccupied? Yes. Is one leg crossing the other? She dawdles. She doesn't when she is walking alone. Then you've seen how she walks. But with me it was as though she had suddenly forgotten how to walk. It used to cause terrible rows. I was always waiting for her to catch up. Then she would ask, accusingly, why I kept walking ahead. I would reply with a question of my own. Why did she have to walk so slowly, so deliberately slowly? She would say there was nothing deliberate about it, she wasn't walking slowly, she was walking how she always walked, so what was I trying to prove? Firmly, but patiently, I would tell her I am not trying to prove anything. I am just wanting to get from A to B and if we walk any slower I will fall over.'

I try to imagine, were the positions reversed, what I would prefer. To be told the boy has left the city or to go on believing.

thirty-four

In June that year Jermayne put the price up to sixty euros. He mentioned the same thing as the blind gentleman had, though in the Jermayne way—'The world is on the brink of sliding into a shit hole of its own making.' I asked him what that had to do with me. Jermayne shook his head. I was back to being dumber than I looked. 'What happens,' he asked, 'when you get caught out in the rain without an umbrella?'

'You get wet.'

'You got it.'

I snuck across to Bernard's that night. In the dark he lay with his coat on, without his trousers. I lay my hand on his chest and I walked my fingers down the way the blind gentleman had walked his across my face. Down to Bernard's navel. Over his boxer shorts until I felt him stir and I whispered in his ear, 'Bernard, I need your tooth. Please. Just this one more time.' He took my hand and put it back at my side. He told me I was confused in my motivation. What did I want from him—to make love or to take his diamond-inlaid tooth? 'Both' was the honest answer.

Now to a different day, a Sunday. I am out with the blind gentleman and Defoe at the market under the railway line in Tiergarten. The same stuff as in the apartment is displayed over tables. Books, paintings, drinking horns, knives, mugs, ornaments of every kind. And people are buying it.

The next morning while Defoe was at the museum I took the vases out of the apartment. I went to a shop in Bernard's neighbourhood. Not the pawnbroker, a different shop. The money I got for the vases paid for two visits with the boy.

I asked myself what difference did vases and paintings make to a blind man who couldn't see them? The blind gentleman could remember what his apartment looked like just as he could remember what his wife looked like. They didn't have to be there.

I went to the shop three times with all the things Defoe wrote to the inspector about. Defoe was now my problem.

According to Ramona addicts behave in the same way that I did. They do not think of the consequences. The world is reduced to what lies closest to hand.

So I had hotel sex with Defoe in order to buy his silence. I also needed the money. I couldn't afford to lose my room or the little money I shaved off the housekeeping. I went down to his room and everything he describes is true. Even the bit about my hunger. The little Frenchman would not make love to me. He was afraid I would lose my mystery. I would turn into familiar hollows and plains. Whenever Bernard tried to prevent me seeing something about him he'd build a cloud of confusion out of words. He could build a wall out of the same. He knew I didn't know the questions to ask that would allow me to see over that wall. So we were left to lie with that wall between us. Me wanting to climb over it. The little Frenchman on the other side nursing his insecurities.

So I had Defoe. I don't like his eel story. And I still remember a visit to the zoo where he couldn't tear himself away from the Cape hunting dogs eating the live chickens. So many in the world are like Defoe. They lean on the safety rail and watch with horror the pain of others. Funny. I don't recall him so clearly as the blind gentleman. The blind gentleman had loose skin hanging off the end of his penis. I was always glad when he slipped on a condom. But I have him to thank for teaching me how to build a picture of the boy. I am sorry it took a lie to learn that skill.

Ramona always says she wouldn't have done what I did. I ask her what she thinks a flower does when it sees the sun. It opens itself up. Isn't that the most natural thing in the world? Her face got that patchy look. I had put her husband back in her thoughts. She is seeing all over again a line of women opening up as her husband comes into their lives. I try not to let her stick around in that thought. I talk about the boy. He is the distant shore I am trying to reach. Defoe is just a buoy to hang onto, to catch my breath, before setting off for the shore again—and again. Now when I look at Ramona she is sitting up on the edge of her bunk. She is nodding. The line of women has gone.

thirty-five

I have nearly finished writing my account. I have read out parts to Ramona. She has tried hard to correct my mind but not the events I have written about.

She wonders if the inspector is soft on me. Why else would he show up as regularly as he does? I tell her I don't see neediness in the inspector. The inspector is a family man. I have met his two daughters—they stared at me until their father whispered in their ears. By the end of that visit they were playing on the floor around our feet. I have not met his wife, Francesca. But I have eaten the bread rolls she gives the inspector to pass on to me.

This afternoon the inspector arrived in a white shirt and tie and black shoes that shone like a waiter's. He'd been to the commemorative service for Ines Maria Dellabarca.

He leant across the table that divides us. I sat forward to listen. And later this is what I told Ramona.

The church sits on a knoll above a shallow bay carved out from a steep hillside of white stone. It does not confront the ocean panorama. It sits at an angle, its attention divided between the sea and the white mountainsides marching inland. In the morning the sun finds the graves of the children of shepherds. By late afternoon the headstones of the sons of fishermen are luminous.

It was a bright day. The last of the summer flowers drooped around the graves. The sea breeze failed to reach the church, said the inspector, but the hillsides trembled with tiny bulbs of colour.

The church was full. The inspector walked to the front to pay his respects to the family. I did not know Ines Maria Dellabarca had a fiancé. She never mentioned him. But it makes sense now. That must have been Claudio on the other end of the phone I picked up out of the dirt. A thin asthmatic fellow, says the inspector, whose shoulders shook with every cough. Her parents sat in front with an older sister, Christina. The inspector looked around at faces of old schoolfriends, work colleagues and neighbours.

The grandfather climbed up the front on crooked legs. When one leg gave way the congregation leant forward ready to catch him. The grandfather raised a hand and smiled. The inspector says he is an old rogue. He may even have stumbled on purpose. Anyway he stood up there nodding and smiling at various faces. Then he settled his gaze out the open doors and began to recount the morning Ines Maria Dellabarca came into the world. He'd never known such happiness. When he left the hospital he stopped by the well above the beach and made a wish, then he carried on up the hill to this very same church, and here he walked around the family graves to break the news of a granddaughter's arrival into the world.

Other people followed the grandfather up to the pulpit. When Claudio spoke each word had to be drawn out of him. In the end the old fisherman led Claudio back to his pew.

When everyone had had their say the inspector rose from his place near the back and walked down the aisle. He spoke with the parents and the grandfather, and with their agreement he climbed up the front to read my letter.

From the church the inspector drove to the beach. There, he said, he sat on the hull of a boat. He smoked a bit and looked out to sea. The horizon was dirty with sand blown off the North African desert. There are days, he says, when nothing on the beach looks ever to have been disturbed. The sand is exactly as it has been for a thousand years with white shells sticking up like ancient ruins. Then along comes a storm and everything that had a look of permanence about it is ransacked.

A year ago, he said, this is where he had found himself, and with the impossible task of trying to piece everything back together again.

This afternoon he asked me if I still think about Ines Maria Dellabarca.

'Yes,' I told him. Although I don't know if she appears as a thought. I remember seeing one of the blind gentleman's beetles trapped in amber. That is how she appears—her face filled with fright, a hand thrown back, and sometimes there is another picture of her and this one I shut my eyes to. I am trying hard to rid myself of that picture and instead insert another, of her looking at me after we climbed out from under the dinghy on the beach.

The inspector listened closely, then he nodded and continued where he had left off.

While he sat on the hull smoking, his thoughts turned to a friend from childhood. He still has a photo of him, a small boy, dressed in a rodeo suit that was sent to him by relatives in America, twirling rope. The boy grew up to become a fisherman. He and the inspector stayed the best of friends. One evening the fisherman was feeding pots over the side of the boat when a rope wrapped around his leg and pulled him overboard, down into the filmy depths, where for days after, months, the inspector continued to see him flopping about like bait, his bright red cowboy shirt shifting in the cold currents, his face all butter and light, gape-eyed, as though struck with wonder and at the same time stalled by thought. He continued to see him like that, he couldn't rid himself of the image of the drowned man, his friend from childhood in the cowboy suit, until one day his memory let go of him, and he rose slowly, like a man in an armchair, rotating up to the white light.

The inspector said, when the time came, when the moment was right to do so, I would have to find a way of letting go.

'Not of the boy,' I said.

The inspector smiled, his eyes moistened in that way I have described to Ramona and which makes her so suspicious.

Those moist eyes were not trying to unlock me. They were setting me up for good news.

Next month, he said, he would be visiting Berlin. A stamp fair, he said. But he planned to see Abebi. He hoped to return with some news. Perhaps more. He didn't want to make promises. I would have to wait and see.

I placed a hand over my heart and I thanked the inspector. Then I asked him the question Ramona always asks. I asked why he visits, why does he go out of his way on my behalf.

He sat back, shifted his head. He looked up at the clock on the wall. I looked too. There wasn't much time left. Fifteen minutes. He got out his cigarettes and laid them on the table.

In the brief time left to us he began to describe a trip he'd taken to Serene. Serene, he reminded me, is near to where I had washed up. It was after my trial. For months on end he'd felt as if he'd walked in my shoes. Sometimes he said he'd felt inhabited by me. He'd spent weeks away from home following my footsteps between Sicily and Berlin. Now he needed a break, so he took his family to Serene.

One hot afternoon he found himself swimming far out from the other swimmers. He swam, he said, with a reckless disregard for his capabilities. Later his wife would tell him he looked like a man swimming towards Africa. As he swam he noted how still the ocean is compared to the shallows. When he stuck his head under and opened his eyes he saw how quickly the blue light turned to coal-black depths. This would have been the place to turn around, but he didn't. He swam on. Several times it occurred to him that he had gone out far enough. But he kept swimming. By now the beach had disappeared from view. The tops of the old buildings that line the beach bobbed up and down. Out there in the sea, far from the shore, removed, he said, from everything he had ever known, he found himself thinking about me. Thinking—this is how it must have been. And, he said, how extraordinary to arrive in this way, without the frozen smiles of cabin crew, to arrive instead wet, numb and fearful.

On his way back to shore his arms felt heavy. His strokes were more laboured. He found himself out of breath. The possibility of his own death mildly entered his thoughts. He found himself thinking about his daughters. Out there in the sea, the inspector said, he began to cry. He forced himself on. Soon the buildings above the beach grew taller. At last the shoreline with its circus effect of air-filled animals and sun umbrellas came into view. He said he was scared more than anything. Scared of never seeing his girls again rather than scared of dying.

The inspector stopped there. His moist eyes smiled back at me. I reached across to touch his moustache. But he drew back. He blinked once or twice at me. His fingers moved to his tie knot. He glanced up at the clock. His hand raked in his cigarettes. He coughed into the back of his hand and stood.

He said, 'I don't know if that was a satisfactory explanation but it will have to do.'

part five: *Abebi*

thirty-six

Jermayne is gone. That's the first thing to know. I don't wish to pretend any longer. I told him to go last year. It was September. He took everything with him. Outside in the street the leaves were falling off the trees. The same wind shook up the apartment. Everything flew out the window with Jermayne.

He was never a doting father. He took on his parenting role as a job. The other thing to know about Jermayne is his obsession with money. He is a dreamer. An ordinary life was never enough. We had to have the best. Now, to have the best, as I learned through my twelve years with Jermayne, requires time and patience and planning. None of those qualities can be said to be Jermayne's. Consequently, we who were destined to have everything, according to my husband, ended up with nothing.

Never did I think he would use Daniel in the way that he did, as a bargaining chip, like a TV you go out and hire.

There is another thing to know about Jermayne. The woman does his washing. That is the unfortunate and arrogant part of my husband. The careless part of him left behind wads of money in his pockets. Money that could never be properly explained. So, I asked myself, what has changed? What is new in Jermayne's behaviour? The question led me to follow him and Daniel to the park. I could not believe that Jermayne had overnight turned himself into a normal loving father. That's where I saw her. In the park. The boy and the 'incubator' woman. I saw the exchange of money. I saw Jermayne walk away. And I saw Daniel leave with that woman. I did not want to believe what I saw, so again I followed, and a third time. There may have been a fourth. It was always the same thing. The woman waiting under the trees. Daniel running to see her. I don't need to say what that did to me.

I always read to the child. I still do. Every night I read to him. His eyelids were beginning to close when I put the book down. I asked him about his play in the park. I asked if he had played with his ball. He nodded. I asked if his father had kicked the ball to him, back and forth the way they do, and he nodded. I ask if there was anyone else there in the park that they met. His chest fell, his eyes closed. He turned himself into a little stubborn ball. I smiled down at him. I stroked his face. I asked if he had a friend, a special friend he meets in the park. When at last he nodded I stroked his hair and face. I kissed his eyes. I thanked God the lying gene had not passed to him from Jermayne.

Now I had his father to confront. I waited two days. I told myself to wait another day, and when that day turned up I was still not ready. I told myself to wait until the weekend. On the

Sunday night I told him. I told him what I had seen, then I told him to get out. He'd turned himself into someone I didn't recognise any more. I could not tolerate that stranger being under the same roof.

I had tried to have a baby of my own. I had tried so hard I lost all reason. I told Jermayne he needed to drink goat's milk. I must have read that somewhere. Someone who knew all about circadian rhythms told us to copulate under a full moon but not after 8pm. Jermayne wanted to know why not after 8pm. We had a row over that. Of course Jermayne assumed the problem had to lie with me. In those days I still listened to him. Jermayne is very clever with computers. He had his own business writing software. This is back when we were still part of the human race and Jermayne had not yet set us on a track apart. We talked about adoption. We even talked about adopting a Romanian or Russian child. But that was just talk. Neither one of us was up for that, but we went on talking as though we were, and I think it was just nice to pretend we had options. We were always going to adopt an African child. Then Jermayne had a different idea. He had been reading up on surrogacy. I listened as I did in those days with an open mind.

One evening he came home and announced he'd found someone to carry our baby. Of course what he really meant was *his* baby. Now there are certain channels you need to go through with surrogacy. It's not as simple as grafting a shoot onto another branch. There is medical advice to heed. There are counsellors to talk to. There are legal matters to work through. Every i to be dotted and t to be crossed. Jermayne said we didn't need to worry about all that—middle-management logjam—that's what he called it. Middle-management logjam. Incredible. I am amazed that I listened to him. Middle-management logjam. Those sorts of phrases just dripped from his tongue like syrup. Anyway, he'd found somebody, a woman in Tunisia.

We had been there on holiday. Jermayne had been there twice on his own on the strength of some software work for a hotel chain. I've forgotten their name, but in those days they were quite big fish in the industry—I imagine they've since been swallowed by a larger fish—so there was a lot of work on. Jermayne was always over there, back and forth, between here and Hamburg, and Cologne, as I recall. The business was going well. We were doing well, as normal people.

Jermayne had met the surrogate and talked with her. I did not want to meet with her. I did not want to know her name. I did not want to know anything about her. I didn't want to think of her as anything more than an incubator for our baby.

When babies are born they could be anyone's. That's the truth—as Jermayne himself might have said. And yet the parents still pick them apart and search for whatever they can find that reminds them of themselves—hair, eyes, ears. But really in those few months a baby is its own whole new thing. There is nothing in that new baby to trace back to anyone in particular. That's the thing I noticed. The next thing I discovered is that that first impression does not last. A baby definitely comes from somewhere. In those first few months it is still getting its colour scheme right, features are still finding their future mould. A baby is really a process, rather than a solidly arrived at thing, if you see what I mean. And after six months or so a baby begins to grow into its own future.

Now with our boy it is easy to see Jermayne. His face set like a little buddha's, a heaviness around his shoulders, just like my husband. But I could find nothing of me, nothing at all, which is not surprising because now I know I wasn't part of the recipe. Slowly however Daniel grows into someone else whom I do not recognise. Perhaps there is still a touch of Jermayne about him, but this other area of character, and of physical character, I just don't know about. There are times when Daniel's eyes turn into shields, they express nothing, absolutely nothing at all, but at the same time they appear to know a lot. I find myself wishing I had taken a greater interest in the surrogate. When Jermayne said the test tube with our ingredients was tipped inside of the woman, supervised of course, I saw people in white coats, I saw a hygienic situation. Jermayne in some sort of green hospital gown and wearing a white face mask. He always used to complain that I watched too much television.

The part of the child that was not my husband remained a mystery right up until I saw the mother standing under the trees in Tiergarten. There it was. It was no mystery after all.

Then she disappeared. I might as well be honest. I was glad about that. Soon after I told Jermayne to pack up his things. I didn't know what the woman had done. I didn't know about the manslaughter charge or the prison term until the visit from the inspector.

I had grocery bags in both hands, Daniel was with me, and I was trying to get the key in the door when someone helpful—someone without a face at this point, just somebody helpful or another tenant in the building, I could have assumed that too, it happens from time to time—relieved me of the shopping as I unlocked the door. Inside, the inspector introduced himself. Very politely he asked if we could talk inside my apartment. He was still holding the shopping and I knew the only way I would get it back was to allow him to carry it up the stairs to the apartment. You see how a man like the inspector can pass through walls.

So we climb the stairs in silence. Daniel has run ahead and left the doors open. Inside the apartment the inspector set the shopping down. I sent Daniel down to the courtyard. I told him we were to be left alone until I called for him. From here on the conversation is in English. The inspector followed me out to the kitchen. I always make myself coffee after the shopping. The inspector didn't want any. He rubbed his stomach—said he suffers from acid. Well, Jermayne used to suffer the same thing. Peppermint tea is good for that sort of condition. I looked in the cupboard but Jermayne must have taken the peppermint tea with him. The inspector was happy with water.

Now the sound of the ball bouncing against the wall in the courtyard travelled up the side of the building. It can be the most lonesome sound in the world. At other times it is irritating. For the inspector it was a matter of curiosity. He admired the pots of Italian parsley, mint and rosemary on the sill and pressed his face to the window. Down in the courtyard the ball bounced against the wall, back and forth, back and forth. He sleeps with that ball. He won't walk anywhere without that ball. He walks to school kicking it ahead of him. He is a quiet boy. Hardly ever says a word. He is obsessed by that ball. He is not interested in other children. I took him to see a doctor. He passed us on to a specialist. The specialist says he has a mild form of Asperger's.

To get away from the ball in the courtyard we returned to the living room. What did we talk about? Nothing much at all. I kept waiting for the inspector to come to the point. He talked about stamps. That's why he'd come to Berlin—for a stamp fair. His father had introduced him to stamps and following his death he had inherited his collection. He had stamps from every country. Some I'd never heard of. Others that no longer exist or do so in a new form and have a new name. I didn't see where all this was leading, until finally he asks to see the 'adoption papers'. I went and got them. I have nothing to hide. The signatures are there. The authorities have stamped the papers. The inspector looked at them, though I could tell he wasn't reading. His Deutsch is not nearly good enough. He asked for a copy. There is a copy shop nearby. I offered to walk there with him whenever he was ready. When it came time for him to depart he forgot about the papers and I did not remind him.

I should add here that before he left he opened his briefcase and brought out a ring folder. A black ring folder which he slid across the table to me. 'They are testimonies, and they will tell you more than I can,' he said. On reflection I don't think the adoption papers interested him at all. He was just hoping to soften me up. Perhaps that is what he thought I needed. I don't know. But this is the order in which our conversation ran its course.

His second request was from the birth mother. She would like a photo of the boy. The inspector said he had thought hard and long about this request. He decided it could only be a good thing. At a glance she would be able to see he is well fed and well cared for. Loved, he thought to add.

Yes, I said. He is loved. He is loved by the only mother he has known.

That was just my nerves speaking out loud. As soon as I said it I knew I was wrong. There were the times in the park, all those times—where Daniel had run across the fields to this woman who I knew nothing about, a complete stranger at that point.

Perhaps I sounded too aggressive. Yes, I think so, because the inspector rose to his feet. He looked ready to leave. But I didn't move from my chair because I had a question of my own.

'How did she know you were coming to Berlin, inspector?'

'I visit her,' he said. 'I visit whenever I can.'

'So you are friends?'

'Not exactly.'

'But you help her?'

'Where I can. My wife Francesca and I. But, as you can see, I am not always successful.'

I told him I wouldn't give her a baby photograph. Then I got up and walked out to the kitchen. I raised the window and called Daniel up to the apartment. When I returned to the living room the inspector was smiling down at himself as he cleaned the lens on his little camera.

Since then I have sent more photographs. I even sent one of myself. A short letter arrived from her. In English. Thanking me. She wished she had a photograph of herself to send. I wrote back to say that could wait. Then she wrote back, and things just evolved from there.

Once I shut myself up in the bathroom. I sat on the rim of the bathtub with a cup of coffee. I wanted to find out what it felt like to be shuttered up in a cell. Then I called Daniel in, got him to bring in his ball as well. Some time after that I received a letter from the inspector to say he'd managed to get her moved from the over-crowded Piazza Lanza in Catania to a nicer prison in Agrigento. In her letters she never complained of the other place, of its over-crowding and general decay and poor amenities.

When Daniel's last birthday came round I asked him what he wanted. What did he most wish for in the world? It was a question I was asked when I was a child and I never had difficulty compiling my list. Daniel shook his head. What about a new ball? He replied with a smile. Anything else? He shook his head. I reminded him of the woman his father used to take him to see. I asked him, 'Would you like to write to her?' I told him I would help with his letter. He turned into a little wooden soldier. I could have tipped him at the shoulder and rocked him back and forth. I had to tell him nothing bad would come of it. Only good. Then I heard myself say this—'I think she would like to hear from her boy.'

Here is another night I find myself alone. I get into bed. I turn on the television. There is a program about retired Britons buying French castles. Men with weary faces who gaze despondently up at high impregnable walls. The jovial women do all the talking. I think, with Jermayne, I should have been more like them. Large and bossy. I switch channels to a game show. For a while I watch surfers on huge waves in the Pacific. I switch to the History Channel. It is D-Day. I must have dozed off because I wake to sand explosions and marines wading ashore.

I used to find myself saying, I can't imagine. But, I've since found out, you can—it's just a case of wanting to.

It is late now. I get up and walk to the window. I picture her crossing the park. Car doors open, they close behind her. Voices carry from the trees. A woman emerges in front of her. They give each other a fright, then politely move around one another. More cars. The electric whine of a window. A man calls after her. For a while there are footsteps behind her—they keep in time with her own, waiting to see if she will turn off into the trees. She concentrates on what lies ahead. The cars peter out. The voices drift away. She crosses the canal and enters the street below. I picture her down there in a doorway. In her letter she told me there are creatures in the sea that blend perfectly into the background. Creatures that look like sand or plants. You can't see them until they move. A car or truck moves along the street and she steps into its shadow and moves with it until the passing shapes deposit her in a doorway on the other side of the canal. It is empty right now. She said she used to occupy it the way a crab will occupy an abandoned shell. It is very late. Perhaps there is ice down the street. The canal has frozen over. Yet she has travelled across town for this moment. She does not hope to see him. But to stand in the same street, under the same lit clouds, to be near.

One day she will leave the prison. I don't know if this is how they do it. But in my head this is how I see it happening. I imagine other prisoners released that day as well.

They will step out of a hole in the side of fortress walls, a small group of women with pasty faces taking big breaths, taking small steps, stopping now and then to look up at the sky. They walk out to the road where there is a bus stop and some kind of pickup area. Some family people will swing by and scoop up the prisoners. One by one they will drift off like dogs retrieved from the pound. Until all that is left is the woman. And then Daniel and I will come by. She will look up, surprised. She's been sitting there with a heavy heart. Now she sees us—sees me and looks confused perhaps, yes, that is likely, but then she will see the boy and that's when she stands up and the rest of the world melts away.

I don't imagine the next part. I can't bear to think about that part.

I'm getting there.

I'm just not there yet.

acknowledgments

I spent a year during 2007 and 2008 in Berlin on a writer's residency and I wish to thank Creative New Zealand for that opportunity—there is nothing like a new place to pull the scales away from one's eyes. Thanks to the Goethe Institute in Wellington and Berlin for its encouragement and collegiality, and to Katja Koblitz, Franziska Rauchut and Ingo Petz in Berlin for their friendship and insight into the city and its past. A special note of gratitude to my publisher Michael Heyward at Text who showed tremendous faith in this project from its beginnings, and to my long-time agent and first reader Michael Gifkins and my editor Jane Pearson.

In chapter ten, Millennium Three quotes from Rainer Maria Rilke's poem 'Fear of the Inexplicable'. In chapter eight, the inspector describes a mother delivering her dead son to his place of burial in a wheelbarrow. I suspect this image owes a debt to a scene in 'A woman in Berlin', a war-time diary which I read during my time in Berlin.